THE WELSH GUARDSMAN

BASED ON A TRUE STORY

ANN BROUGH

To Kath

With love,

Ann Brough

September, 21 2018

Thicket Books

To my sister, Christine

PROLOGUE

*L*onely! Is that the word for feeling displaced, unwanted, unloved?

Hope! Is that the word for holding onto a dream, a promise, a memory?

Early in life Dorothy knew both. She spent her young life balancing the two opposing feelings of despair and elation.

She had been abandoned twice in the same year by her mother, Gertrude. Her father, Edward, had no legal right to his daughter. He lived in London, but had promised Dorothy he would never forsake her and that she would be able to join him one day when she was old enough. Dorothy kept each letter from him in a tin box beside her mattress. The toy soldier her father had given her was hidden behind a brick in the fireplace.

Memories of a lovely life flooded Dorothy's dreams. A life filled with warmth and love. A house nestled in a garden of roses with a white fence and a gate. A room of her own, with clean sheets, a real pillow and a fluffy bedspread covered with rosebuds. Mrs. Medwin, who would come in every day to cook and keep house. Just the thought of the raspberry muffins she used to make for Dorothy would fill her mouth with the taste of them. Father coming home every night to lift her up high and swing her around, declaring "My beautiful girl, how I love you." Mother, so beautiful in her silk dresses and her dark hair drawn up off her face, her lips always ready to plant a kiss on Dorothy's cheeks.

But life was different now.

"Keep out o' me way."

"Shut bloody up."

"Bloody nuisance."

"Get from under me feet, now, ya little bugger."

"Bastard."

These were the remarks aimed at Dorothy by her grandparents, with whom she now lived. They said her mother was never coming back. Emma and Tom Bryan would never forgive their daughter, Gertrude, for landing them with her bastard child. Hadn't they enough to take care of with four offspring still living at home? Life had dealt them another blow—another girl to feed and provide for. They were stuck with her.

A LETTER ARRIVES

Dorothy waited at the top of Mercy Street for her Aunty Dolly. It was March 2nd, 1927. It was cold and drizzling with rain and Dorothy shivered inside her threadbare coat. She pulled her headscarf tighter under her chin to keep the rain from running down her neck. Her boots were leaking, so her feet grew colder and colder as the wetness crept in. Two tears escaped her eyes and joined the moisture from the rain to roll down her cheeks. She was five and a half years old and still remembered her life before coming to live with her grandparents. She remembered being warm and well cared for; how her father had adored her and dressed her like a princess. It made her present life seem all the more difficult to bear, living with a family who only tolerated her but didn't love her.

Her only comfort, the letters which arrived each second day of the month from her father via Aunty Dolly.

There she was, trudging through the puddles, head down against the wind, scarf pulled tightly around her head, like

Dorothy's. She seemed to walk slower lately and her coat didn't quite meet at the front.

"Aunty Doll," greeted the little girl, running to meet the rain-soaked woman. "Do you have my letter? I've been waiting for ages, I thought you weren't coming." Dorothy still spoke with the distinctive accent of the home counties—the counties which surrounded London. People in the home counties called it the 'king's English,' people in Longton, Stoke-on-Trent, Staffordshire, called it 'stuck up' or 'snotty nosed.'

"Here ya are," Dolly said, taking the envelope out of her coat pocket and handing it to her niece. "Now don't go getting it all wet duck, or we won't be able to read it. Did ya tell ya Gran ya were coming to meet me?"

Dorothy pushed the precious envelope down the front of her coat and held it there with her arm.

"I told her I was going to your house for a cup of tea, but she didn't answer me, so I ran out of the house, before she could stop me."

The two of them made their way to Dolly's tiny terraced house at the bottom of the hill on Mercy Street. It was the same as every other house in the streets of Neck End. Two-rooms-up, two-rooms-down. Dolly lit a coal fire in the frigid kitchen, counting out the pieces of coal. If she didn't ration the coal each day, she knew the coal would run out before pay day.

"Keep ya coat on duck," she told Dorothy. "It'll take a bit to warm this place up."

Dolly was kind to her little niece, feeling sorry for her and the life she could have had if her mother, Dolly's sister Gertrude, had left the little girl with her father, instead of bringing her back to the Potteries and the squalor of the terraces of Longton. Dolly struggled with the guilt she carried that Dorothy's father, Edward, didn't know Gertrude had, once again, abandoned her daughter and left to live in Sheffield with another man. Dolly knew she should write to tell Edward, but she also knew it would cause problems in the family if Edward learned that Gertrude had left their daughter with her parents, Emma and Tom Bryan. Edward sent a money order every month to pay for Dorothy's school fees and living expenses. It was a generous amount and gave Emma and Tom extra money to spend at the pub. If Edward stopped sending the money, Dolly would be blamed for spilling the beans. So she kept quiet.

The fire started slowly, as Dolly held a piece of newspaper over the front of the grate to help draw a flame from the damp coal. Once the embers were glowing she added more coal until the smoke grew finer and lighter and flames licked the sides of the black coal, sending out a ray of warmth into the cold kitchen. Dolly filled the blackened kettle and hung it on the hook over the flames.

"Come on, duck," smiled Dolly, "Now we can read your letter."

Dorothy drew the slightly soggy letter from under her coat with a smile. Dolly sat beside her on the horse hair sofa facing the fire and covered their knees with a small grey blanket. Then she opened the envelope and drew out the treasured letter and began to read.

My Dearest Dorothy,

I thought about you while I was walking through the park this morning on my way to my business. The tulips and daffodils were poking their heads through the cold soil and will soon be showing their lovely colours. Spring came early this year and I already feel the warmth of the sun getting stronger each day. I wish you were holding my hand as I walk around London, so that I could show you all the wonders of this great city. One day you will be here with me and for that day I cannot wait.

Then we will do all the things I dream of us doing together. There will be a long, long list and a lifetime to discover everything.

I dined at Claridges last evening, with a good friend, Miss Eleanor Preston, who is headmistress of an elite girls school near London. It was the school you attended for a short time before you left to live in Staffordshire. I hope you remember her. She remembers you well and wished me to give you her good wishes and kind thoughts.

We ate a fine meal of lamb cutlets, with asparagus and new potatoes. You would have liked the dessert—chocolate souf-flé, it used to be your favourite.

The storms, which pummelled the entire Island in January, left poor London with trees downed and streets inches deep in rain water. I didn't leave my flat for a whole day, but watched the wind and rain through the window, wondering if it would ever stop. Hopefully, you were safe and dry my precious princess. The intensity of the storm must have scared you, but I'm sure you held on to the Prussian Captain and were very brave.

Soon you will be able to read my letters all by yourself, but I will still send them to your Aunt Dolly. She is a good friend to both of us and you must always remember to thank her.

Until next time I send you my hugs and all my love,

Daddy.

"There now, duck," smiled Dolly, putting her arm around the little girl curled up beside her. "What a nice letter from your dad. He's the best dad of all the dads I've known. He never forgets ya, not for a minute."

"I wish I could have been at dinner with him and Miss Preston," sighed Dorothy, looking intently at the words on the page as though she saw a picture. "I do remember her. She was very kind and very pretty. The school was lovely and I shared a room with three other girls, who shared their sweets with me. I didn't want to leave, but mummy came to get me."

SURVIVAL

For Dorothy, everything she knew was turned upside down. She struggled to find her place in the family and the community she had been thrust into.

"Come get ya chips," came a loud voice from the kitchen.

Emma had thrown a large bag of chips wrapped in newspaper from the chippy into the centre of the kitchen table.

"A treat tonight," she continued. "Ya can 'ave a wad o' bread and butter with ya chips."

Tom Bryan was always fed first. As breadwinner and master of the house, it was his right to eat his fill. His right was also to eat any meat, usually sausage or a bit of fish, because he needed his strength for work. Tom always favoured the boys in the family, sharing his ration of meat with them.

"Come on over 'ere then Bill," he'd call to his eldest son. "'Ave a bit o' this sausage. You as well our Tommy, and there's another bit for Eddie."

He'd cut chunks of his sausage for each of his sons, ignoring his youngest daughter, Madge, and his grand daughter Dorothy, as though they were invisible. Not even giving any meat to his wife, Emma, although she was wise to him after twenty some years and saved an extra sausage for herself without Tom ever knowing about it.

Tom wore a white silk scarf around his neck, winter and summer, which was used as a napkin to wipe his greasy moustache and fingers. The scarf was rarely washed and carried the stains of many meals, not to mention the stains from using it as a hanky.

The kettle was always boiling on the hob over the fire. Tea was brewed constantly, and when Tom's cup was empty he clinked the side of his cup with his teaspoon to let Emma know he needed a refill.

Dorothy thought her grandfather was a very rude man. She had grown up living with her father, Edward, whose manners and genteel ways were ingrained into her memory. She learned quickly to keep out of Tom's way, to keep her mouth shut, to make herself invisible.

The three boys fell on the chips, grabbing handfuls, then quickly cutting chunks of bread off the loaf and slapping on the butter. They lined the chips up on the bread, with a generous sprinkle of salt and dashes of malt vinegar, then folded over the bread to make a chip butty. The butter and vinegar ran down their chins as they stuffed the food into their mouths as quickly as they could.

Dorothy grabbed a few chips for herself, but missed out on the bread and butter because it was all gone by the time she reached for the last crust. Nobody noticed. She took her chips and stood at the back of the kitchen, nibbling on the fatty, greasy fried potatoes and wishing she was with her father in the cottage, sitting at the table and eating chicken in orange sauce from a china plate.

Although mealtimes were a cause for anxiety, Dorothy's biggest fear was the toilet, which everybody called "the lav." It was dark and damp and smelled bad. The plank with the hole that spanned the width of the tiny closet was too high for Dorothy to sit on. The only way she could get over the hole was to take off her bloomers and climb up on her knees, carefully turning over to move to where she could use the lav. She had to remember to take a piece of newspaper off the nail before her climb, because she couldn't reach it from where she sat, and was always scared she would fall into the bottomless dark hole. The whole process was even more difficult in the dark, when she had to manage a candle to light her way. There was a thick candle, set on an old saucer placed on a shelf beside the back kitchen door, along with a box of matches.

It took Dorothy several attempts and a few burnt fingers to strike her first match, all the time jigging around trying to hold in the urge to pee. Too late! Then she had the added problem of drying out her bloomers, socks and shoes without anybody knowing. She carried the lit candle up the yard and used the lav, then, carrying her wet clothes, she pushed her feet into her damp shoes and went out the back gate.

The candle wobbling around, she made her way down the dark entry between the houses and across the street to Aunt Sarah's house, where the wet clothes and shoes were dried out with no fuss and Dorothy was given a cup of tea and a broken biscuit.

"Gramma's going to wonder where I am," worried Dorothy.

"Don't you worry now, duck," Aunt Sarah said. "I'll go back with ya."

"Don't tell her I wet my bloomers," begged Dorothy. "She won't understand and will be very annoyed with me."

"There's no need to tell 'er anything. I'll take 'er a bit of seedy cake. She won't even know you were missing." Aunt Sarah's house was Dorothy's sanctuary. A safe house. Somewhere to run when she needed comfort.

Aunt Sarah walked across the street with Dorothy and delivered the seedy cake to her sister. Dorothy stayed in the parlour, where Madge and the three boys sat on the sofa staring at her.

Madge had seen Dorothy's precious toy soldier hidden by the fireplace in the parlour and when she told Eddie about it, he and his two older brothers took it. Billy had tied a string around the Prussian Captain's neck and drew it out of his pocket, dangling it in front of Dorothy.

"Look at this," whispered Billy. "It's a bloody toy soldier. Let's throw it down the lav 'ole. Ya can always go down the 'ole and try to reach it, ya little bastard."

If Sarah hadn't come through from the kitchen at that moment, Dorothy's Prussian Captain would have been lost forever.

"Stop that, you lads," Sarah shouted to her nephews. "I'll shove the three of ya down that lav 'ole if ya don't stop ya bullying. She's just a little lass. Ya should be ashamed. Now give it back this minute."

Dorothy's eyes stung with tears as she removed the string from her precious soldier.

"Ya're still a little bastard," muttered Tommy, as the boys went into the kitchen.

"Bastard" was a name called after Dorothy wherever she went. She had no idea why they called her that, no idea what it meant. It sounded horrid. She learned not to show the tears that stung her eyes, because any sign of weakness only increased the teasing.

LEARNING THE ROPES

"**C**ome on, you girls," yelled Eddie. "We're already late."

It was Saturday morning, which meant errand running on the streets.

Errand running was in high demand. Very rarely did the women do their own shopping, unless it was a once a week trip to the market. Mostly, food purchases were the result of errand running.

There was a definite pecking order for running errands. The older children had first dibs and would have their regular customers, calling on them daily to ask if there were errands today. The younger ones had to depend on casual errands, when a woman would stick her head of the front door and shout "Errand," and half a dozen youngsters would be at her door in seconds. Then she'd choose one to run the errand.

Bargaining was done on many levels, younger children offering to run the errand for half the tip; older children employing half a dozen younger ones to run the errands for a small share of the takings.

The going rate for errands was one penny—the cost of a scotch cake. Scotch cakes were big dough cakes and were full of raisins. Every errand child would run to Mrs. Jones' shop at the top of Edward Street clutching their penny and ask for a scotch cake. Mrs. Jones would reach into the shop window, brush all the blue bottle flies off the cakes and hand one to the waiting child. It filled hungry stomachs like nothing else.

The older children taught the younger ones how to stay out of trouble and how they could find some comfort, food or shelter around the streets they lived in. It was a tight-knit community, with large families, low wages, and dire poverty evident in every house, every street.

Food was always the most sought-after commodity, and there were several venues where food was often available. Aunt Sarah's house was one such venue. Although she had enough children of her own, she would often find a line at her front door. She opened it up to the knock of the bravest child in the group.

"Got any broken biscuits, Mrs. Marshall?" the brave child would ask.

Sarah would look at the eight or so bedraggled children and ask them to wait. She would always find something for them to eat. Sometimes the broken biscuits at the bottom of the tin would be emptied out onto a piece of newspaper and shared between the group. They were fiercely fair about sharing and would count out the broken biscuits, making sure each child had the same amount, down to the crumbs.

On particularly cold days, Sarah would let them troop into her kitchen, noses sniffling and being wiped on grubby sleeves. She'd line them all up in front of the fire and cut up crusts of bread, dipping each piece into the lobby pot, she would give each of them a wad of bread juicy with the rich broth. That was a good day, when they had lobby dips.

Other days, Sarah sadly turned them away. She didn't have anything to give.

The Sally Army (Salvation Army) was another great resource. They had a meeting place on the corner of Edensor Road which was open every night and Saturday mornings. They gave out little paper bowls of hot sloppy peas while showing magic lantern shows about the dangers of alcohol and reading stories from the Bible. The whole meeting place used to be full of children all eating peas. Every night ended in the same way, with a rousing chorus:

"Dare to be a Daniel,

Dare to stand alone,

Dare to pass a public house,

And take your money home."

The children would skip home after the meeting singing the chorus over and over. Dorothy always thought it was a great pity the words were never heard by her grandfather and the other men drinking in the pub.

Saturday nights were busy for Dorothy and the other children. The market closed at six o'clock and they had to be there to shop for broken biscuits, fish heads and bacon ends. Once the shopping was done and safely stored in paper bags, they would all make for the fruit stalls. The girls would hold out their skirts, the boys untucked their shirts or jumpers and make a pouch, and the stall holders would tip bruised pears into their makeshift carriers. They would walk home to deliver the food, filling themselves with the juicy, over-ripe fruit.

Saturday night was also bath night. Emma didn't bother to heat the boiler to fill a bath for Eddie, Madge and Dorothy. Instead she sent them to Sarah's to have a bath with the Marshall children. Aunt Sarah heated the water in the boiler in the back kitchen and put two half barrels out in the back yard in good weather, in the back kitchen in poor weather. The hot water was carried from the boiler to the barrels in two buckets, adding cold water until the temperature was just right.

The children lined up in order of age, beginning with the youngest, who were jammed into the first barrel two or three at a time. Aunt Sarah, helped by Aunt Mary-Ann, rolled up their sleeves and put on an extra apron, then scrubbed off the dirt amid squeals and giggles. Aunt Sarah was always gentle, even giving each child a piece of rag to hold over their eyes when she doused their hair to rinse out the carbolic soap. Then each child was lifted into the rinsing barrel, where the sting of the soap was rinsed away.

Dorothy hated lining up with all the other children. Even at the girl's school, before she came to live in Longton, she had been given a big white fluffy towel and escorted to a private bathroom, where the house prefect ran the water for her. Perfumed bath crystals were added to the water, and the prefect helped Dorothy wash her hair and rinse out all the soap.

Now, she had to strip off her clothes and leave them on the drying rack in Aunt Sarah's back kitchen, then wrap the rough grey towel around her and wait her turn. The soap stung her eyes and nose and made her head itch. The old towel didn't dry properly and she had to hand it to Madge right away, leaving her running naked into the back kitchen to drag her clothes on over her still wet skin.

It seemed to Dorothy that she was always cold, hungry and sad. Crawling onto her straw mattress at night, she shut her eyes tightly and reached for her tin soldier.

"I'm so grateful that I have you for a friend," she whispered. "I know I won't always live here, but while I do you make me feel good. You remind me that my daddy loves me. You remind me that somewhere there are warm, lovely homes where people are happy. That will be me one day, I'm sure of it."

AUNT MARY-ANN

*D*orothy enjoyed visiting her old aunts. She often wondered if her grandmother, Emma, was really a part of their family. She seemed so different from her sisters.

Emma had a family of sisters, four in all. The Thursfield sisters were admired by all who knew them for their strong family loyalty, their integrity, their social responsibility. Their mother was an expansive woman, in size and in soul. She was the cornerstone of the community, always the first person to help in a time of need. Whether it was caring for children when a mother was sick or collecting donations for a family whose breadwinner had suddenly died, Margaret Thursfield was the woman everybody relied on. She brought up her four girls to follow in her footsteps, and three of them did.

The only disappointment for Grandma Thursfield was Emma, who married Thomas Crossley Bryan, a drunk. Emma became a bitter, unhappy woman who struggled through married life from one crisis to another. She succumbed to drinking stout and neglecting her family.

The other sisters remained true to their mother's example, becoming generous, caring women who were loved and revered by family and friends.

The eldest sister, Mary-Ann worked in service at an estate in Trentham, from the age of fourteen. She married William Finney when she was twenty-two. She lived at the big house, beginning as parlour maid and working her way up to lady's maid over the years. She spent her days off and annual one week holiday with William at their little terraced house in Lower Spring Road, Normacot, about a fifteen minute walk from her mother's house in Neck End, Longton.

Her younger sisters gathered around Mary-Ann like bees around a honey pot, confiding in her, asking her advice. She was the first to know about Emma's pregnancy, and baby Gertrude always had a special place in her heart. Even when Gertrude grew up and left the family to live with Edward, Aunt Mary-Ann defended her and the choice she had made.

"She's grown up with nothin' all her life. I don't blame 'er for wanting something better. Don't tell me ya all wouldn't 'ave done the same, given the chance," Mary-Ann would nod and point at each sister, including Emma.

Life had been difficult for Mary-Ann, who had endured many miscarriages over the years, losing sixteen babies during the first trimester of each pregnancy. She never gave birth to a live baby. Yet Aunt Mary-Ann was devoted to her nieces, providing what assistance she could when they were growing up. The girls in the family all knew the days of the week when Aunt Mary-Ann would be at home. She would make sure she brought special treats home from her employer's kitchen to share with them—an apple pie, or sugar cookies, or a quick bread. Although money was never plentiful, she bought each one of her nieces a pair of navy blue bloomers at the beginning of each new school year. That one pair of bloomers was worn every day, washed on Saturday mornings—when the girls went without bloomers until they were dry. Little navy blue pills from the bloomers would stick to the girls after a few days wear, to be washed off in the bath at Aunt Sarah's on Saturday night.

When Aunt Mary-Ann retired from service at the big house to settle down and enjoy the little home—which she had only ever lived in for a few days each month--her husband left her for another woman. It felt more of a shock than losing the sixteen babies. There had never been any hint that William was involved with somebody else. He had always seemed dependable, even loving towards his wife. Yet he had deceived Mary-Ann for six years. There was ample opportunity for the affair during the days when the house was only occupied by William.

"What am I to do?" sobbed Mary-Ann, laying her head on her sister's shoulder.

Selina, or Lena to everybody, sat beside her sister and let her cry herself out. It was a shock to the whole family and Lena couldn't begin to answer the question her sister had asked.

"I don't know what to say, duck," she whispered, stroking Mary-Ann's head. "I wish I could 'elp ya. Ya don't deserve it, I know that. A kinder woman I don't know than yaself. I know what I'd say to that William if I 'ad 'im before me, I can tell ya."

The sadness seemed never-ending for Mary-Ann and she decided she couldn't live in the home she'd made with William without him. So she went to live with Selina, a widow with only one daughter.

Every Sunday afternoon Dorothy and Marion Marshall had

to meet Mr. Finney outside the Central Hall and collect money from him to take to Aunt Mary-Ann.

Dorothy loved visiting Aunt Mary-Ann. She was the only person in the family who would talk about Gertrude. She would tell Dorothy stories about her mother, how beautiful she was, what fine clothes she wore, how she was thrown out of the house by Emma, because of a scandal. This information was always spoken in a whisper and the scandal was never disclosed.

"Will my mother ever come to visit me?" Dorothy asked.

"I don't expect she will," answered Aunt Mary-Ann. "She doesn't want to see 'er parents, ever again. But I know she thinks about ya all the time, duck."

"Can I go and visit her instead?" persisted Dorothy.

"She lives a long way away, in Sheffield," replied the aged aunt. "Ya'd best just make the best of livin' with ya grandma Bryan while ya're little. Maybe when ya grow up ya can visit your mam."

Even as she said the words, Mary-Ann wondered if Gertrude would ever send for her daughter. It seemed Gertrude had always looked after her own interests, and her little girl had been discarded in the process.

Aunt Mary-Ann always talked about Gertrude in a kindly way, giving Dorothy a picture of a lovely, caring mother. Why, then, hadn't she taken her daughter with her to Sheffield? Why hadn't she come to collect her at a later date? Why didn't she love her own little girl?

LIES AND SECRETS

Gertrude's obsession was to get away from the poverty of Neck End, where she had been unfortunate enough to be born. She saw her second chance of a new life with George Owens, an 'older' gentleman from Sheffield. This time was different though, because Mr. Owens was a career soldier, a sergeant in the British army, and Gertrude planned to marry him. She would never have to live in poverty again.

There was just one problem—Dorothy.

Why did I go get her from that posh girl's school? I should have left her there, even though Edward would have spoiled her rotten. She needed to be with her own kind, not that snooty lot in the south. Well, she'll have to make the best of it, like I did.

Gertrude tried to reconcile her decision, but knew deep down she was not considering her daughter. She didn't want to jeopardize her romance with George Owens, who didn't know about Dorothy. Once they were living in Sheffield, Gertrude would tell him, and maybe he'd agree to send for the little girl. But for now, she would play her cards close to her chest and keep that secret until her future was secure.

With Mr. Owens, Gertrude followed the same path as she had with Edward six years earlier—she planned to get pregnant! The time restriction to accomplish the plan was tight as George was stationed in the Longton area for only four months, before returning to Sheffield. He was a quiet, considerate man who enjoyed the company of the young dark haired beauty. He wondered why she hadn't been snapped up by somebody, being twenty-four and still single, but he didn't pry into her past, content with her companionship while he was working away from home.

At first George Owens had no intention of becoming romantically involved with Gertrude. Well into his forties, he had already been down that road and had regrets of his own. But Gertrude was persistent. She didn't have to pretend she liked George. She had to admit he reminded her of Edward physically. Tall, greying hair, handsome and old enough to be her father. The physical resemblance was where the similarities ended. George was quieter, more thoughtful, less confident, less passionate. He stole glances at Gertrude when he thought she wasn't looking and thought she was the most beautiful girl he'd ever seen, with her high cheek bones, creamy skin, full lips and glossy dark hair.

Gertrude arranged for Dolly to watch Dorothy so that she could spend the afternoon and evening with George. They walked to Longton Park and rowed around the lake, Gertrude sat facing George and lifted her skirt to show off her shapely legs. They went to the pictures together, Gertrude making sure her knee touched his. They ate fish and chips out of a newspaper, sitting on a bench in the church yard by the railway bridge. She boldly brushed his lips with hers as they moved from the bench, tasting the oil, salt and malt vinegar from the chips. George tried to think of other things, the cold air of the evening, the drizzle beginning to fall, but all to no avail. Gertrude was too beautiful, her lips too full and luscious. He hadn't kissed a woman for a long time and he responded to Gertrude's flirting, pulling her close and kissing her back, only this time it was more than a brush of the lips.

George was billeted in one of the more spacious houses on Trentham Road, which had its own private entrance off the main hallway. It was a comfortable bed-sitting room, with a double bed in the corner covered in a green silk bedspread. A small green sofa and cosy armchair created a small sitting room around the fireplace. Under the window a long narrow table contained a gas ring, a few cooking pots, a kettle and two china place settings in blue and white. A warm dark green rug covered the sitting area, giving the room a home-like atmosphere.

"Don't worry Georgie," Gertrude whispered in his ear as she snuggled beside him on his bed. "Don't worry about a baby. I have everything under control."

By the time George was packing to return to Sheffield, Gertrude had him trapped and her period was ten days late.

"Gert, you said it would be alright," George began. "How can you be pregnant? I can't begin a family at my time of life."

"I can't think 'ow it 'appened, Georgie," Gertrude lied. "It's not the end of the world though is it? A baby will be nice for us. We'll be a family. You, me and the baby."

George looked like he had turned to stone. His jaw set, and his lips pressed into a thin line, as he turned to Gertrude. His eyes never left hers as he whispered, "I already have a family."

Gertrude could feel a sense of panic creep in.

"You never said anything about a family. You mean you 'ave a wife and children livin' back in Sheffield? What about me? What about our baby? You can't just throw us aside."

Now she was crying and clutching at the front of George's shirt, desperate for him to take back the words he'd just said.

"Gert, it's not like that. It's complicated," he tried to explain.

"Complicated. Well uncomplicate it."

George paced the room, trying to think. What a mess! What was he to do? He wanted to do the right thing. Gertrude was beautiful, and he was at a loss to understand why she would want to even consider spending the rest of her life with him. When he told his story, she would probably regret her pregnancy and the path they were presently on. But he had to tell her.

"I have three grown children Gert. You see, I'm a grandad. I'm old. It's not fair to begin life again with a young lass like you."

Instead of being angry and screaming at him, Gertrude ran to him, clinging to him as though she were drowning. She kissed his cheeks, holding his face between her hands, looking deeply into his eyes.

"Yes we can begin life again," she assured him. "I love ya. I love ya more than any man I've known. Ya're kind and quiet. I love how ya look at me. I want to spend my life with ya, Georgie."

She stopped, quietly holding onto him, knowing she had to ask the question hovering between them.

"What about ya wife?"

"I don't have a wife, Gert," was the reply.

A great sigh escaped her.

"Then we can get married. Ask me to marry you George. I'll say yes. I'll come and live with ya and care for ya. We'll be so 'appy."

George needed time to think. There was one more secret he hadn't told Gertrude. Maybe she would change her mind about going to Sheffield with him when she knew the whole truth.

But he wanted her to be with him, to make a home and start a new family. The thought of another baby coming into his life suddenly filled him with joy. A new beginning after all the heartache. A new family, even at this late stage of life. He'd had more than his fair share of grief and worry for so much of his life. He deserved some joy. Some happiness.

"All right luv. Don't fret now," he said, wrapping his strong arms around Gertrude, kissing her forehead. "You pack up your things and come to live in Sheffield with me. You're right. It'll be a new start for both of us."

He didn't want to risk losing Gertrude, there would be another time to tell her about his past.

The following Sunday, in the middle of the night, Gertrude packed her belongings quietly in the dark so she didn't disturb Dorothy. As she was leaving in the early hours of the morning, Gertrude looked down at her daughter sleeping in the parlour on her straw mattress. She still looked like a baby, with her thumb part way in her mouth and her lips moving as though still sucking. Gertrude felt a physical tug at her heart, knowing she was leaving her little girl behind in the care of her parents. She would send for her soon. When she had plucked up the courage to tell George about her. Once they were married everything would work out.

She met George at the train station and they were in Sheffield before noon. A new life had begun—Gertrude was out of Longton and planned never to return.

SHEFFIELD

The military house in Sheffield was roughly the same size as the house in Edward Street, Longton. George had lived there for a number of years and took pride in the work he had done to make the little home comfortable. Every room showed signs of a well cared-for home; the carpet squares in the kitchen and front room, made the space quiet and cozy; the front room was furnished with a cushiony floral sofa, two small arm chairs and a fireplace that was obviously used often. A doorway led out of the kitchen into a small indoor washroom equipped with a flush toilet and a small sink. There was tissue paper on a roll and a hand towel by the sink.

Gertrude was well pleased with her new home. She slid into life with George effortlessly, enjoying the peace and quiet of living with one other, and not having to share space with four others. She loved the big bed, cuddling up to George, warming her feet on his calves. She loved his gentle words and loving caresses and love-making. She lay beside him thinking about becoming his wife, spending her life with him, raising their baby.

But plans don't always turn out the way they should. The secret George carried with him would prevent such a union and he knew he had to tell Gertrude before somebody else did.

It was evening. The fire was burning in the black kitchen grate, filling the tiny room with warmth. After being at the barracks since early morning, George stretched out his long legs in front of the fire, his belly full of the pot roast they'd eaten for dinner.

"That was a good meal, Gert," he said, reaching out to touch her hand. "You spoil me, truly you do."

He paused, considering how to tell her his secret. There was no easy way.

"I have something serious to tell you luv," he began. "You know how you've talked about getting married? You know I have three grown children. I told you I didn't have a wife, but that's not exactly true. It's not a lie either, really."

George rose from his chair, unable to sit any longer. Gertrude rose with him, grabbing both his hands and forcing him to look at her.

"Explain," was all she said.

"We can never be married, luv. I know it's going to be hard for you to hear this. The last thing I wanted was for you to be hurt, believe me. I still have a wife, but she hasn't lived with me for a number of years. I can't divorce her either, because…" George paused, seeing the hurt and fear in Gertrude's eyes.

"She's in an asylum, luv. She's sick; mad. The last few years she lived with me were a nightmare. We all suffered with her as she deteriorated, especially the children, who couldn't understand what was happening. In the end she was a danger to herself and to us. She had to be taken to the asylum. There was no other choice. I wish with all my heart things were different for us. You know I love you and want to marry you. It's just impossible. Insanity isn't recognized as a reason for divorce—God only knows why."

Gertrude's face was pale. She couldn't answer him. No marriage for her—again! Another baby born out of wedlock. No future.

"Don't look like that Gert," whispered George, taking her into his arms and trying to warm her suddenly cold body. "I'm telling the children that I want to spend the rest of my life with you. That as far as I'm concerned we are married. We can have a life here, with our baby. You are, and always will be, the centre of my life. I'm begging you Gert, stay with me. A piece of paper saying we're married doesn't make any difference. We are a couple. We can be a family. Promise me luv! Promise me you'll stay."

Gertrude allowed him to embrace her, but her mind was reeling. What he said made sense didn't it? This wasn't like it was with Edward. Edward had a wife, whom he visited regularly; he refused to ask for a divorce. He always put his rich wife and the money before her. Hadn't he moved Gertrude and Dorothy to Cobham just to be closer to Amy, his wife? George was different. He really loved her. He would divorce his wife if he could, so that he could marry her.

She stirred in his arms, pushing him away so that she could see his face, but still holding onto him.

"I love ya George," she choked between tears. "I promise to stay with ya. Yes, we will be a family. I know folks'll talk, but I don't care about that. We'll brave it out together, me and you."

Their tears mingled as they held one another. As he held Gertrude close, George knew his secret wouldn't destroy them. They could begin again.

George's daughter, Joan came to the house with her two small children the following Saturday morning. She usually visited her dad on Saturday mornings, so that he could see the little ones. Gertrude stayed out of sight in the back yard, to give George a chance to break the news.

Joan's reaction wasn't the expected one. George thought she would be upset with a younger woman coming into the family home and taking her mother's place.

"Dad, I'm so happy for you," Joan said. "I have prayed that you would meet somebody else. You have been so lonely and unhappy and me and the boys worry about you. So what if she's young? If she's good to you and wants to stay with you and care for you, good for her. She's got herself a good man. I hope she knows that."

George hugged his only daughter, and the two little ones joined in, grabbing their granddad's legs.

"Just one more thing, Joan," George confessed. "We're having a baby."

"What?" gasped Joan. "You're kiddin' me! A baby? You? Dad, you've got grandchildren. What are you thinkin'? You can't be havin' a baby. You're too old, aren't you?"

She knew she was babbling, but couldn't stop herself. The baby would be younger than her two children. She'd be a step sister to this new baby. Suddenly she wasn't sure about this young woman dad had attached himself to.

Gertrude crept into the back kitchen to listen in. She peeked around the door and, seeing George with his arms around Joan, thought everything was going very well. She caught George's eye and moved into the kitchen to greet the young woman in his embrace.

"I'm pleased to meet you, Joan," said Gertrude.

"Same, I'm sure," answered Joan. "Dad's just told me there's a baby on the way. Well you haven't wasted any time have you?"

"Now now, luv," George interjected. "We're both very happy about the baby. We hope you'll be happy for us. I'm sure Gertrude will look to you for advice, having two little ones yourself."

"Well, I can't say I'm exactly happy," Joan said. "More shocked, but I dare say I'll get over it. I'm not going to stand in your way. If you're happy with each other, that's every-thing. Dad's had enough heartache in his life. I wouldn't want to make him feel bad about the new life he's chosen."

With that said, Joan held Gertrude's two hands in hers. "Good luck to you both," she said.

Joan told her two brothers the news about their dad and Gertrude. Like their sister, they were relieved to know their dad was in a relationship with a woman who would care for him and love him.

Now there was only one secret left between George and Gertrude. A secret Gertrude had no intention of disclosing—yet. She would wait until the baby was born, then she'd tell George about Dorothy.

The midwife who attended Gertrude realized this wasn't a first baby, and asked about other children. Gertrude didn't answer and the midwife didn't push it. She was used to being discrete. A baby girl was born after five hours of labour. She was a lucky baby. Born in a lovely clean home, a real baby crib with spotless linens, a layette rarely seen in her experience, even real nappies made of thick soft towelling. The father waited anxiously in the kitchen until he was called to see his baby. He kissed his wife first before taking the tiny girl into this arms in wonder, planting a kiss on her wet head.

"She's a beauty, Gert," he smiled at the happy mother. "Look at her, she looks like me."

George laughed in delight as the newborn waved her tiny fists in the air and opened her mouth in a wide yawn.

Life in the Owens house was busy with baby Joyce taking up much of Gertrude's time. She loved her baby girl. Surprising herself, she took care of the house, the cooking, and the baby with ease. Joyce thrived and grew. She was a happy baby and only added to the joy her parents had found with each other.

Gertrude thought about telling George about Dorothy, but there didn't seem a right time.

Soon, Gertrude was pregnant again and a second daughter, Barbara, was born. The two little girls were a delight and Gertrude poured every ounce of love into taking care of them. Again, she considered telling George the secret she was keeping. Bringing Dorothy to Sheffield now would be a major change for the family. Dorothy was already seven years old; after two years, she was used to living with her grandparents, and they were used to receiving the money from Edward towards her upkeep. Gertrude thought it best to wait a few years until the girls were older. Then she would explain everything to the two of them and to George.

When Barbara was four, a baby boy arrived—they called him Geoffrey. George had turned fifty and the three small children left him exhausted, while their mother seemed to keep gaining energy with each baby.

George had retired from the army and gone into the civil service. The family had moved out of military housing, and rented a terraced house on the outskirts of the city. Gertrude was thrilled with the three bedrooms and indoor plumbing. It was everything she had dreamed of. She was content.

Somehow, life had become so busy there never seemed to be a right time to mention Dorothy. Her mother didn't even think of her often any more. The child was part of her past, being raised in a different city by different people.

BEST FRIENDS

"*I*'m going to leave Staffordshire when I grow up," was Dorothy's motto. Like her mother before her, she vowed she would leave the Potteries and live some-where, anywhere else.

When she was almost eleven years old, Dorothy had to move from the Church School, where she had been since she was five, and attend the local secondary school like everybody else, Edensor School, where she would stay until she was fourteen. She was ahead of the other children in every subject and was teased and bullied because of it. How she hated school! How she hated that Madge, two years older, walked to school with her and then ran off to join her friends, who taunted Dorothy.

"Where's ya mam, then?" they jeered. "Gone off with some bloke." They broke into fits of giggles as they watched Dorothy turn red and walk away.

"Where's ya dad, then? Lives in London, does he? A toff is he? Why don't ya go live with 'im?" they shouted after her, accompanied by more giggles, which sent Dorothy running to the opposite side of the playground.

She was always relieved when the school bell rang and she could line up in the playground with her class. Quiet fell on the playground then, as talking was strictly forbidden, and all the children concentrated on being exactly behind the person in front. To be 'out of line' meant a swift flick on the head from the teacher's whistle, which would leave a sore spot for the rest of the day.

Dorothy made a good friend in her first year at Edensor School with a small, thin, quiet girl named Dora Jones. She sat across the gangway from Dorothy in class, and after a few mutual smiles, the two girls began meeting in the playground before school and at playtime. Dora had five older siblings, three girls and two boys, who all went to work. Her oldest sister was getting married soon and Dora was to be a bridesmaid. She lived in one of the corner houses of Neck End, which were roomier, most having three bedrooms. Dora always wore good clothes, not jumble-sale clothes like most of the girls. With a house full of workers, there was more money for new clothes and, as Dorothy got to know her better, she learned that Dora's mam and dad were chapel goers and had signed the pledge against drinking.

Soon the girls were firm friends, even though Dora's mam forbade her to visit Edward Street. However, Dorothy was a constant visitor at Dora's house, the two of them walking home together every day after school. Dora's mam didn't work and there was always a drink of tea ready and waiting when they arrived, along with the baking of the day, which was either pie or biscuits or scones with jam. Dorothy had her first glimpse of what life was like for a family whose parents—or grandparents in her case—didn't spend all their money on stout or beer.

Dorothy wished she could live with Dora's family. It seemed the more time she spent at Dora's house, the worse her situation with Emma and Tom Bryan became. The constant shouting and swearing, the dirty house, the crowded conditions, the poor food, the drinking, the fear of what Tom would do when he was drunk. Life at number twenty-seven Edward Street was about survival. The three teenage boys, Billy, Tommy and Eddy, all now working, filled the tiny kitchen with their big work boots and dust covered clothes. They demanded more than a pennyworth of chips and sloppy peas for their tea, after turning up their pay packets to Emma.

"Buy some sausages, mam, why don't ya?" Billy whined one night, after several days of chips. "We've been workin' all day, and want somethin' in our bellies. We turn up our money, so stop spending it all on booze, and get some food in the 'ouse."

Although Emma was upset by Billy's outburst, she knew he was right, and sausages were bought along with cheese and bacon. The young men sliced off thick wedges of bread and wolfed down their grease-soaked meal with relish—this was more like it, something to get your teeth into. Madge and Dorothy both benefitted from the extra food, although their servings were pared down in comparison to the boys.

Tom still favoured the three boys. He had never liked girls and had shown his disapproval with each girl born to him and Emma. The first of his girls had been born quickly, only six months after their marriage, and then came Dolly two years later. Then there were the two stillborns—both boys. Tom blamed Emma for both deaths, and swore there would be no more babies. When the next baby was a boy, Tom was

37

delighted, and even more so when two other boys followed. Madge, the last of the babies, was another disappointment. After that, they certainly hadn't counted on Gertrude bringing her bastard girl back to live with them.

How Tom hated that girl Dorothy. Some toff's kid, and Gert taking off to Sheffield, leaving the girl behind for him to raise. The money Dorothy's father sent every month was no compensation for what he had to put up with, and Tom didn't feel any guilt about spending it at the pub.

Gertrude had never been in touch with her parents or her daughter since walking out six years before. Neither had Tom or Emma ever tried to contact their daughter to ask her intentions regarding Dorothy. Life slipped by in a blur of stout and drudgery. No hope for the future, and no ambition to change or strive to make a better life.

Edward, on his part, continued to send support cheques to Longton. He never tried to visit Dorothy, but waited patiently for her to grow up in her mother's care. He knew Gertrude's name was on Dorothy's birth certificate and that beside "Father's name" was the word, "unknown." Gertrude had made it absolutely clear at their last meeting, when he had tried to recover Dorothy and take her back to live with him, that he had no rights as far as the law was concerned. He never asked about Gertrude, and Dorothy never wrote to him about her mother. Edward was convinced that one day Dorothy would choose to live with him in London, and he clung onto that dream.

Dorothy wrote to her father about her new friend, Dora. She didn't write often, only when she had something good to say, as she knew that it would worry Edward if he knew her circumstances. Aunty Doll mailed the letters for her, buying a stamp from the shop at the top of Mercy Street on her way to work. Dolly also provided the paper and envelope, taken from the wooden writing lap desk, left to them by Norman's mother when she passed away. Dorothy's handwriting was neat and she took a great deal of time writing to her father. Edward loved receiving a letter from his beloved daughter, although infrequent. He had seen the changes over the years, from awkwardly spelled words written with a pencil stub, to well-formed sentences, written carefully in a rounded, attractive style. Dorothy was growing up, and Edward delighted in the thought of her travelling to London to visit very soon.

He wrote a letter addressed to Dolly suggesting that, now Dorothy had turned eleven, they should plan for her first visit to the capital city.

FEELING BEAUTIFUL

*T*he joy of graduating from Aunt Sarah's bath night to going to the public baths was a highlight in Dorothy's life. It cost a penny and she had to take her own soap and towel.

Every Saturday morning Madge, Dorothy, Eileen Meredith, Marian and Gladys Marshall set off for the baths at the bottom of Edward Street. There were ten separate bath stalls. The woman in charge of the baths ran things like an army barracks. She was a severe woman, named Doreen, and all the girls were afraid of her. Doreen took the money and said who was to go into which bath stall.

"Fill the water up to the line," were her instructions. "Don't you dare fill it one inch above that line, or you'll be banned from the bath house for ever."

Dorothy wondered how she knew how much water was in the tub, but didn't dare fill the water above the thick black line drawn on the bath tub.

Doreen also monitored the time allowed for each person and would bang on the door and yell "Out you get. Ya time's up," sending the girl inside into a flurry, trying to dry off quickly and get dressed.

Dorothy was amazed the first time she went, seeing the hot running water come out of the tap. The sheer luxury of lying in the warm water with nobody there felt like heaven. She loved the feeling of being clean—she felt beautiful!

Emma thought the cost of the baths was a disgrace and every Saturday she made a fuss.

"I suppose yaw two want a penny each for the bloody baths? Well, it's daylight robbery. What do ya get for a penny? Just water? Ya 'ave to take ya own towel and soap. Bloody thieves them bath 'ouse folks. Takin' me 'ard earned money for a bit o' bloody water."

Madge and Dorothy waited patiently while Emma ranted on and on, eventually digging into the pocket of her apron and producing the two pennies, tossing them at the girls with a scowl.

"Never been to the bloody baths in me life," Emma still continued to complain. "Wonder ya don't catch somethin' usin' a public bath. Ya don't know who's been in there before ya. Could be some old man with fleas."

The girls were used to the arguments, and it didn't deter their pleasure of going to the baths.

Life was changing for Dorothy. She was growing into a tall, slender, beautiful girl. She walked with confidence, head held high, even in the cast off clothes and jumble sale shoes she wore. She had a best friend. She didn't have to run errands any more, but earned her pennies by babysitting or cleaning the bath tubs at the public baths on Tuesdays and Saturdays. She was saving to buy a hat. She had heard all the ladies in London wore hats, and she wanted to be ready when her father sent for her.

A NEW BEGINNING

*E*dward lived in the cottage in Cobham for several years after Dorothy had left, savouring the memories of his little girl. Reliving the few years when Dorothy was growing from a baby into a little girl; watching her run in from the garden with a chubby fist full of flowers she had picked from under the hedge; seeing her sitting on the rug in front of the fireplace with books spread around her, seriously studying the pictures of cats in the book on her lap; cuddling her close after her bath, when she smelled of soap and shampoo, her hair wet against his chest. He wanted to hang on to every memory and the house helped him do that.

When the cottage lease came up for renewal, Edward decided it was time to move on. Not only away from the cottage, but away from his job, away from the small village. He was tired of the engineering profession in all its various forms—the numerous positions he had held over the years. He wanted something completely different. But what? He definitely did not want to live with his wife, Amy, permanently in Maidenhead. He wanted to maintain his independence. He also wanted to move into the city. What could he do in London? It was 1932 and society was changing. The world was coming out of a deep international depression. London was bustling with life—people from all over the world pouring into the city to pursue their dreams.

The answer to Edward's dilemma came unexpectedly. He had moved in with his sister and her husband in a quiet area of Knightsbridge. His brother-in-law took the tube into the middle of the city every day to his job at Barclay's Bank. Sometimes he would ask his wife to meet him after work so that they could enjoy dinner together, followed by a show in the west end. After a night out on the town it was always difficult to make the trip home. It was late and the tube ride was inconvenient at best. The few hackney carriages available were so busy with customers, who had booked them days before, that it was impossible to get a ride. Edward usually offered to pick them up at a designated spot, so that the evening wasn't spoiled by the effort of making the journey home in the dark, often wet, night.

The Austin Motor Company had designed a new hackney carriage, a sleek motorized beauty which glided around the London streets offering fare service for people who needed a ride. Inspired by the lack of taxi service and encouraged by the number of acquaintances who asked him for rides, Edward thought it would be a very good idea to start his own taxi service.

After a myriad of bureaucracy, Edward finally had the licence to begin his venture.

The first thing to do was to find accommodation with garage space. He found the perfect spot in Chillworth Mews. Close to Hyde Park and Paddington Station, it had two garages below the flat. The flat itself was large and comfortable.

There were three large bedrooms, two bathrooms, a kitchen with adjacent pantry, a dining room and a spacious living room.

Edward was ready to begin a new phase of his life. Everything had fallen into place and he only needed to ask his wife, Amy, for the money to buy the two new Austin motor vehicles he needed.

Edward and Amy had been married for twenty-three years. Amy was an heiress and had inherited the family fortune when her father died. Edward had benefited financially from the marriage. Amy had always been generous, supplying her husband with the finer things of life.

He broached the subject of the taxis on his weekend visit to the house in Maidenhead.

"What do you think you are doing, Edward?" Amy asked, her eyebrows arched in distaste. "A common taxi driver! I cannot believe you are contemplating such a venture. I am ashamed of you. I would rather you come and live here in Maidenhead. Boredom would not be an issue. I have many genteel friends who would welcome you into the society. Indeed you could play bridge every afternoon at the Armstrongs. We are often short of a fourth to make up two tables."

"Heaven forbid, Amy," laughed Edward. "Me, play bridge? I would sooner go pheasant shooting, which I abhor. This will be a great adventure. I want to try something completely different. Engineering has become a bore, especially my last position with the petroleum company. I like people. They like me. I would set my own agenda, my own hours of operation. I plan to hire another driver to do much of the everyday work, keeping the more interesting clients for myself."

"Edward, I am not about to sink money into such a harebrained scheme," Amy insisted. "I have a plan of my own, which I wanted to discuss with you. Something I hope you will agree to."

Edward and his wife had lived separately for their entire married life. It suited them both. Amy was the partner with all the money, residing in the large house in Maidenhead. Edward lived wherever was most convenient for him. The weekends and occasional vacations were spent together, as husband and wife, with Edward escorting Amy to society functions, or going into town to an opera or a symphony concert. To the outside world it was important, to Amy in particular, that there was a "happily married" persona. Privately the marriage was in name only.

"My doctor thinks I need a change of air. I have struggled through the last two winters in this damp climate and am dreading the thought of another season of coughing and wheezing. I think it's time I took his advice and invested in an extended vacation," Amy began. "We haven't been anywhere for years, except for a few days in Paris and that ghastly week we spent in Spain. I have a mind to travel and see some of the world. We are both getting older and I want to spend some of Father's money while we're in relatively good health. What do you think?"

"Couldn't you go alone?"

"No, Edward, I could not go alone. A woman has a great disadvantage travelling alone. Anyway, I may become ill. You love to travel, darling. You are the perfect companion for me. You let me have all my own way and I close my eyes to your indiscretions. You have nothing to keep you in England. We could stay away for as long as we liked."

Edward did have something to keep him in England.

Dorothy. Although he couldn't see her, he felt he wasn't far away from her—only a few hours by train. Somehow leaving England was moving too far away from Dorothy. She had just turned eleven and he had already told her he would make plans to bring her to London for a visit.

"I'm not at all sure I can fall in with your plan, Amy," he finally blurted. "I've just signed a lease on a very nice flat in Chillworth Mews. I don't want to give it up. It's perfect for me."

"You don't have to give it up," countered Amy. "Rent it until we get back. It will just sit there waiting for you. You can put your life on hold and pick up where you left off."

Suddenly Edward saw his opportunity. How he could gain an advantage.

"Well now, you are right, darling," he said, sitting beside Amy on the chaise lounge. "Do you think you would agree to buy the two Austins when we return? If I am to pick up where I left off, it would be here asking you for the money to buy the motor vehicles."

"You are impossible!" Amy laughed.

Charming Edward! Amy would have her extended vacation and Edward would have his taxi cabs. What more was there to discuss?

Dorothy would have to wait to visit London.

ST. MORITZ

*A*my planned the trip with great enthusiasm. Edward stayed at his sister's house in London while the preparations were in progress, preferring to be out of the way. He would leave the flat in Chillworth Mews vacant until he returned to England.

The letter he wrote to Dorothy was difficult for him to write. He still had the heart-wrenching feeling that he would be too far from her. Not able to reach her if she really needed him.

My darling girl,

I have to leave England for a few months. I will be travelling to Switzerland and France. I will write to you about all the places I visit, and will think about you every day. I know we planned for you to visit London soon, but I will have to delay your trip until my return.

I urge you to talk to your Aunt Dolly if you are scared or need help.

I promise to let you know as soon as I return to London.
The time will go by very quickly. I long to see you, Dorothy.
Be brave.

Love always,

Father

Edward felt guilty that he had postponed Dorothy's visit to London in order to procure two taxis. Was that the worth of his beloved daughter?

Edward packed his trunk and left it in the foyer of the house in Knightsbridge for collection later, then headed to Maidenhead to assist Amy with last-minute details.

They headed for Switzerland first, to spend the summer months at The Palace Hotel, St. Moritz. With panoramic views of the Engadine Alps and Lake Sankt, the hotel was renowned for its beautiful surroundings and its excellent cuisine. Edward was impressed with Amy's choice of hotel, which included adjacent rooms, giving them both the privacy they had been used to.

The autumn months were spent wandering the many pathways in the extensive gardens of the hotel, Edward venturing further afield to trek into some of the foothills. He became lean and fit and enjoyed himself immensely, arriving at the hotel from his adventures hungry and tired. He dined with Amy each night, keeping up the intended impression of a devoted couple. They sometimes went to the ballroom for after-dinner dancing, attracting the glances of other guests, who couldn't help staring at the tall, elegant, attractive dance partners. Letters to Dorothy were written regularly, describing the Alps, the lake, the crisp clean air. Always ending with words of affection and encouragement.

Amy enjoyed sketching. She took her pencils and sketch pad to the edge of the lake each morning after breakfast, when the light was at it's best, and happily sat in the shade of a willow tree drawing the nature surrounding her.

Edward didn't hike the foothills every day, but browsed around the town, exploring the unusual shops and small cafes in the narrow streets. Always with an eye for a lovely lady, Edward caught the glance of a woman drinking coffee in a small cafe he had stopped at. She looked around forty and had soft, fair hair framing her face. Edward smiled at her as she stole another glance at him. He moved over to her table and introduced himself, and invited himself to sit at her table.

Her name was Mia and she was from Germany. Edward talked to her about his trips to Germany as a boy and how his father had loved her country. Before they realized it, they had sat for over an hour and let their coffee get cold.

"Please, let me buy you a fresh cup of coffee," offered Edward.

He never mentioned he was there with his wife, but arranged to meet Mia the next day at the same cafe and maybe browse the streets together.

Mia was flattered by the older gentleman's attention. What harm would it do to meet him again? She wasn't attached to anybody and had enjoyed Edward's company. In fact the chance meeting had come at a very good time for Mia. She was assisting with a photographic shoot of the area for the company she worked for in Munich, and hadn't made any friends in the two weeks she had been there. She hadn't intended to make friends with Edward, he just popped up unexpectedly. Mia had recently sworn to herself that she was better off without a man in her life, having just ended a relationship after five years of anguish with a selfish and jealous partner. However, Edward was so handsome and charming, she simply couldn't resist him.

There was a bounce in Edward's step as he walked along the lakeside the next day. His mind was on meeting Mia at the coffee shop later that day. Once the light was past it's best, the photographer would let Mia go for the day, so at four o'clock she was seated by the window sipping her coffee when Edward joined her.

"Thank you for meeting me," said Edward. "I've been thinking about you all day."

"Have you," Mia said, smiling at the handsome man sitting across the table. His steel grey eyes wrinkled at the corners as he gazed at her. He was tall and elegant, with hair greying at the temples, and Mia had to admit to herself that she was flattered by his attention. "You promised me a walk through the town after coffee."

"I haven't forgotten. We will walk and browse together."

Coffee and a walk became a daily routine for the couple. By the end of the week, Mia invited Edward to her tiny apartment on the third floor of a small hotel on the outskirts of town. She found Edward attractive and wondered if the feeling was mutual.

Edward followed Mia up the winding staircase to the room under the eaves. He was in no doubt as to the reason for the invitation, and he was flattered. As he took Mia into his arms he felt the familiar surge of passion flood through him.

Edward had made love to many women, each one unique and beautiful in his eyes. Mia was no exception, with her fair hair and pale skin, her long shapely legs and bountiful bosom. He lay beside her, caressing and exploring her, then moving above her as she spread her legs to invite him in.

Mia was surprised and excited by Edward. She had not expected an obviously older gentleman to be so fit and agile. He was an attentive lover, concentrating on giving Mia pleasure with every touch and stroke with his expert fingers. He was gentle and strong. He had the stamina and virility of a much younger man, and he enjoyed making love to Mia.

The affair lasted for the next two months, with the couple meeting in Mia's tiny love nest several times each week. They were both ecstatically happy with the arrangement.

Amy suspected there was a new love interest in Edward's life. The subtle change in his demeanour was enough of a hint for the wife who had seen it all before. He was happy. He was discrete. Amy loved his company and closed her eyes to the obvious indiscretion.

When Mia went back to Munich, she went with joy, having enjoyed her two months loving Edward.

Edward missed Mia's company. As he hiked into the hills, or strolled around the town, his thoughts returned to Dorothy and he imagined how wonderful it would be if she were with him. There was so much he wanted to show her. So many places he wanted her to see. It made him impatient to return to London, but Amy had planned to be away for the winter and he had made a promise he would stay with her.

MONACO

The weather was cooling in Switzerland and it was time to move to their next location. After the few months of restful, lakeside culture in a quiet town, Amy had accepted an invitation from her cousin, Henry, to spend some time with him in the south of France. It was a cousin she hadn't seen in over ten years, but with whom she kept in touch, writing usually to his wife, Carole, several times a year.

Carole was born in France and had met Henry while she was at the London School of Music. They were both accomplished musicians and had both worked at the Conservatoire de Paris after graduation. Henry taught piano, occasionally performing as a solo artist. Carole played flute with the symphony and gave lessons at the Conservatoire.

They retired to Nice on the French Riviera and enjoyed their lives in the sun.

Amy and Edward travelled by train from Switzerland to the south of France. They looked forward to a winter spent without the drizzle and damp of England. Amy's cousin welcomed them warmly, showing them into a lovely bedroom on the second floor of their home. A small balcony looked out over a tree-lined street, and in the distance the sea sparkled through the king palms. There was only one difficulty—one large bed!

When they were alone, Amy stood gazing at the bed.

"What are we to do about this?" she asked. "This won't do. We haven't shared a bed since we were newly married."

Edward smiled, thinking the situation very comical.

"Well dear, we could try it out. I promise not to touch you."

"That's not the point. I wouldn't sleep. I'm used to being on my own. You probably snore."

Amy set off to find Carole and explain to her that, due to her respiratory difficulties lately, she would feel more comfortable if Edward slept in a different room—so that he would have a good night's sleep!

"Oh my dear, I quite understand," Carole said. "I will make up the bed in the small guest room. It's at the back of the house, with no view, and is quite tiny, but I hope Edward will be able to cope."

"Edward will be fine, and forever grateful. He needs an uninterrupted sleep, which he would not have if he slept beside me."

The rooms were settled and Edward and Amy relaxed. How could they help but relax in such a city! The tall king palms lined the streets and waved back and forth in the blue sky, the warm air was filled with perfume from the profusion of flowers and shrubs. Edward wrote to Dorothy to tell her about the beauty of Nice.

Henry and Carole were attentive hosts, escorting their guests to see the sights. Henry and Edward climbed the three hundred steps to Castle Hill, which offered a spectacular view of the city and its coastline. Carole and Amy settled themselves at a table in an outdoor cafe in the shade of Castle Hill, to sip their cafe au lait and watch their husbands make the long climb.

"Edward," Amy began, as they sat sipping their tea in the garden one particularly lovely morning. "I could live here for ever. I have never felt better. I think the climate suits me."

She smiled warmly at Edward. At more than sixty years of age, she was still a strikingly beautiful woman, still slender, with wrinkle-free skin now slightly tanned from weeks in the shaded sun.

"Does that mean I should move into your room, darling?" laughed Edward.

He was met with a frown from Amy.

Fortunately they were good companions. The intimacy in their marriage was short lived and they had both found other avenues to find love. Amy with her life-long love, Alice, who had died in a tragic accident several years ago, and Edward with several insignificant affairs, until Dorothy's mother, Gertrude, whom he had loved passionately. Now, after twenty three years of marriage, they were happy with the arrangement between them. Edward would never share Amy's bed, but he enjoyed teasing her about it on occasion.

"We will stay until April, and then I have a special treat for you," Amy continued.

"What?"

"No, no! I am not telling. It is something you will love though."

"Do tell Amy," begged Edward. "You know I hate surprises."

"I will tell you before we leave here, so that you can prepare yourself for the excitement."

Edward's curiosity was peaked, but he knew better than to press his wife. He would wait and contemplate what the secret might be.

His imagination couldn't match the reality. At the end of March, Amy announced that they were leaving the following Tuesday, April 1st, to spend three weeks in Monaco.

Edward hurled himself across the room and hugged his wife.

"I am dumbstruck," he announced. "Monte Carlo for the Grand Prix! Not in my wildest dreams would I have imagined such a trip."

"Then I am happy. Because I've managed to surprise you," laughed Amy.

She really was extraordinarily fond of her handsome husband. It was a great pity she couldn't love him in the manner he wished. But she could make him happy. He was like a boy who had just opened a gift of such enormity that he couldn't contain himself. Henry and Carole joined in Edward's laughter, and the four of them linked arms, forming a circle and dancing around together.

Amy had planned for them to stay at The Hotel Hermitage in Monaco. All glitz and glamour.

The hotel was magnificent. Their suite consisted of two

bedrooms, two bathrooms and living room. The windows looked out over the Mediterranean Sea, bringing the breeze through the balcony's french doors. It was paradise! The Belle Epoque dining room was designed by Gabriel Ferrier, renowned winner of the Rome Prize and gold medalist at the Universal Exhibition of 1889. The glass roof in the Winter Garden was designed by Gustave Eiffel, whose tower in Paris bore his name.

Edward wrote to Dorothy the day after arriving to tell her all about Monte Carlo.

My Dearest Dorothy,

Monte Carlo is like fairy land. Like an imaginary world on the edge of the turquoise Mediterranean Sea. The majestic white buildings, surrounded by king palm trees, are built on the hillside around the harbour, where many sailboats are moored.

The hotel is very splendid and my room looks out over a beautiful flower garden. It seems every night there is a party at one of the hotels, and I dress in my finery and join in the fun. I wish you could see the lovely evening dresses the ladies wear.

I am very excited about the big car race next week. You know how I love horseless carriages! I have found the perfect spot to watch the race and hope to see an Austin Motor cross the finish line in first place.

I think about you every day, darling, living with your grand parents in such poor conditions. It will not be forever. One day you will join me in London and your life will be changed. As soon as I return to London I will send for you to come for a visit.

Until then, I am your ever-loving father.

Life in Monte Carlo was extraordinary. Every morning the waterfront was alive with visitors walking the promenade in the warm sunshine. Edward loved to walk, striding along in his cotton shirt and slacks, wearing a straw hat and sunglasses. Amy preferred to sit at the outdoor cafe at the end of the promenade, sipping her iced pink lemonade as she watched the parade of fashionable women wearing the very latest Parisian creations.

Casinos were in every hotel, but the place to be for night life was the Hotel de Paris. Amy dressed in her finest haute couture, Edward in a white dinner jacket and bow tie, looking the very essence of high fashion and culture. A great deal of money could be lost at the tables in the casino; more money than Amy was prepared to provide. Edward was given a strict limit on his gambling, and he never took advantage of his wife's generosity. He enjoyed the atmosphere, particularly the exceptionally beautiful women he found himself surrounded by.

The entire community was dedicated to providing entertainment for its visitors, who flocked there in thousands to enjoy the amenities. Sports clubs, bathing clubs, spa treatments, yacht excursions, motor vehicle trips into the mountains, all available—for a price!

They both continued to enjoy the temperate climate, being able to be outdoors for much of the day without a raincoat or warm jacket. Amy was good company in the evenings when they dined together, and if Edward felt the need for female company there were numerous ways of engaging a beautiful woman to spend time with. Edward did not feel the need, with the memory of Mia still fresh on his mind.

As the days flew by the city became fixated on the Grand Prix.

Edward was particularly excited to watch the latest automobiles go up against each other, especially as there were two Austin vehicles involved. The streets of Monaco were prepared weeks before the race, the route marked very clearly, so that by race day everybody would know where the cars would be racing. Edward had rented a car a few times and driven Amy into the area around Monaco, where they had spectacular views of the ocean far below them. He imagined what it would be like to drive in the Grand Prix, and thought if he was a younger man that is what he would have done.

Edward walked the route a number of times and chose where he would stand to watch. He tried to persuade Amy to go with him, but she found the noise and fumes too distasteful and preferred to stay in the hotel.

The excitement was palpable on race day. Edward took his spot alongside hundreds of other spectators and waited in the warm sunshine for the first signs of the race. He heard the engines growling in the distance, before he saw the automobiles. Then under the archway burst the first car. Was it an Austin? No, it was an Italian Bugatti. Now others followed, close on each other's tails. The noise was terrific. The fumes choking. To watch such a spectacle, such speed, such skillful drivers, was exhilarating for Edward. How he wished he was behind one of those wheels, going so fast.

The evening of the race was one long party in the city. Fireworks filled the sky, champagne flowed. Edward and Amy dined on the terrace dining room in their hotel where they had a panoramic view of the celebrations.

Monte Carlo was unforgettable. A once in a lifetime experience.

Edward couldn't thank Amy enough for planning such a great secret trip, knowing it was entirely for his pleasure.

However, a few weeks of such decadence was enough for both of them and they packed their trunks longing for quiet rest.

The summer was about to start in northern Europe and they both agreed that England was calling them home. Home, where Dorothy lived.

TAXI

*A*my was, once again, settled at home in Maidenhead. Edward broached the subject of taxis, the other half of the bargain made before their vacation.

"Now we're home, I want to go ahead with my idea for the taxis," Edward reminded his wife. "Treat it as a loan, dear. I promise I will repay it quickly. The time is ripe for such a business. London is bursting with people, all looking for a ride. I know London like the back of my hand. Imagine being paid for something I consider to be so much fun."

"Oh, you are hopeless," Amy declared. "I only hope nobody I know hears of this outrage. What would people think?"

"My dear, I will do my best to keep the news away from your society friends," Edward said, still not being able to keep the smile from his lips.

"I know you, Edward," Amy said. "You will not be happy until you have tried this ridiculous venture. I will have my bank extend you the money for your automobiles, but if it flops, you had better have other ideas about how to pay me back."

Edward re-signed the lease for the flat in Chillworth Mews and proceeded to hire a housekeeper. Mrs. Arnold had worked for Lady Carnworth, and had now retired. She came highly recommended by Peter Chartrand, the chef at Edward's club, who had worked with Mrs. Arnold at the Carnworth estate.

"I don't know if she's lookin' for a position Mr. Wrightson," Peter said. "But I know she's stayin' with her sister in Watford for the time bein'. Her and Mr. Arnold aren't young, but good workers, both of 'em. He's a painter and decorator, but just does odd jobs for folks now. Used to do all the maintenance and stuff at the big house."

Armed with the address of Mrs. Arnold's sister, Edward drove out to Watford the following morning. It was a nice neighbourhood. Terraced houses of light-coloured sandstone lined the streets. He found number fourteen, a wooden door with a shiny brass knocker. Mr. Arnold answered the door and when Edward explained why he was there, invited him into the cozy kitchen, where Mrs. Arnold sat knitting.

Mrs. Arnold didn't take much persuading to work for Edward. Housekeeping a flat would be a piece of cake for her after the work in the country house. Edward said they could come and go as they pleased, as long as the flat was kept clean and the shopping and food was prepared as needed. The Arnolds would have one of the bedrooms, a bathroom and the full use of the flat; Edward wanted them to treat it as their home too. The couple were both delighted with the offer, particularly as Ethel, Mrs. Arnold's sister, had become irritating lately, making it obvious they had outstayed their welcome.

Edward purchased two of the new Austin Motor vehicles. He

would drive one himself and the other would be driven by John Goodwin, a polite and pleasant young man with an impeccable driving record, hired by Edward. John would be the driver for casual fares, picking up people from the theatre, or station, or business section of the city, driving around to be hailed by a customer, or contacted by telephone at Chillworth Mews. The two vehicles were garaged under the flat and Edward had a separate telephone line installed to take the business calls, which Mrs. Arnold answered.

News of the taxi business spread through Edward's acquaintances, and the phone kept Mrs. Arnold busy, with Londoners who preferred to ride rather than walk in the rain, ride the bus, or face the crowds and noise of the underground tube.

Through Edward's contacts at his men's club in Pall Mall, he was introduced to Phillip Manfred from The British Picture Company. The newly created company was formed in direct competition with the growing American market for talking motion pictures. The Americans dominated the market and only five percent of movies had been made in England in recent years. The British Picture Company intended to reverse that trend. They were making two movies, based on successful novels, in the City of London, and Phillip Manfred offered Edward a contract with his company for the use of his taxi. Driving cast members, directors, technical experts and also using his taxi in the movies. It was a lucrative contract and Edward happily shook hands on the deal.

The new venture gave Edward what he had hoped for, something completely different, a chance to move on with his life.

Mrs. Arnold helped Edward furnish the flat to his liking, choosing beautiful mahogany furniture for the dining room and Edward's bedroom. Lush dark red velvet drapes were hung at the windows, Persian rugs covered the wooden floors. The kitchen was already well equipped, with Mrs. Arnold adding a new refrigerator and butcher block kitchen table.

Everything was prepared. Dorothy could come for a visit.

JOURNEY TO LONDON

*I*n Longton it was a cold day for May. The wind whistled through the dark, smoky station, finding its way inside coats that were old and worn. People huddled in small groups as they waited, finding comfort being close to each other, blocking out some of the gusts of dusty wind. The sound of the oncoming train reached their ears long before the swirling smoke blew under the high roof of the station, filling their eyes and noses with acrid stinging fumes.

The engine came into view behind the mask of smoke, looking like an enormous dragon coming into a cave. It hissed and squealed and puffed as it came to a grinding stop, causing the people to instinctively step back on the platform. Then, surging towards the carriages behind the engine, carrying their bundles and bags and children, the passengers pushed and shoved their way onto the train in the hopes of finding a window seat, or at least a seat near family or friends.

Dorothy stood on the platform with Aunty Dolly, holding her small bag in both hands and shivering against the cold and because she was scared. Scared of the journey ahead—her first time travelling anywhere. Aunty Dolly pushed her forward to the nearest carriage, giving her arm a squeeze of assurance, and Dorothy clambered up the steps and onto the train. She was small and thin and could wiggle her way through the line of adults filling the corridor. Seeing a carriage full of women and children, Dorothy squeezed through the door and crammed herself into a small space beside a sulky-looking older girl dressed in a navy blue coat.

As the train pulled out of the station, Dorothy's head was full of questions. *What lies ahead? Will I recognize him? It's been more than six years since I last saw him. Will he like me? How long before we get to London? What if I need to pee—where's the loo?*

Sitting crammed beside the corridor window, she couldn't see outside. The windows were all steamed up anyway. The girl beside her blew her nose on a dirty hanky and continued to stare at the floor. The two small boys wrestled and pinched each other, falling onto the floor, then being yanked back onto the seat to sit on either side of their frustrated mother. The time went by at a snail's pace. Dorothy watched the rivulets of moisture making their way down the glass near her face. She sucked on the bitter lemon drops that Aunty Dolly had tucked into her bag before she'd boarded the train. Her tongue grew sore and pimply from the tart candy and she wished she had some water to soothe it.

It was many hours of stopping and starting between Stoke-on-Trent and London; people bustling on and off the train with their bundles and packages, shouting at dawdling children and old folks. The family in Dorothy's carriage exited at Watford, the boys still pinching and shoving each other and the sulky girl still blowing her nose and looking at the floor.

Sliding over to the window seat, Dorothy rubbed her sleeve

over the wet window and made a hole in the moisture big enough to peer through. She watched as the train flew past green fields with cows, miles of hedge rows, towns full of brick houses clustered together. She sucked another lemon drop, wishing she hadn't once the acid lemon bit into her sore tongue again.

Now there were no more meadows, or trees, or hedges, just grimy buildings and smoky chimneys. Not like the black smoke of Longton, but smoke from tall chimneys reaching into the sky, and house chimneys belching out the smoke from the coal fires warming the thousands of homes lining the railway tracks.

Oh no! Oh no! The train's slowing down. It must be London. Euston Station. Will he be there to meet me? What if he isn't? What if I'm all alone in the capital city, not knowing where to go?

Dorothy felt sick as she thought of being alone and lost. She licked her fingers and ran them over her hair, straightening the red ribbon. She grasped her small bag tightly in her fists as the smoke covered the carriage window. Legs wobbling from sitting for so long, maybe from fear, Dorothy edged her way into the corridor to join the throng of people moving towards the door. She squeezed her legs together, trying to stop the feeling of needing to pee. Now wasn't the time to find a loo, but it added to her discomfort.

Down the steps onto the platform amid a sea of people, she was swept along, not able to see anything or know where she was headed. Porters loaded their carts with luggage and bags of mail, the passengers flowing around them like a river around rocks. Then, as the crowd began to thin, using several exit gates to spill into the station, Dorothy could at last see her surroundings. Euston Station was immense! The biggest building she had seen or even dreamed of, and people everywhere. How would she find her father? Nobody noticed the small person as she weaved in and out between families, businessmen, smart women, all hurrying and all seemingly knowing where they were going, except her.

She sat on a nearby seat to catch her breath and gaze at the constant human traffic streaming past. She opened her bag and pulled out the paper Aunt Dolly had given her. There were the instructions; look for the big clock on the station platform—Father will be waiting there.

Edward had reached Euston Station early, having barely slept. Today was the day he had waited for, had longed for. Today he was meeting Dorothy, his only child. His stomach was knotted as he dressed, looking at himself in the mirror and acknowledging he looked more like a grandfather than a father of an eleven-year-old girl. His hair was grey at the temples and his face, although still handsome, was lined around the eyes. He had turned 64 years of age on May 2nd.

He had last seen his daughter Dorothy when she was five years old. Her dark curly hair and big brown eyes, her round dimpled cheeks and rosebud lips were burned into his memory. Now she was coming to London to see him. To stay with him for two days.

Edward was shocked Gertrude had given her permission to let Dorothy visit. Although he always communicated through Dolly, he imagined it would be Dorothy's mother who must give her final consent. He was amazed that there had been no attempt to prevent the visit.

Edward had written to Dolly several weeks earlier and arranged for Dorothy's first visit to London. He knew nobody in Longton would buy a ticket for Dorothy or arrange the journey, so he had sent Dolly the cost of a railway ticket and the dates and times of the trains.

"Our Doll, have you lost ya bloody mind?" Emma had screamed at her daughter, rising from her chair at the kitchen table to stand face to face. "She's not goin' to no bloody London, I'm tellin' ya that."

"Mam, don't get into a state now," Dolly said, standing her ground and staring into the older woman's wild pale blue eyes. "'e's sent the money for the ticket and 'e's expecting 'er. Anyroad, ya don't want 'im to stop sending ya the money do ya? 'e will if ya push 'im."

It was always the ace in the hole for Dolly—threatening for the money to be cut off.

"Well, I don't bloody like it," continued Emma, sniffing and wiping her nose on her sleeve. "'e's no right to send for 'er and expect us to let 'er go just like that. She's only eleven for God's sake."

"She'll be all right Mam. I'll put 'er on the train in Longton and e'll meet 'er in London. Piece o' cake. Ya know she's got a good 'ead on 'er. It's not like our Gert ever asks about 'er or wants to see 'er."

Emma sat down at the table and took a swig at the bottle of stout. No good would come of her visiting her dad, she thought. Him a toff, living in London, showing her all the glitz and glamour of a different world. She'd come back with her head full of all kinds of nonsense. Yes, Emma thought, there was trouble ahead.

"I'm still not likin' it Dolly. But, ya'r right, 'e's 'olding the purse strings. That young madam's 'ard enough to 'andle as it is, always bloody cheekin' back. I regret the day that little bastard of our Gert's got dumped on me to bring up. Well, she'd better not bring those bloody London ways back 'ere."

Dolly had written down all the information. Time of the train, where Dorothy was to meet her father at the station called Euston in London. Dorothy's full name and address in Longton and the address in London where Edward lived. Dolly had been to the chapel jumble and bought a nice skirt and blouse for her niece. As suggested by Edward, Dolly tied a red ribbon in Dorothy's hair, so he could recognize her. The threadbare coat would have to do, as would the scuffed old shoes, which were a size too small.

Edward had a vision of the little girl he last saw seven years before. He adored her. She was the child he had longed for, born when he was middle aged and had given up all hopes of becoming a father. She was his delight and joy and his heart had never recovered from the loss of her.

Would he recognize her now? She would be changed. Grown up into a tall girl, maybe skinny and gawky like most eleven-year-olds. How would her hair look? Was it still curly? Had her little pearly teeth been replaced with straight or crooked ones?

At the flat in Chillworth Mews, near Paddington Station where Edward lived, he had asked his housekeeper to make up the bed in the guest room and prepare it for Dorothy. Mrs. Arnold had enjoyed shopping for new sheets and blankets and had purchased a small dresser for Dorothy's clothes.

As the train from the north pulled into platform twelve, Edward took a deep breath and stood under the tall station clock. He scanned the crowd of people streaming from the train, hoping for a glimpse of the red ribbon. He clenched his fists as he felt his stomach rolling and pitching, his breath coming in short gasps. As the crowd began to dissipate, Edward peered through the bodies in search of his illusive little girl. Then he spotted her, slowly rising from a bench, looking anxiously around. The same beautiful dark curls, tied with a red ribbon, the same almond shaped dark brown eyes and a way of holding her head that reminded him of Gertrude. His eyes filled with tears as he choked for control. He wanted to rush forward and gather her into his arms, but knew she would be looking for the clock and he didn't want to frighten her. He stayed where he was, his eyes never leaving his daughter as she searched the busy station.

Dorothy felt very small as she moved slowly into the vast station. Where was the clock? She craned her neck to see over the adults in front of and around her, then looking up towards the roof she spotted the clock, hanging from a high support post. She stopped for a moment to catch her breath, praying there would be a tall gentleman wearing a trilby hat standing beneath the clock with his hand raised in the air.

Edward smiled as she came closer. His hand raised in the air. He would have known her, even without the red ribbon. She was his baby still, with dark curls, beautiful brown eyes and ruby lips. Dorothy stopped in front of her father, looking up into his smiling grey eyes.

What now? Should she shake hands?

Edward bent down to her level. He reached out and touched her cheek gently.

"Hello Dorothy," he whispered, drinking in everything about her.

Then she was in his arms, holding onto him with all her might. Now he couldn't stop the tears as they spilled from his eyes. The years since he had last held her close dissolved and Edward's heart filled to the brim with love for his daughter. She was thin and he could feel her shivering as he held her. He kissed her forehead and held her face in his hands, smiling through his tears.

"Hello Father," she finally managed to say, feeling suddenly warm and loved.

THE BIG CITY

*L*ondon! The capital city!

Dorothy had spent the most wonderful day of her life, with her father.

She awoke, in the warmth and safety of her downy soft bed, to delicious smells coming from the kitchen.

Mrs. Arnold had run a bath for her and sprinkled lavender bath crystals into the water. Dorothy sank into the perfumed warm water up to her neck, watching the steam rise, closing her eyes and enjoying the fragrance. Lavender remained Dorothy's favourite perfume!

Edward was waiting at the breakfast table, drinking coffee and reading a newspaper, which he folded and placed on the table immediately when his daughter came into the dining room. It was bacon she had smelled, for there it was on an oval plate surrounded by scrambled eggs. Fingers of buttered toast and orange juice, two kinds of jam, a dish of fresh fruit (not even dinged) made up the feast they called breakfast.

Edward had asked John Goodwin to bring the taxi cab around to take them to Brompton Road after breakfast. He sat beside Dorothy in the back seat and held her hand. He had checked with Mrs. Arnold on the best place to buy clothes for an eleven-year-old. It was an immediate and necessary errand—Edward could barely believe the dilapidated condition of Dorothy's clothes. They followed the housekeeper's recommendation and the taxi cab dropped them at the Harrods Department Store.

Dorothy thought the shop must be a palace. The imposing five-story stone building, topped by castle-like turrets, towered above Dorothy as she stepped out of the taxi. Edward still held Dorothy's hand as he guided her to the entrance and into the vast interior. The small hand grasped the large hand tighter and tighter as they made their way to the lifts.

Other shoppers turned to watch the tall, elegantly dressed gentleman accompanied by a skinny, shabbily dressed waif walk through the shop. Whispers and questions passed between the sales staff as they saw the pair head towards the centre of the main floor where the lifts were located.

"Don't worry darling," whispered Edward. "This will be fun. Have you ridden a lift before?"

"Never," replied Dorothy, biting her bottom lip.

"Third floor please," announced Edward as they stepped into the lift together.

"Certainly Sir," replied the lift operator, trying not to stare. He could see out of the corner of his eye the little girl's scuffed shoes and shabby coat. But he had also noticed her twinkling brown eyes and excited smile as she had skipped onto the lift beside the old gentleman.

Maybe her grandfather? Thought the lift boy.

The morning was spent in a whirlwind of shopping for Dorothy. Two ladies, working in the children's clothing department, were more than happy to help choose everything from underwear and socks to dresses and a warm coat. Two woollen hats, a scarf and two pairs of gloves were selected in shades of cherry red to compliment the coat's soft slate grey colour. Added to the new clothing were a pair of black patent leather shoes and lined brown ankle boots. Soon there were bags and boxes piled beside the armchair where Edward sat giving instructions, giving his opinion on the outfits he liked, and helping his daughter decide which she should take.

Edward discretely asked the two sales assistants to dispose of the clothing Dorothy had worn into the department store. She was to leave the store dressed from top to toe, undergarments to outer garments, in new clothes.

Am I dreaming still? Dorothy looked at herself in the long mirror, dressed in a blue dress covered in tiny white flowers, with her new T-strap shoes shining, and ankle socks gleaming white. *What would Madge say if she could see me now?* The thought of if almost made her burst out laughing. *What would me grandma say?* Now she did laugh out loud, making her father laugh along with her even though he didn't know why she was laughing. He was elated to see her so happy, looking so lovely.

"Let us take our parcels home darling," he said. "We must show Mrs. Arnold what we have bought."

Mrs. Arnold was treated to a parade of the new outfits, which she approved of with many Oohs and Aahs.

The afternoon was spent wandering around Hyde Park,

which was a few minutes walk from Edward's flat. Dorothy had never been into such a place, full of endless green grass and hundreds of trees, all newly leafed, some covered in pink blossoms. Edward took his newspaper with him and settled down to read on one of the park benches littering the maze of paths.

Dorothy was content to sit beside her father and watch the strange world around her. She was fascinated by the number of horses and riders trotting or cantering through the park, the riders dressed up in their finery. Even small children, younger than herself, were riding with their families. Everybody looked happy, well fed, well dressed. There were no groups of ragged children huddled together; no bleary-eyed men staggering out of the pub; no tired, downtrodden women carrying heavy shopping bags, with babies on their hips. This was London. So far removed from the town in the Midlands where people strived to make it through each day, with no expectations of anything good or beautiful happening.

The excitement of the day hadn't ended with Hyde Park.

After a rest in the late afternoon, Edward gave a light tap on Dorothy's bedroom door.

"Are you well rested darling?" he asked. "Mrs. Arnold has prepared dinner for us, so tidy up and come into the dining room."

Dorothy didn't recognize any of the food laid out for them, but her father named the different dishes, encouraging her to try each one. Mushroom soup with tiny croutons floating around, declared delicious by both father and daughter, chicken cordon bleu with tiny roast potatoes and something called asparagus covered in onion sauce, and fluffy chocolate mouse served with sponge fingers.

Dorothy thought she would burst. How would she ever tell Dora about all of this?

"Now my dear girl," began Edward. "I have saved the best surprise for after dinner."

"What?" said Dorothy, her eyes wide, wondering what else could possibly happen that would be more of a surprise than the rest of the day had been.

"Come. Put on your new coat. It will be chilly now that the sun has gone down."

"Where are we going, father?"

"Ah! I told you it's a surprise. There is a taxi cab waiting outside, so hurry along."

Dorothy was back a few minutes later, dressed in her new grey coat, her red hat placed jauntily on her dark hair.

"Ready Father," she smiled up at Edward. "Now can you tell me where we're goin'?"

"Shhh! All will be revealed," Edward smiled back.

It was terribly exciting to travel through London in the dark. Well, it wasn't really dark because lights were everywhere. As earlier in the day, Edward sat holding his little girl's hand in the back of the taxi. She stared out of the window, her eyes dancing with delight. All questions gone from her head, she watched the lights whiz by and watched the people scurrying along the pavements, window shopping, chatting, laughing.

When the taxi stopped, Dorothy looked up at the words in

bright lights on the building in front of her, "Music in the Air", and above it "His Majesty's Theatre."

"Father? What is this? Are we going to a real theatre?" Dorothy gasped as she stepped out of the taxi onto the crowded pavement outside the theatre doors.

"It is His Majesty's Theatre, and we are going to see the very newest musical production," said Edward, taking her hand and guiding her through the main doors. He was dressed in black evening dress, with white bow tie and tall top hat. Dorothy felt so proud to be holding his hand and walking beside him. *This is my father!* She wanted to shout it out to everybody.

How would Dorothy ever describe what she saw when she went back to Longton? The theatre itself, with tier upon tier of red upholstered seats, the beautiful red draped curtains with gold tassels covering the stage, the orchestra down in a special dark room in front and almost underneath the stage. Music filled the theatre and drew tears of joy from Dorothy, who seemed to be trapped in the dream-like state she had been in for the whole day. One of the songs from the musical remained in her head long after they had left the theatre. "I've told ev'ry little star …….. mmmmmmm," she hummed as she sat in the back of the taxi with her head on Edward's shoulder.

Laying in bed, staring out of the window at the starry sky, Dorothy played the day over and over in her mind. A day she couldn't have imagined. A day she would never forget. She picked up the Prussian Captain, who stood on the table beside the bed and planted a kiss on his helmet.

"Isn't this a magical place?" she asked him.

BACK TO REALITY

With her bag packed with new clothes, Dorothy caught the train back to Longton. She waved to her father through the carriage window until he was out of sight. She looked down at her shiny new shoes and smiled. For as long as she could remember she had never had such a pair of shoes nor a warm coat, hat or gloves in warm wool. As the train made its way north Dorothy thought about the weekend in London and what she would do when she went back to her real life in Longton. Although she was only eleven, she realized that if she told her family and friends about the flat in Chillworth Mews, the new clothes, the food, the theatre, it would be seen as bragging; trying to be a "cut above." She decided she would say as little as possible. That way they wouldn't judge her as a snob or a toffy-nose.

Nobody met her at the station but Dorothy knew her way to Edward Street. She walked slowly down the soot-covered steps of the station and took her time as she made her way past the shops in Market Street. It was late in the day and the streets were quiet. A group of boys played football in Mercy

Street using milk bottles as their goals. The lamplighter was doing his rounds, lighting the gas lamps one by one with his long lamp-lighting pole.

When Dorothy reached number twenty-seven, she paused at the door for a moment, before pushing it open and going into the house, trying to prepare herself for her grandmother's bitter tongue.

"Well, well, look who's 'ere then!" Emma looked up from her cup of tea. "Little Miss Muck. Bin to London 'ave ya? All dolled up are ya? Coat, shoes. New bloody everythin'."

Dorothy took off her new coat and laid it on the horsehair sofa. She went over to the table to look what was left to eat, and picked up a piece of bread, spreading it with butter and biting into it with relish. She was hungry after her long train ride, even though Mrs. Arnold had packed her a lunch of ham sandwiches.

"Can I 'ave a cuppa, Gramma?" asked Dorothy.

"A cuppa? You? Ya can 'ave water, and don't think ya'll be gettin' more bread and butter either. That bread's needed for Tommy and Billy's snappin' tomorra'."

Dorothy finished her bread and butter and filled a mug with water from the back kitchen. She flipped into her real life situation, yet savoured the two days of wonder she had spent with her father, already looking forward to going again in a few weeks' time.

Madge had sat on the sofa watching Dorothy, envying her new clothes. Tom sat in his chair by the fire drinking his beer, puffing on his pipe and glaring with distaste at his young granddaughter. Silence fell in the Bryan kitchen. Nobody asked how Dorothy had enjoyed her trip. Nobody said a kind word to her. Tommy and Eddie came in carrying more beer and stout for Emma and Tom.

"Nice frock, Dot," commented Tommy. "Where'd ya steal that from eh?"

"Shut ya gob," Dorothy retaliated. "Me father bought it for me."

"Oooooo, father!" teased Tommy. "I bet that cost a pretty penny."

Dorothy felt the tears sting her eyes and quickly headed up to the backyard lav to hide from her family. Nothing changed here. She would be all right. She knew how to stay out of trouble.

Madge didn't say anything to her about her trip to London, but pinched her a couple of times when they went into the parlour and unrolled their "pally arses" to get ready for bed. Dorothy found her old nighty in the cardboard box pushed under the sofa and took her new clothes off with care, folding them into a neat pile. Tomorrow she'd wear her new clothes to school.

The following morning, the only clothes Dorothy could find were the old ones in her box. Even her shoes were gone and she had to borrow a pair Madge had grown out of.

Dorothy didn't talk about her trip to London to any of her friends at school, except Dora. She told Dora about going to the theatre and how nice her father was, but not about the new clothes and shoes, because she was ashamed that her clothes had disappeared overnight. Somehow she felt she had let down her father by not taking care of the gifts he had bought for her.

After school, Dorothy wandered over to Aunt Sarah's house

to see the girls and have a cup of tea and broken biscuit. She told Aunt Sarah about her clothes. Her Aunt's lips squeezed together and her eyes closed.

"Never you mind, duck," she finally said. "Ya got to wear those nice things for a few days. You'll get to see your dad again in a couple of weeks. You just keep ya head down and ya mouth shut at the Bryans. Don't give them reason to treat ya badly. Ya can always come over 'ere to get out of the way."

When Dorothy had left, Sarah went through her backyard to Dolly's house to tell her about Dorothy and the disappearing clothes.

"We both know where the clothes are, don't we Doll?" Sarah said, looking at her niece sadly. "Gone to the pawn shop, that's where. They'll have extra beer money now. I don't know 'ow our Emma can be like that—it's Tom's influence, always 'as been."

After tea Dolly went to her mother's house and picked up Dorothy.

"Come on our Dorothy, duck," she called to the young girl. "We're off to get ya something to wear, bein' as your nice clothes are gone."

Dolly cast an accusing eye on her mother, Emma, sitting at the table drinking a bottle of stout. The older woman didn't look at her accuser. No point. They both knew the truth about the nice clothes from London.

Dolly and Dorothy walked to the Central Hall Methodist Chapel on Market Street, entering the building by the side door along the alleyway. There were people coming and going inside the large building. Squeals and shouts could be heard from the large meeting room at the top of the short flight of stairs off the main foyer. Dolly was looking for one particular person.

"Hey," she hailed a young man hurrying past them. "Do ya know where Nelly Tart is?"

"Yeh, she's running the Girl Guides in the big room up there," he said pointing to where the noise was coming from. "She won't want to be disturbed though. Nobody interrupts her Girl Guide meeting for nothin'."

Dolly and Dorothy sat on the stairs and waited.

Nelly Tart was a short plump woman, with curly greying hair and a smile to light up the world. She stood at the door as the girl guides left, giving each one the left handshake of friend-ship, used by every girl guide as a sign of friendship to another guide—the left hand being closest to the heart. She saw the woman and girl sitting on the steps outside the meeting room and, when the last girl had left, she called out to them.

"Come on up here. Have you been waiting long?"

"No, not long," said Dolly. "Doreen Bradbury, who works with me, said to ask for ya if there was a need."

"Oh, I know Doreen. She's a gem. Always here at the chapel working away at something. What can I help you with? Firstly though, what are your names?"

After introductions, Dolly spoke up.

"I know it's not jumble day Missus, but me niece 'ere needs some clothes and shoes. Particularly a warm coat. We'd be ever so grateful if ya could find a few things in 'er size."

Nelly's eyes warmed with sympathy for the young girl before her. She was a pretty little thing. She had heard similar stories many times. Fortunately, the chapel benefited from the patronism of several wealthy families who lived near the town, who donated their out-of-fashion clothing. Many articles were little worn and of good quality and were always in high demand on jumble day.

"Come with me," Nellie said, opening a door at the back of the room. "We'll find something nice for you."

The room behind the guide meeting room was lined with shelves, containing boxes and boxes of clothing.

Nelly pulled down two of the boxes marked "GIRLS 12 -14".

"Here we go, let's start with these," she said. "I'll root around for shoes while you're looking."

It didn't take long for Dorothy to find what she needed. The coat was too big, but warm and not frayed on the cuffs. The two skirts, jumpers and socks would be good for school and Nelly found two pair of shoes in the right size.

"Thank you Nelly," said Dolly, as she pushed the new clothes into a brown paper bag, except the coat, which Dorothy kept to wear for the walk home.

As the threesome walked towards the outside doorway leading to the alley, Nelly Tart turned her attention to Dorothy.

"Well now, Dorothy. Why don't you come to Girl Guides on Monday nights?" she asked. "I think you would enjoy it very much. All the girls are from around here and you'd make many new friends. You'd learn a lot as well. Cooking, sewing, local history as well as play games, and there's always a snack. I could easily find you a uniform to fit. We keep extra ones for new girls."

"I don't know," hesitated Dorothy. "I have to ask me Gramma first."

"No ya don't," Dolly butted in. "I'm sayin' ya can go to guides. I'll talk to ya Gramma."

"Well then. I'll expect you next Monday at six o'clock," smiled Nelly.

Even though her new clothes and shoes were gone, Dorothy felt happy inside. She thought Nelly Tart was a lovely lady. She seemed to really care about her.

Although she didn't realize it at the time, it was a pivotal day for Dorothy. She would spend many years as a girl guide at the Central Hall Chapel and Nelly Tart would become her mentor and advisor.

SUMMER TRAVELS

The next journey to London was a month after the first one. This time Mrs. Arnold knew what to expect and was waiting for Dorothy when she arrived at Chillworth Mews with her father.

"Hello Dorothy," Mrs. Arnold greeted the shabbily dressed girl. "You must be tired after your long journey. I've already run a nice hot bath for you and laid out new clothes on your bed."

The hot bath and new clothes were always waiting for Dorothy every time she went to London. The clothes she had travelled in always disappeared while she was in the bath, replaced by silk underwear, pure white socks and fashionable dress. Mrs. Arnold never said anything to Dorothy about the state of her clothes or the need of a bath, but quietly made her way downstairs to the furnace under the flat and burnt the small pile of shabby clothes. The clothes Dorothy wore from the chapel jumble already showed the signs of two weeks of not being washed, and had taken on the odour of the dank house Dorothy lived in.

Edward was usually busy during the day, especially on Saturdays, driving his taxi. Mr. and Mrs. Arnold spoiled their master's young daughter. Having no children of their own, they enjoyed Dorothy's company. The three of them ate breakfast and lunch together, chatting about school and Dorothy's family. Mr. Arnold shared stories about life in service and how much they liked living in the flat and taking care of Edward. Dorothy went shopping with Mrs. Arnold after breakfast. She was fascinated with the street markets and asked dozens of questions about the fruits and vegetables she didn't recognize.

"Get your apples 'eeeeeeeeere," the street vendors yelled out in their wonderful cockney accents. "Fresh peas and carrots. C'mon missus, taste this pear—a bit o' heaven this is."

Mrs. Arnold cheerfully bought her groceries, bartering for the best prices as did all the shoppers. She then took Dorothy to a small cafe on the corner of the street for a cup of tea and a scone, piled high with butter and jam. Sometimes they would go further afield, to Covent Garden market or Billingsgate fish market, where the constant similarity was the street vendors and their loud verbal advertising.

On the first Saturday evening of Dorothy's second visit, Edward took her to a cozy Italian restaurant close to the flat. His eyes glistened with emotion as he sat opposite his beautiful daughter, remembering Gertrude and how much their daughter looked like her. The same dark hair and almond-shaped eyes, high cheek bones and full lips.

"I don't understand anything on this menu," Dorothy said, gazing at the list of food with wide eyes.

"I'll help you, darling. Do you like pasta?"

"What's pasta?"

"It's very good. Made with flour, like bread, but a much different consistency. I'll order for you. Something not too spicy. You will love it."

Edward ordered a linguini dish with rosé sauce for Dorothy, and his favourite dish for himself—ravioli florentine.

"Dorothy," Edward began, while they were waiting for their food and sipping their drinks. "How is your mother? I was very fond of her, in fact very much in love with her, and I still think about her very often."

"I don't know how she is," declared Dorothy, staring into the bottom of her glass. Her Pottery dialect slipping away, as she tried to talk more like her father.

"What do you mean?"

"I never see her."

"Why not? Don't you live with her?"

"No."

Edward thought about stopping the conversation right there, but he had to find out what had happened.

"Dorothy, look at me," he began, and she slowly raised her eyes over the rim of her glass.

"Put the glass down, darling. I need you to tell me where your mother is and who you live with."

"She lives in Sheffield, but I don't know where, and I live with my grandparents, Emma and Tom Bryan. There are three boys and Madge, whose two years older than me living there as well."

"When did she leave?" Edward whispered.

"When I was a little girl. A long time ago. I don't remember what she looks like."

Edward gulped his glass of wine down in two swallows. Why hadn't Dolly let him know? Why hadn't Dorothy told him in her letters? Gertrude had abandoned her daughter for the second time, leaving her in the very house, and with the very people she had loathed.

Edward couldn't think straight. He could no longer look at his daughter sitting across the table with her eyes searching his face. He fought for control, his anger threatening to overwhelm him.

"I'm sorry, father," Dorothy said. "I thought you knew."

"You have nothing to be sorry for. You are the innocent victim. The adults in your life have let you down, Dorothy. Including myself."

Of course, they didn't let me know when Gertrude left. I would have stopped the money. I would have stormed up to Longton and taken my child away. Now I know, and that's exactly what will happen. That family will no longer receive a monthly allowance and they will no longer be responsible for my daughter. I must tread carefully though. I do not want to scare Dorothy, or upset or worry her. Until plans are fixed, things must seem to be as normal as possible. But I will resolve this and put it right.

"Now, darling," Edward smiled. "Let's put all this aside and enjoy our dinner. We will talk of other things. You have to tell me all about school and your friend, Dora. I want to hear all your news."

Dorothy enjoyed the linguini and the iced raspberry dessert. The conversation about her mother had been odd, but they had happily moved on and the rest of their evening was full of lively talk on both sides.

"I have a question Father," Dorothy said, a line forming between her eyebrows. "Why do all the working people leave school early? Their education is over by the time they are fourteen. Why aren't they educated according to how clever they are?"

"Those are big questions for such a young girl," smiled Edward. "I believe, as most do, that education would be wasted on the working class. They would be discontented. Besides who would empty the dustbins?"

Dorothy stared at her father. He really believed his answer was correct and it took her aback to hear his viewpoint. She couldn't debate the issue with him, but knew she thought differently. She tucked it into her mind, and hoped the future would bring changes for the working people of Britain.

Sunday morning became their Hyde Park morning. Dorothy loved the park and never tired of watching the horses and people, or sitting beside her father while he read the Sunday paper.

When it was time to go home, Mrs. Arnold didn't pack any of the new clothes into Dorothy's bag.

"We're going to keep your clothes here now, Dorothy," she explained. "They'll stay here so that you can use them on your next visit. You can wear these clothes for your trip home, and here are the shoes and coat you arrived in."

Mrs. Arnold handed Dorothy a small brown bag with cotton underwear, socks and a plain green knitted dress.

It became routine. When Dorothy arrived in Edward Street, she made a neat pile of her London clothes and left them outside her bedroom door, to make it more convenient for Emma to pick up and take to the pawn shop. Emma was not impressed with the plain dress and cotton undies as she only collected a few pennies for them.

Edward called his solicitor on Monday morning to talk about the situation in Longton and what his legal rights were in regards to his daughter.

The case was clear. Edward had absolutely no legal right to his daughter. His name did not appear on Dorothy's birth certificate. Gertrude had entrusted her daughter to the care of her parents and she had a legal right to do that. The advice given to Edward was that he could probably invite his daughter to live in London with him once she had finished school, at age fourteen, unless the mother objected strongly and sought a court order to send her back to her family, Dorothy could choose for herself where she would prefer to live after her eighteenth birthday.

Three more years of living with the Bryans! How can she bear such a thing? She's already lived with them since she was five years old, heaven forbid. I can only make sure that every summer, every Christmas, every Easter will be spent with me. That each month she will be with me for a weekend. Somehow this will have to work. I worry about what it will do to my precious girl emotionally, having her foot in two such different worlds. At the very least, she will have a taste of a better life. My Dorothy will stay strong.

So the life of travelling back and forth between Longton and London began, and Dorothy was strong. She adjusted to each location when she was there. What other choice did she have? Her life with family in Longton was one thing, and her life in London with her father was another. As simple as that.

BILLY

*B*illy was only twenty when he met and married Nancy Poole. She worked in the decorating shop at Ainsley's factory, where Billy was a plate maker. He had noticed her sitting outside on the low wall at the front of the factory, eating her sandwiches at lunch time. She was plump, with dimples in her cheeks so deep he could have put his finger into them. Her hair was a rich auburn colour and her eyes pale blue. Tommy thought she was lovely, but couldn't pluck up the courage to speak to her.

Nancy noticed the attention. As Billy walked passed her every day while she was eating her lunch, he blushed a deep red as he glanced at her from under his cap. One bright Friday afternoon as Nancy worked at painting daisies onto six-inch plates, a note was dropped on her work bench by a lad from the clay shop. It was from Billy, who had decided he would never be able to talk to her, so had written to her instead.

It had taken him several nights, sitting at the kitchen table with the gas lamps giving off a meagre light, to write and rewrite the short note.

Dear Nancy,

I would like to take you to the pictures. If you would like to go with me, could you make it on Saturday night? I could meet you outside the Empire at 7 o'clock if it suits you.

Yours sincerely,

Billy Bryan

Nancy giggled as she read the note. *Nice writing,* she thought. *What harm would it do to go to the pictures? Billy's pretty good looking, although he's very thin. I bet he'd pay for me.*

Nancy turned over the paper, and wrote with her pencil to say she would meet Billy at the Empire on Saturday. Her heart was racing as she called over the errand girl in her factory shop, and gave instructions to take it to the clay shop, and give it to Billy Bryan.

Billy didn't remember much about the pictures they went to see that Saturday. He counted himself a lucky young man to be there with such a pretty girl, and he even rested his arm on the wooden rest between them, and brushed against the top of her arm a couple of times. When the pictures were over, and they were outside the theatre, Billy walked beside Nancy, trying to get the words out.

"Can I walk ya home?" he stuttered quietly.

"Alright, ya can if ya like," Nancy replied, not looking at him.

They walked, in silence, neither of them daring to begin a

conversation. They finally arrived at Fenton Old Road, where Nancy lived with her mam.

"I had a nice time." Nancy said, when they reached her front door.

"Me an all," mumbled Billy. "Will ya go out with me again?"

"Alright, I'd like that."

They arranged to go to Longton Park the following afternoon, then for a cup of tea at the pavilion. After that, they ate their lunch together every day, and went out for fish and chips after work on Fridays.

Kissing Nancy was like flying, Billy thought. Her lips were so soft and her hair smelled of flowers. He wanted to live with her forever, and asked her to marry him after only three months of walking out. When Nancy told her mam Billy had proposed, she expected a lecture on her being too young and him being unsuitable, but Nancy's mam did neither.

"He seems like a nice young man, duck," she said. "You can live 'ere with me if ya like. It will save you 'aving to find somewhere and buy your own stuff, and it will be company for me. You're both so young, and you'll be able to save some money if you live 'ere."

"Mam, thank you," Nancy said with tears in her eyes. She knew it had been a struggle for her mam after her dad had died so young. She and Billy would be able to help out with the house expenses, and they could be married quickly now they had somewhere to live.

Billy was delighted with the arrangement. He liked Mrs. Poole. She didn't drink like his mam, and she did some cooking—just plain food, but better than chips and peas every night. Mrs. Poole said they could have her bedroom with the double bed, and she would sleep in Nancy's bed, which made Billy turn red to the roots of his hair just thinking about sharing a bed with Nancy.

All these plans had been made before Billy mentioned anything to his parents.

He blurted it out one night as they were gathered in the kitchen eating their chips.

"I've met this girl named Nancy, and we're getting married in two weeks at the chapel. We're going to live with 'er mam in Fenton. Everything's arranged. You can all come to the wedding if ya like." He paused for breath, trying not to look at his father, who suddenly choked on his chips.

"Married? You?" gasped Emma, dropping her chips back into the newspaper. "Who'd 'ave you? You're only twenty! Whoever this Nancy is must be daft, takin' you on. Living with 'er mam? 'er mam, takin' the money from ya every Friday? Money that's rightfully mine." She took Billy by both his arms and shook him with all her strength. "You bloody fool. Is she knocked up? Is there a bun in the oven? That's the only reason you would be gettin' married."

Billy cast his mother's hands away and took a step back.

"Nancy's the best thing that ever 'appened to me. She's lovely, and innocent, and no, she's not pregnant. I can't wait to get away from this 'ouse, but mostly away from you, you old cow." He aimed this last remark straight into his mother's face. "I take it back that you're welcome to come to the wedding. I don't want any of ya there."

Billy stormed out of the house, grabbing his coat on his way through the door. Why had he expected anything else? All his mam ever did was make things seem seedy and disgusting. Well, he would soon be rid of the whole lot of them.

The wedding took place as planned. Tom, Tommy, Eddy, Madge and Dorothy all walked to the chapel together, and at the last minute Emma came through the side door and sat on her own at the back of the big sanctuary, her face like stone. After the short exchange of vows, Reverend Black, the minister blessed the young couple and they walked out of the church with Mrs. Poole.

Two weeks after the wedding, Nancy persuaded Billy to take her to his family home to meet his parents. He begged her not to persist in this, but Nancy was adamant. She didn't want a cloud hanging over their marriage. She wanted him to reconcile with his mother and the rest of the family. Billy reluctantly agreed, and walked to Edward Street with Nancy on his arm, one windy Sunday morning.

Dorothy saw them coming down the street as she polished the front step with the red polish. She was relieved that the other two boys were at home, so that Billy wouldn't have to face Emma on her own. She was worried about the reception the young couple would receive from her grandmother, who constantly ran down Nancy as a money-grabbing harlot.

"Gran," Dorothy shouted, jumping up from the step, rag in hand. "Our Billy 'ere with Nancy. They're coming down the street."

Emma jumped at the sound of Dorothy's announcement. *How dare he bring that Nancy 'ere, when 'e knew 'ow she felt. Oh yes, she knew alright. A young woman with only one thing on 'er mind—catching a nice young man like our Billy. She would just sit at 'ome now, not bother to work, with 'im bringing in the wages to cover the living expenses, which is probably more than 'e should pay, being it's 'er mam whose benefiting. Well, I'm not giving an inch. If our Billy thinks I'll make them feel at 'ome, 'e can think again. Getting married when 'e's just a boy, doing me out of 'is wages every week, and giving money to some bloody unknown woman in Fenton.*

But things were very different once Billy and Nancy walked through the parlour and into the kitchen. Nancy, with her warm smile and dimples, greeted Emma with an affectionate hug, not knowing that nobody ever touched Emma—not even her own family.

"I'm so 'appy to meet ya at last," smiled Nancy, making her way over to Tom standing with his mouth open by the fire. "Nice to meet ya too," she continued, placing a kiss on Tom's cheek before he could back away. Nancy was so full of smiles and dimples that Tom and Emma couldn't think of a word to say. Billy took it as a very good sign and stepped forward to shake his father's hand, touching Emma on her shoulder as he reached around her.

"Well, I'd better make some tea," mumbled Emma, clattering the cups together and busying herself with the ritual of tea preparation.

From that day onwards, Nancy was a firm favourite in the Bryan household. She was like a ray of sunshine on a cloudy day, bringing her lovely personality into a depressed and downtrodden family.

TRAGEDY

*D*orothy and Dora encouraged each other through the first year of senior school, spending as much time together as they could. Madge had left school when she turned fourteen and was working at Ainsley China as a trainee lithographer (putting decorative transfers onto china). She was paid very little for her ten-hour days and all she earned was given to Emma.

Emma sat at the kitchen table waiting for her three working children, Tommy, Eddy and Madge, to come in from work and hand her their pay packets. She opened each one, and gave the bearer pocket money from their wages—enough money for the boys to have a few pints at the pub, go to the pictures, bet on the dogs. Less to Madge, who didn't need money, according to Emma.

It was a hot summer in 1933 and everybody in the Potteries counted the days until wakes week, when the whole pottery industry took a week-long holiday—the first week of August. Apart from Christmas day and Boxing day, it was the only time off for the hard-working people living in the industrial

Midlands. Dorothy could hardly wait, because she would be going to London on Monday to visit her father for a whole week of bliss.

On the Friday night at the beginning of the wakes week, Emma sat at the kitchen table as usual, waiting for the money to roll in. The boys were excited about the week's holiday coming up and came into the house in good spirits.

"Mam, can we 'ave extra pocket money this week?" asked Tommy, the spokesman for himself and Eddy. "We want to meet our Billy at the marl 'ole for a swim tomorra' and then 'ave fish and chips and then go to the pictures."

"I suppose you're takin' girls out," Emma grunted. "Money for girls, that's what ya want. I can see right through the both of ya. Well, me rightful 'ouse money isn't goin' on bloody girls I don't even know, I can tell ya that." But she gave them an extra shilling each anyway.

"Thanks Mam," they both said at once, not believing their luck to get the extra money without more of a fight. Now they'd be able to go to the Brown Duck tonight for a pint as well as their big day out tomorrow. There would even be enough to go to the town hall dance on Monday night. What a great wakes week they were going to have.

Dorothy went to Dora's house on Saturday morning, before the people at number twenty-seven were stirring. Friday night had been a late night for all, with wakes celebrations at the pub going on until the early hours of Saturday morning. She left a note on the kitchen table for her grandmother, Emma. *Gone to Dora's all day.* She skipped up the steep hill and ran along to her friend's house. Dora's family was going to Trentham Gardens on the bus and had invited her along.

There was a new open-air swimming pool in the Gardens

attracting people from all over the Potteries, even though you had to pay to swim there. During wakes week the buses streamed into Trentham Gardens carrying the would-be swimmers, their bags packed with towels and food and drinks, ready to make a day of it.

Dora's dad, Mr. Jones, had told Dorothy to be at their house early, because the swimming pool would only take a set number of people, then the gates would be closed and they would have to wait for people to leave before being allowed in. Dorothy was so excited, even though she didn't know how to swim and didn't own a swimsuit. Dora's mum had borrowed one for her from her sister, who had girls a bit older than Dorothy.

The day was warm and sunny and, as predicted, there was already a queue for the swimming pool when Dora's family arrived. They joined the throng of holiday makers waiting for the pool to open, knowing by their early arrival and their position in the line that they were among the lucky ones who would gain access. They filed into the changing rooms, where Dorothy pulled on the black swimsuit she had borrowed, feeling embarrassed as she undressed with Dora, her two older sisters and Dora's mam. Mrs. Jones gave Dorothy a bag to put her clothes in and offered her a blue towel to wrap around herself. Then, carrying their bags, and gripping their towels tightly, they paraded out of the change room and onto the pool deck.

"Look at this," gasped Dorothy as she stared at the scene before her. "It's beautiful. How huge it is, and look at the diving boards, and all that water."

It was indeed a sight to behold, and the five of them hurried over to join Mr. Jones and the two boys, where they had staked out a spot under the shade of a large oak tree.

"Well girls, what do you think of this then?" Mr. Jones beamed. "This will be a grand day. Come on Mam, let's be first in the water."

He took Mrs. Jones by the hand and they both jumped into the blue water, laughing and shivering as they splashed each other, then calling for the others to join them.

Dorothy held back, she was nervous and didn't want to make a fuss. Tears sprang to her eyes, not because she was scared, but because Dora's family were so happy and her mam and dad were having such fun together, something Dorothy never saw in her own family.

"Come on, duck," shouted Mr. Jones to Dorothy. "Take the plunge. I'm 'ere to 'elp ya. You can touch the bottom just 'ere, so don't worry. We'll 'ave ya swimmin' in no time."

He came to the side of the pool and held his arms out for Dorothy, as she sat on the edge of the pool and lowered herself in beside him. Mr. Jones held onto her arm with a strong hand until she was used to the water, then all the older Joneses came to help, teaching her how to float and how to move her arms and legs. Soon she was having fun, splashing and laughing like everyone else. It was a perfect day.

Mrs. Jones had made cheese sandwiches and sweet home-made pickle, with lemonade to wash them down. Sugar and butter tarts were handed around after the sandwiches. They all sat on their towels under the shade of the big tree and ate their picnic. Dorothy thought it was the best day she could remember. She would tell her father all about it when she saw him on Monday.

At the end of the day, they piled onto the bus, tired and sunburnt and happy.

Dorothy waved goodbye to the Joneses at the top of her street and dragged her feet down the hill towards her Grandma's house. Why was the door open? Why were there neighbours hanging around outside? Why were people crying and shaking their heads?

Dorothy quickened her step and ran past the people and into the house, where there were more people in the parlour and crammed into the kitchen. Emma sat with her head in her hands leaning on the table. Tom sat in his chair by the fireplace with his eyes closed. Tommy and Eddy stood in silence by the kitchen door. Everything was very quiet, except for Madge sobbing in the corner, with Dolly standing beside her hugging her close.

"What's the matter, Gramma?" asked Dorothy.

Emma didn't look up or answer her.

Dolly came over to Dorothy and took her hand. "It's our Billy, duck," she explained. "He was swimming in the marl 'ole and there was an accident. Billy was drowned."

"Is he dead?" asked Dorothy.

"Yes, duck. He's passed on, and 'im so young. Now yow, Madge and Eddie go over to Aunt Sarah's, she's expecting ya. She'll give ya some lobby. All three of ya stay with her until we fetch ya back. This is no place for young 'ns tonight."

With that, Dolly ushered the three youngest Bryans through the parlour and across the street to Aunt Sarah's.

Dorothy couldn't help thinking about the beautiful day she had spent with the Joneses. How much fun they had had in the pool splashing and playing, while all the time Billy was dead. Her head was full of thoughts of Nancy and what she was going through. They had only been married for a few months, and now she was a widow. Poor Nancy. What would she do now?

Aunt Sarah found a place for them to sleep, not wanting to send them home that night. Madge and Dorothy squeezed in with the other girls, the double bed crammed with bodies at the top and bottom of the bed. Eddy squeezed in with the boys in the other bedroom, happy to be given a small space rather than go home.

The funeral service was at the Central Hall Methodist Chapel, the church of choice and preference for the working class in Longton. Dorothy walked, with the family, behind the coal man's wagon, pulled by Old Jessie, the shire horse. Mr. Meakin, the coal man's father, sat next to the casket on the back of the wagon, looking appropriately somber. He had a black top hat, which he used for funerals, to give an extra touch of sobriety to the occasion.

The casket was carried into the chapel by six men, all sweating from the heat of the day. Nancy walked behind the casket, with two of her uncles supporting her, one on each arm. Her legs were wobbly and she felt sick. She felt trapped inside a dream, a nightmare, that wouldn't end—she longed to wake up and see Billy standing beside her.

The family sat in the front pew, dressed in their begged and borrowed funeral clothes. Dorothy's black dress was provided by Dora's mother, who went to the chapel storage room and chose a dress from the box marked 'mourning clothing.' It was a bit big for Dorothy, but she was grateful to Mrs. Jones, as Emma would never have bothered to kit her out with a black dress. Madge was wearing a black skirt from Aunt Sarah, pinned in at the waist to make it fit and a black shawl from Mrs. O'Neal, who lived two doors away, covering up her only blouse, which was dark blue.

The entire population of Neck End attended the service, all genuinely sorrowed by the loss of a young man of twenty-one in the prime of his life.

Dorothy sat gazing at the organ pipes at the front of the chapel and listened to the mournful, haunting sound they made. The hymns were all sad. The women sobbed their way through the words, the men didn't sing at all. The minister looked weary and spoke about the better life in heaven that Billy had gone to.

The following day Dolly walked to Longton station with Dorothy and Madge to put them on the train to London. Dorothy already had the money for her ticket and the family had taken up a collection for Madge's ticket.

"Best send our Madge to London with Dorothy," Dolly had said to the rest of the family. "Edward won't mind when 'e knows what's 'appened. It'll do the girls good to be out of the way. I'll go to Ainsley's China factory and tell them Madge won't be at work next week. I think the girls should stay away for a bit, just 'till things 'ave settled 'ere."

Edward had been at the station on Monday to meet Dorothy, but she hadn't arrived. He wasn't particularly worried, as there had been other times when the trip to London was cancelled for one reason or another. It seemed to him that the people his daughter lived with had little regard for his expectations, but changed plans to suit themselves. This was probably the case in this instance. He hoped Dorothy was only delayed and would arrive the next day.

It wasn't Tuesday, but Wednesday when Dorothy finally made it to London. Edward was there to meet her—he intended to be waiting every day just in case. He hardly noticed the sulky girl accompanying her.

"This is Madge, Father," announced Dorothy. "She came with me because our Billy drowned and Gramma didn't want us around. I 'ope you don't mind."

Edward was taken aback at the casual way Dorothy announced Billy's death. He needed a few minutes to gather his thoughts before turning his attention to Madge.

"Hello Madge," Edward welcomed the strange girl who wouldn't make eye contact with him. "You are welcome to stay as long as you like. You have both been through such a terrible tragedy and we will make sure you rest and recover while you are with us."

TOMMY

$\mathcal{I}$t was a dreadful time at the Bryan house. Billy, being the first-born son, had been Tom's pride and joy. Tom sat in a state of stupor for days following the funeral, staring into the unlit fireplace. He didn't talk to anybody; he didn't go upstairs to bed, but just dozed in his chair. Even his drinking mates from the street couldn't get him to go to the Brown Duck for a pint to "ease the grief."

Tommy, who felt he had lost both a best friend and a brother, rode his bike into the countryside around the town, disappearing for hours at a time. He wanted to be as far away from the memories of Billy as he could get. After the wakes week, he went back to work and didn't talk to anybody about the tragedy.

The house was an unhappy, silent place, where the misery seemed to cling like a fog.

Tommy would never fill his brother's place. His father, Tom, seemed to have shrunk overnight. He had always been a man of few words. Now it was almost impossible to involve the old man in a conversation.

"Come on, Faytha," Tommy tried his best to raise some kind of response from the shrivelled man sitting in his chair glaring into the fire. "Let's go up the pub for a pint. Ya can't just sit there. Come on out."

"Sod off! Leave me alone. Bloody botherin' me. Can't a man sit and think?"

Tommy shrugged and walked through the parlour and out the front door, slamming it behind him. He was struggling with Billy's death himself. The flashback of the morning they had gone swimming in the Daisy Bank Marl hole played over and over in his mind. Him and Eddie setting out early to walk the two miles to the next town of Fenton, just under the railway bridge and then another fifteen minutes to Mrs. Poole's house, where Billy lived. It was a fine day! Everything they could have hoped for to begin the wakes week holiday. The two brothers were in high spirits, with money in their pockets, their swimming togs on under their trousers.

Billy was sitting on the doorstep waiting for them, a big smile lit up his face as his brothers walked towards him.

"I'm off then Nance," Billy had called out. "See ya later on, duck."

Nancy came to the door, smiling at her two brothers-in-law.

"'Iya lads," she greeted. "'ave a good time swimmin'.' Come back for some oatcakes and cheese after. Mam's making an apple pie as well. Ya'll all be 'ungry after your swim."

"Thanks Nance," Tommy and Eddie said in unison as they walked off towards Daisy Bank.

There were lots of lads on the rim of the marl hole when the three young men arrived. Billy led the charge down the thick piles of broken china covering the sides of the upper part of the marl hole, jumping and leaping down the steep slope. At the rim of the clay hole, the three brothers tore off their outer clothes, anxious to join the dozens of other lads in the warm, clay-coloured water. They had swam there dozens of times before. The day was particularly fun because of the rain the week before, which had filled the swimming hole deeply. The slimy sides of clay were slippery, making the slide down into the water excitingly fast. Boys from twelve to twenty whooped and yelled as they made the journey from rim to water in a matter of seconds, the Bryan boys joined in enthusiastically.

Billy and Tommy kept an eye on their younger brother Eddie as the water play was always wild in the marl hole, pushing each other under the water, jumping onto each other's backs, diving down and tugging at legs to bring the swimmer down. All part of the fun! Tommy saw his big brother Billy in front of him, swimming away to duck one of his mates, and hurled himself on top of his back. He felt the air leave Billy's lungs as he disappeared under the water. Tommy threw back his head and laughed—he had got him good that time. Except Billy didn't pop to the surface. He was obviously trying to give his brother a scare by holding his breath and staying under water, probably swimming away to come up in a crowd of swimmers where he wouldn't be noticed.

Tommy scanned the surface of the marl hole, searching for signs of his brother. Where was he?

"Bill, show yaself, ya big codger," Tommy yelled.

The other swimmers suddenly stopped their revelry and became silent and still, treading water as they all looked over at Tommy. Eddie was the only one moving as he swam towards his brother.

"What's up Tom?" he said, his face full of worry.

"Our Bill, stop mucking about," yelled Tommy, desperate now. The water seemed suddenly cold, the clay coloured murkiness denser, as the realization that more than a few minutes had passed and Billy hadn't surfaced.

Tommy went over it and over it. He'd hit his brother pretty hard. It was his fault. He'd killed him. All the young men in the marl hole had started to dive down, searching the depths of the clay hole with their hands. Tommy and Eddie remained on the surface, suspended in time, dreading each swimmer emerging from the water. It took more than thirty minutes before a shout went up from Walter Green. Walter dove again, accompanied by two other lads. Billy appeared on the surface supported by the three divers, his head lolling forward onto his chest. He was a funny grey colour. He was completely still.

Tommy didn't remember how they got out of the water. He remembered somebody helping him, grabbing him under his arms, lifting him onto the side of the hole where a wooden trellis provided foot holds.Billy was ahead of him, being carried by two of the divers who had found him. Too late. Billy was dead and it was Tommy's fault.

How does a young man of nineteen deal with the horror of causing his brother's death? How could he stop the recurring nightmare of the cold water around him, scanning the surface for his brother's face? The guilt settled on Tommy like a physical rock he carried around inside him. He thought of little else, only finding some solace when riding his bike into the countryside.

When Tommy wasn't thinking about his brother, he was seeing Nancy's face as she stood beside the grave. She had looked across the freshly dug grave, straight into Tommy's eyes, as the casket was lowered into the earth.

She knows! Why else would she be looking at me like that? She knows and she hates me.

Tommy would never be able to look into Nancy's eyes again. Never be in her presence without feeling the weight of guilt crushing him. Nancy was only twenty years old and a widow. He had been the cause of her grief, of her tears and heartache. He had destroyed her life as well as Billy's.

Nobody talked about the drowning at home. Eddie kept out of Tommy's way as though he didn't want to remind his brother, or remember himself. People at work wouldn't meet his eyes and avoided sitting with him. Even Dolly, his older sister, stayed in her own home in the next street being comforted by her husband Norman.

Tommy had wheeled his bike out of the backyard and set off into the country, escaping from the memories. He had eaten his tea, standing in the kitchen in silence as Emma dished out the lobby Aunt Sarah had brought over. Now he couldn't wait to leave the dirty streets behind and head towards Trentham where there were trees, green grass, flowers and pretty houses. He always imagined he lived in one of those pretty houses, with a wife who cooked for him and made things like apple pie.

Tears sprang into his eyes as he peddled further into the countryside. He wanted to keep peddling for ever until he was so far away from Edward Street that he couldn't find his way back. Because then he wouldn't have to remember. Tommy knew that he didn't have the courage to follow through on his dreams, and it made turning around to head back the way he had come even more pathetic.

As he neared the old toll house, sitting at the crossroads where four roads met, Tommy saw a Bedford lorry travelling on the opposite side of the road. It was the only vehicle anywhere in sight. As the truck drew nearer, the solution to all the misery of the last two weeks appeared clearly to Tommy.

"I'll always luv ya Bill," he whispered as he drove his bike into the front of the lorry.

A KNOCK ON THE DOOR

*I*t wasn't unusual for Tommy to be out after dark on a Friday night. He often took his bike and went for a joyride into the country. Eddie sat at the table in the kitchen reading a comic. Emma sat silently on the horse hair sofa drinking a bottle of stout. Tom was in his usual chair, bottle of beer in hand, staring into the fire, his pipe balanced between his teeth.

The loud knock on the front door made them all jump. Eddie was the first to the door.

"Is this the Bryan house?" asked the bobby, and when Eddie nodded the young policeman didn't wait to be invited, but walked through the parlour and into the kitchen.

It was like a replay of two weeks before, when another young policeman had knocked at the door and brought bad news. Neither Tom nor Emma moved. Both frozen like statues in their seats as the bobby told them Tommy had been killed in an accident. The few simple words ripped into their already crippled lives.

Eddie ran to Dolly's house, and then to Aunt Sarah's house, and soon number 27 Edward Street was full of people all in disbelief that another son had died. Tom had soiled his pants, so Norman helped him to the back yard lav to help him clean up, Eddie brought his father's other pair of trousers from the bedroom. Pots of tea were made, sweetened heavily to help with the shock. Emma still sat on the sofa, supported on either side by two of her sisters.

The following morning a telegram was sent to London, by Dolly, urging Madge and Dorothy to come home on the earliest train. Not telling them the bad news, but just that they were needed at home.

Edward read the telegram and suspected a tragedy had probably occurred. Otherwise the family would have been happy to leave the girls with him for the agreed time. He drove Dorothy and Madge to Euston Station to catch the eleven o'clock train, which would get them into Longton by four thirty.

As the two girls arrived home and saw the house full of people, they were instantly aware that something terrible had happened. The crowd parted, letting the girls through to the house. The whispers around them, "Poor girls, poor Tommy, poor Emma and Tom, what a tragedy........."

Another funeral, another burial. Sleepless nights, tears, tea. More tea.

Dorothy stayed at Aunt Sarah's, rather than be anywhere near her grandparents. She slept in the double bed with Aunt Sarah's four girls, three at the top and two at the bottom, their legs interlacing in the middle.

Some memories are not easily recalled. Pushed into the far recesses of recollection, covered in thick layers of protection and shame. Dorothy knew why Billy and Tommy had died so tragically, but she would never tell. She had "prayed them dead," when she was a little seven-year-old girl. The two brothers thought it was a lark and had dismissed it long ago as "lads will be lads." Neither of them had given it much thought over the years. For Dorothy, the two deaths triggered the deeply buried memory of the boys laughing as they pulled down her knickers and forced her legs wide. Emma and Tom were at the pub. Eddie was playing football with the boys on the street. Madge sat watching with a smirk on her face as her brothers "played" with Dorothy.

Dorothy's "peepee" was sore for days afterwards. She hated Tommy and Billy. She prayed they would die. She knew she couldn't tell anybody. Nobody would believe her. Madge had even threatened her about not telling. Why had the big boys wanted to do that to her? Would they want to do it again? Dorothy had to have a plan, so that it never happened again. There was ample opportunity. The children were often left unsupervised and Madge couldn't be counted on to help her. Eddie, however, hadn't been a part of the abuse. He was already eleven years of age and Dorothy thought of him as almost grown up.

"Eddie, can I ask you something?" Dorothy began.

They were sitting on the front step watching other children kick stones up and down the street.

"All right, what?" asked Eddie.

"Can you make sure I'm not on my own with Billy and Tommy?"

"Why?"

"They're very bad boys," Dorothy whispered.

"What do ya mean?" persisted Eddie.

Dorothy took the plunge and decided to tell.

"They pulled down my knickers and touched my peepee," she blurted out.

Eddie stared at his little niece in horror. She wouldn't make it up, he thought. She's just little.

"When was this then?" Eddie asked.

"When you were playing football on Tuesday," the little girl answered. "I'm scared they'll do it again, or something worse."

Eddie didn't know what to say, or do. Tommy and Billy were his heroes, his big brothers. Why had they done something like that to a little girl? He'd heard the lads in the street talking about what they'd done, or would like to do to girls, but this was different—this was Dorothy. He was ashamed for his brothers. He needed time to think.

"Don't worry Dorothy," he said. "I'll deal with it. They won't bother ya again."

"Thanks Eddie," Dorothy said. She was absolutely sure Eddie would take care of it.

Eddie thought about nothing else all day. What was he to do? As he watched Uncle Felix, coming home from work, walk down the street, he knew exactly what he would do. Uncle Felix, the most moral, God-fearing man he knew—that was the answer to this problem.

Eddie waited outside the house for Tommy and Billy. As they reached number twenty-seven, Eddie stepped forward to meet them.

"A word with the two of ya," Eddie said.

"Oh yeah. What kind o' word, big shot?" Tommy smirked.

Eddie plunged in with both feet before he lost his nerve.

"If either of you ever touch Dorothy again, I'll tell Uncle Felix. You keep your hands off 'er."

Tommy and Billy looked at him in disbelief. They couldn't believe Dorothy had told Eddie about their bit of fun. They both started laughing at the same time.

"I'm bloody serious," said Eddie, not backing down. "She's just a little lass. Ya both should be ashamed."

"It was just a bit o' fun, Eddie," Tommy said. "We were just 'aving a look, like."

"No more, or so 'elp me, Uncle Felix will deal with the two o' ya."

It was no idle threat. The brothers never went near Dorothy again. She ignored them and pretended they didn't exist. The memory of what they had done was buried deep.

She had lived with Billy and Tommy for more than six years, but after Eddie's intervention they had never paid her any attention. She had been as invisible to them as she was to her grandfather, Tom, and she felt guilty about her lack of grief at their deaths. It made life more difficult for her because the atmosphere at the Bryan house was more toxic than ever. Her presence even less wanted than before. To lose their two sons so tragically, two weeks apart, but still have Dorothy was the burning unanswered question in their minds.

Aunt Sarah talked to her sister, Emma, and persuaded her to move Eddie's narrow mattress into the bigger bedroom with herself and Tom, and let the girls move upstairs into the small bedroom and out of the parlour. Dorothy and Madge were both happy with the new arrangement, which gave them some privacy and a place to call their own.

Life was never the same after the deaths of the two oldest boys. A pall hung over the house, dragging the already depressed inhabitants down to an even darker place. Tom never recovered from the loss. He never spoke to Emma directly again, as if somehow it was her fault. Emma went through the motions of making meagre food, half-heartedly brushing the dirt out of the house, visiting her sisters and drinking her stout.

Dorothy kept busy, helping Aunt Dolly with her little ones. She had two rambunctious boys and was pregnant again. Her husband, Norman, was always sick and often couldn't work, so Dolly would have to pick up what work she could at the pot bank on Market Street. The two boys were left with Emma and Tom during the day, but when Dorothy came home from school she would take them both home and give them something to eat, staying to watch them until her aunt came home from work. Dolly worked until she went into labour, then hurried home to give birth to a baby girl, she called Gladys.

Times were very tough for the young family. Aunt Mary-Ann moved in with them for a few months, supporting them with food and rent money. She was the aunt everybody sent for when life became intolerable.

The one shining light in everybody's life was Nancy Bryan, Billy's widow. She gave birth to a girl eight months after Billy's death and called her Nancy, ever to be called "Young Nance," by the entire family. Nancy was a faithful daughter-in-law and visited Tom and Emma every week, bringing her smile and loving nature into that dark, sad place. Dorothy loved Nancy more than any other member of the family and looked forward to her weekly visits, when she would hold "Little Nance" and sing quietly to her. The baby was like her mother, happy and smiley with deep dimples in her cheeks and fair curly hair. The few hours they spent with the Bryan family each week was like a sprinkle of sunlight showered onto the house. Even Tom perked up and said "thank you," to Nancy who always brought some of her mother's baking with her.

Emma took the money donated by family and neighbours to help the Bryans through their hardships, and ordered large oval photographic portraits of their two dead sons. They were hung in the kitchen alongside the portrait of Queen Victoria. A reminder every day of what they had lost.

Tragedy hadn't finished with the family. Life dealt a cruel blow to Aunt Dolly. A year, almost to the day, after Tommy's death, Norman Cooper died. Dolly would have to continue her work at the pot bank, but worse, she would have to leave her three small children with her parents.

JUBILEE

*I*n April of 1935 Edward made absolutely sure that money was sent to Dorothy for the train fare to London. Dorothy was thirteen years old and was very used to making the journey by then. Enclosed in the envelope with the postal order was a letter to the school, asking permission for Dorothy to be excused from classes for three days. Dorothy took the letter to school and handed it to her teacher, Mr. Donkin, who frowned as he read the contents. He looked over his glasses and glowered at Dorothy.

"Mr. Wrightson must think it is common practise for students to miss school, but I declare it is not. I realize he is your father, but what possible reason could he have that would be more important than your education?"

"I think it's a surprise, Mr. Donkin," explained Dorothy. "My father knows 'ow important education is, and 'e would never ask me to miss school unless it was somethin' really special."

"This will have to go to the headmaster. I will let you know by the end of the day if permission has been granted."

As promised, Mr. Donkin asked Dorothy to stay after her last class.

"The headmaster has reluctantly given his permission for you to miss three days of classes, though I would not have given my permission."

Three days extra in London! What was it all about?

Euston was a blaze of flags hanging from every available part of the vast station. Dorothy ran to where her father was waiting below the clock.

"What's goin' on?" she asked, panting from the zig zag run through the other passengers. "There are flags everywhere and look at that enormous picture of the king."

"Pretty exciting stuff," laughed Edward. "King George the fifth has reigned for twenty five years on May 6th, which is Monday. The whole country is having the day off by order of the King. London will be celebrating for days. Wait until you see the Mews decorated with Union Jacks. Mrs. Arnold couldn't wait for you to arrive, she is so excited and has the whole weekend planned."

Edward was constantly busy for much of the weekend driving his taxi, but, as promised, Mrs. Arnold had planned ahead and knew exactly where Dorothy and herself would have the best view of all the events.

There were new clothes for Dorothy laid out on her bed. A beautiful blue dress, trimmed with lace around the neckline and sleeves and a cozy white bolero jacket. The drawers and wardrobe were still filled with the everyday clothes Dorothy kept in London.

"We have to get you a Dorothy bag to go with your new outfit," said Edward, smiling at his daughter as she paraded around in her new dress. "A lady must always carry a bag for her personal items."

It had become a tradition, Father buying a bag. He insisted on calling each bag a "Dorothy bag," and there were quite a collection of different ones stored on the shelf in the wardrobe.

"I doubt I need another bag, Father," Dorothy laughed. "I'm sure there's several I could use which would look good with this dress."

"Ah, but it's not like having a new one, now is it?"

Between taxi customers, Edward picked up his girl and took her to Harrods to shop for the perfect bag. A white puffy bag with a silver clasp and a long strap to wear on her shoulder. Dorothy loved it.

Her new outfit was worn on Saturday night, when Chilworth Mews held its street party. Tables and chairs were brought out of everybody's flats and houses and lined up down the middle of the road. Food seemed to miraculously appear, as many trips in and out of the homes were made to cover the table with every imaginable tempting dish. Mrs. Arnold had made individual chicken pies, with cranberry sauce, an enormous sponge cake decorated with "Silver Jubilee" across the top, and her famous rum punch.

Chairs were filled as the people gathered, chattering and laughing in the warm spring evening. Many toasts were drunk to King George as the people of Chilworth Mews celebrated. "God Save Our King" could be heard, not only from the people in the mews, but echoing from the streets around them. Dorothy had never seen such a feast in her life, nor people enjoying themselves so much. She ate until she couldn't eat another bite and

ANN BROUGH

even tasted some of the rum punch, with Father's permission.

Barney Millward, who lived at the end of the mews, played the piano accordion and everybody sang along to the old favourites. The tables were moved to the side of the road to make room for the dancing. Mr. and Mrs. Arnold led the dancing, encouraging everybody to join in, which they did— spurred on by the many toasts they had drunk. Dorothy felt like a princess as Mr. Arnold whisked her away in a polka, his face glowing with excitement, his feet nimble as a young man.

What a party! And the weekend had only just begun. How she wished her father had been able to be there, but he would be driving his taxi late into the night.

The best place to see the King and Queen on Sunday was Hyde Park. The royal couple were to take a carriage ride through the park at three o'clock and Mrs. Arnold, Dorothy in tow, was in the park by ten in the morning to stake out their spot. A picnic lunch had been packed, although Dorothy thought she would never eat again after Saturday night's party. However, the cold chicken sandwiches with watercress were welcome as they stood guarding their territory.

As three o'clock approached, Mrs. Arnold handed Dorothy a Union Jack to wave. There were thousands of people in the park waiting for the King's carriage and Dorothy was so relieved that they had a spot at the front of the crowd. The anticipation grew as murmurs spread through the crowd that the carriage was in Hyde Park. Soon, soon, Dorothy would see the King. She could barely breathe.

122

"Wave your flag Dorothy!" yelled Mrs. Arnold. "Here he comes!"

Dorothy stood on tiptoe and waved her flag like mad.

"God save the King!" she yelled, with the rest of the people. "Hooray, hooray!"

There was the carriage. There was the King. He seemed to look right at Dorothy, waving his hand backwards, very slowly. He was very small—not like a king in her imagination. She thought a king should be imposing and grand, but this king was slight and old and sour looking. He looked tired and sick and his uniform and hat looked too big for him. They had waited five hours for a five-second glance at a shrivelled-up little king.

As the crowds dispersed, Mrs. Arnold clasped Dorothy's hand and headed home.

"Wasn't he wonderful, Dorothy?" she said.

"Oh, he was Mrs. Arnold," agreed Dorothy. She would never have hurt Mrs. Arnold's feelings by saying what she really thought.

Monday was the BIG day. The regal procession from Buckingham Palace to St. Paul's Cathedral for a worship service. Dignitaries from all over the world would be there. The whole royal family would also be there and Dorothy hoped she would catch a glimpse of the two little princesses.

Mrs. Arnold was up early, preparing the picnic lunch again. This was to be a long day out for them. They made their way to Buckingham Palace after breakfast and joined the already growing crowd. The King and Queen would ride in an open carriage to give the people a good view of them as they made their way down the Mall through Marble Arch and across London to St. Paul's. Because of the crowds, Mrs. Arnold and Dorothy had to stake their spot behind three rows of people already lining the Mall. It would have to do! At least Dorothy was tall for her age and would be able to see over the heads of the people standing in front of them, with the help of a small wooden stool, made by Mr. Arnold for the very purpose.

Dorothy never forgot the Jubilee celebration that day. The flags and buntings strung along the route, the guard bands, the horse guards, the dozens of carriages, led by the King's carriage. He still looked small to Dorothy, but on such an occasion how could she not cheer and shout like everybody else. The other carriages sailed by, but they didn't see the princesses, only multiple military uniforms and elegantly dressed ladies and so many horses it was sometimes hard to even see the carriages.

As soon as the procession had passed, Mrs. Arnold grabbed Dorothy's hand, put the stool into her big canvas bag and ran towards the palace, following the crowds. All were trying to find a good view of the balcony at Buckingham Palace, where the King would appear later that day. This time they managed to get a spot only one line back from the people at the railings surrounding the palace. A great place to see the balcony. They were all in for a very long wait!

Dorothy sat on her stool and nibbled on the snacks in the canvas bag, an apple first, then butter biscuits and crisps, washed down with ginger beer. She was hot and needed the toilet, but no chance of that. She squeezed her eyes shut and tried not to think about it.

"Mrs. Arnold, I really need the lav," muttered Dorothy, when she could wait no longer.

"Oh dear. I don't know what to tell you, luv. I could do with going myself, but we don't want to give up our spot do we?"

The lady standing in front of them was a pearly queen, from the east end of London. She had a big hat covered in pearls and feathers, and there were hundreds of pearls sewn all over her dress.

"If you save my place, I'll take the girl over to Bird Cage Walk, then you can go when we get back," she said to Mrs. Arnold. "They've put up screens between the barracks and the road. One for men and one for women. Makes sense doesn't it luv? Can't go all day without a pee."

Dorothy went with the pearly queen, pushing their way through the crowds to the far side of the Mall, where the toilet screens were set up. Behind the screen was a long trench dug into the grass between Bird Cage Walk and the railings around the guard's barracks. The railings had a screen of green canvas tied to them, to give extra privacy. Women were squatting beside the trench relieving themselves, all in good humour as they shared the community experience. Embarrassment put aside, it was a case of use the trench or have wet knickers. Dorothy squatted between a large redheaded woman and an old lady dressed all in black, who seemed to be having a great deal of trouble holding up her skirts. It felt very good to pee!

The pearly queen and Dorothy found their spot by the palace railings and Mrs. Arnold set off on her toilet run.

Then it was a matter of waiting and waiting for the royal family to return from St. Paul's, have a meal together, then finally come out onto the balcony to wave. The carriages entered the gates, but were too far away for Dorothy to see them. She could see only the wheels as they disappeared through the archway into the inner courtyard. She hoped it would not be too long before the King appeared on the balcony. She let Mrs. Arnold sit on the stool for a spell, as her legs were very tired. They had eaten all their food and drank all their ginger beer. Dorothy hoped the wait was worth it.

A cheer began in the crowd as they saw the large glass doors open onto the balcony and the King and Queen step through to greet their people. They were joined by the rest of the royal family and Dorothy stood on tiptoes on her stool to see the princesses. There they were! Princess Elizabeth and Princess Margaret! They were very small, only nine and four years old, but they waved and smiled and looked so beautiful. Dorothy was thrilled beyond words. It was worth the wait.

That night, even though it had been such a tiring day, Edward insisted on taking Dorothy to dinner to hear all about the day she had spent watching the Jubilee. The Criterion Restaurant was on Piccadilly Circus, where Jubilee celebrations were in full swing throughout the night. Music and dancing in the streets made it almost impossible for Edward to drive to the Criterion and park the car. Once inside he ordered a wonderful meal of cream of tomato soup with goat cheese for them both, followed by roast lamb, baby potatoes, fresh peas and mint jelly for Dorothy and a seafood risotto for himself. Dorothy was almost sleeping by the time her dessert of white chocolate mousse arrived.

"What a wonderful day you have had my darling," Edward said, leaning forward to take her hand. "Now I think it's time I took you home to bed. I hope you will always remember what you have seen today, especially the two little princesses. You saw history today, Dorothy."

She lay in bed that night, the moon shed a pale light onto the

Prussian Captain as he stood at attention on the bedside table. Dorothy touched the top of his worn helmet.

"What a day I've had," she whispered to him. "But you are the smartest soldier of them all."

As her eyes closed sleepily she hoped that one day she would stay with her father and this bed would be hers forever.

LEAVING SCHOOL

*T*he last day of July was sticky and hot. The boy and girls in the top class at Edensor school watched the big clock on the wall of their classroom slowly ticking off the minutes. It was their last day of school. They would have to go out into the world and find a job. For some it was a day of celebration, having tolerated the lessons, the teachers and all the rules; they couldn't wait to be done with it. To be able to earn money, and be grown up. For others it was a day of despair. These students had enjoyed learning, even admired and loved some of their teachers. Where would they work? What would they do? Would they see their friends?

Dorothy, at almost fourteen, had mixed emotions. She had been a good student, well liked by her teachers. She felt she was only beginning to learn about the world she lived in, had only scratched the surface of mathematics, science, history and geography. Yet she had a good idea of where she was going and what she would do. The plan had been set many years ago. When she left school, she would go to London to live with her father.

Life was hard for Dolly since Norman's death. She worked hard providing for her three youngsters, managing to pay the rent on her small house. Dorothy helped out with the children when she could, feeling sorry that they were with Emma and Tom during the day while Dolly was working. Dolly's Aunt Sally had sent money for the train fare for Dolly and the children to visit her in Blackpool for the wakes week holiday. If anybody deserved a holiday by the sea, it was Dolly.

Tom Bryan's sister, Sally, had married up in life, and she owned a small hotel in Blackpool. Sally had completely disowned her brother because of the life he led. But family roots went deep and Sally was fiercely loyal to her brother's children, knowing their lives had been miserable because of her brother.

"Dorothy," began Dolly. "Can ya come with us to Aunt Sally's in Blackpool? The young'ns love ya and it'd be such a 'elp for me. Ya'd like to see ya Aunt Sally wouldn't ya?"

"I'm supposed to go to me Dad's in London, ya know," explained Dorothy. "But I know 'e'll understand if I go a bit later on. I'll 'ave to ask Aunt Mary-Ann for the train fare though."

Dorothy ran to Aunt Mary-Ann's to ask her for the money for her fare.

"You're a good girl Dorothy," her aunt said. "Dolly needs a holiday. It will do 'er the world of good and I know Sally will take good care of you all."

She reached into an old tin on the sideboard and handed the money to Dorothy.

"Take this now. There's enough for the train and a few bob

left over for some fun. 'ave a good time, duck."

"Thank you, thank you," smiled Dorothy. "We'll 'ave a great time, thanks to you. I can't wait to see the sea and sand. The little 'ns are goin' to love it."

On her way home, Dorothy called in at the Central Hall Chapel to use the phone. Reverend Oliver was preparing for an evening service, but greeted Dorothy warmly.

"I need to phone me father Reverend Oliver. Can I please use the phone?"

"Go ahead Dorothy. Remember, only in an emergency."

He looked over his glasses at the young girl, gathered up his prayer books and hurried away.

"Thank you," shouted Dorothy through the open door.

Edward was expecting his daughter for the month of August, when they would discuss her permanent move to London. But once she had explained why she wouldn't be there for the first week, he smiled to himself. Of course, she wanted to help her aunt and go to Blackpool. He remembered the last time he was in Blackpool, when Dorothy was born. One of the happiest moments of his life.

"Thank you for letting me know, darling. Have a very good time and I'll see you next week. I'll be there to meet the train on Monday. And Dorothy, enjoy Blackpool—you were born there."

As she hurried to tell Aunt Dolly she had the money for the train, Dorothy pondered her father's last words. Born in Blackpool? Why had she been born in Blackpool? She tucked the words into the back of her memory. She would ask Aunt Mary-Ann. She would tell her why.

WORKING GIRL

*A*fter the holiday in Blackpool with Dolly and her three children, Dorothy went to London as planned. The routine was so engrained by now, that she automatically dropped her clothes outside the bedroom door and plunged into the warm, lavender-scented bath water.

I'm free! I'm free! No more school. I can stay in London. I can begin a new life here with my father. I don't have to think about working at a pot bank. I don't have to worry about Grandad and what mood he's in. I don't have to go up the yard to the lav or pay to have a bath in the bath house, I don't have to eat chips every night. I can stay here.

Only one thing lay heavily on Dorothy's mind.

What about Aunty Doll? What about the boys, Albert and Stanley? What about little Gladys? Who would help out now?

The week in Blackpool had been such fun. They had spent every day on the beach, even in the rain. The boys with their socks and shoes off running in and out of the cold water, with Gladys chasing after them, her skirt tucked into her bloomers. Aunt Sally had made them feel so welcome. They had one big room between the five of them. A double bed for Dolly and Dorothy and a double bed for the three children. The sheets were spotless and they each had a pillow to themselves. They also each had a towel. There was an indoor bathroom down the hall, shared by all the guests, but they didn't care. Having an indoor lav and running water was luxury for them all.

The air in Blackpool was clear and fresh and after a few days their cheeks were rosy and their eyes sparkling. Aunt Sally served a hearty breakfast each day and gave them a bag full of sandwiches to take with them for lunch. They all arrived back at the house in the late afternoon, starving hungry from spending the day outdoors. They sat at a proper table, with a tablecloth and ate the plentiful food before them. Steak and kidney pie, fish and chips, sausage and mash, and shepherd's pie. Every night a different meal.

Dolly looked and felt better than she had in years. She dreaded going back to her real life, working long hours to try and make ends meet.

Emma was hostile when they arrived home.

"Back are ya?" she sniffed. "Bin on 'oliday 'ave ya? Well, well, well, muckity mucks. Somethin' I've never done. What makes the two o' ya think ya should 'ave 'ad a bloody 'oliday? Should a bin me, that should. Not the likes of ya two bloody no-goods."

Reality hit them quickly listening to Emma's tirade. Dolly quickly gathered the children and headed home to the next street. Dorothy followed to help her and to get out of the house she'd only just stepped into.

"Dot, don't go to London tomorra," begged Dolly. "Ya know I can't manage without ya. The young uns'll miss ya. There's no food in the 'ouse either."

"Me father's expecting me Aunty Doll. I 'ave to go. I'll go ask Aunt Sarah for some bits and pieces of food to tide ya over, all right?"

As Dorothy lay in the warm bath in the flat, she saw Dolly in her mind, trudging home from work in the rain, head down, shoulders drooping. She saw the boys and Gladys with their noses pressed to the window in the parlour at number 27 Edward Street, waiting for her to pick them up. No Dorothy to take them home early and rescue them. She saw Dolly opening the door to her cold, dark terrace house, the three children running in ahead of her. No fire made, no kettle on the hob, everything damp and cold.

"Father," said Dorothy when she sat down for dinner with him at the dining table. "I need to talk to you seriously."

As always, on her trips to London, Dorothy's midland accent disappeared.

At fourteen, Dorothy was already tall and slender. Edward was amused by her grown up demeanour, but hid his smile with a slight frown of concern.

"Yes darling, what is it?"

"I know we've talked about my moving to London permanently now I've finished school, but I can't help feeling very badly for Aunty Doll. She relies on me to help with the children and I don't think she will be able to manage without me. She has very little money, even though she works very hard, and the boys are rambunctious and hard to handle."

"Your Aunt's predicament is not your concern, Dorothy," Edward butted in.

"No, please. Let me finish. I think if I stayed to help for one more year, Dolly would be on her feet and able to cope better. Gladys will be almost old enough to go to school by then. My plan is to learn a trade and live with Dolly. That way we can share the expenses."

"Darling," Edward interrupted again. "Please think about this carefully. We've talked about you coming to live with me for so long. I would be so disappointed if you decided to stay in Longton. So would Mr and Mrs Arnold."

"Father, don't do this to me," Dorothy said, her voice firm, her eyes boring into his. "I have thought about it and it's the right thing to do. One year won't make a big difference to you or me, but it will to Aunty Doll. Don't make it more difficult, please. I will still come every month and for the holidays." The little girl living inside her adding, "Anyway, I still have my cooking badge to complete in Girl Guides. Nellie Tart would be so upset if I didn't finish it."

Edward realized it was futile to argue with his strong-minded daughter. He tried to cover his bitter disappointment. He had waited years for Dorothy to live with him permanently. She had a beautiful room of her own, all the food she could eat, stylish expensive clothing and people to take care of her who loved her dearly. Yet she chose to stay in the grim poverty of Longton to help her Aunt. So much like her mother in many ways. She would have her own way.

Dorothy was determined not to work in the clay, which was dirty and very hard work. She chose to work as a pottery decorator. She heard through her cousin, Stan Marshall, that there may be a chance of jobs at the Phoenix works in the

High Street. The owner of the Phoenix works was Thomas Forrester and he employed hundreds of workers. Dorothy made her way to the office at the factory entrance, where other girls were waiting in line. She had her school leaving certificate with her, showing her excellent marks and good teacher comments. She had washed her hair and shined her shoes and because of her height and confident manner, she looked older than the other girls. The applicants were asked to wait while the assistant manager looked over their papers. He came into the waiting area, to look over the girls, asking them to step forward as he called their names.

Success! She was hired as an apprentice gilder. She would learn how to put bands of gold around the china ware, a skilled and delicate art.

"I'm moving in with our Dolly," Dorothy informed Emma. "I've got a job at the Phoenix works and start on Monday. I'm helping Dolly with the rent and food until she's on her feet."

"Over my dead body, my girl," yelled Emma. "Ya will do no such thing. Living 'ere all these years with us keepin' ya and now ya want to turn ya money up to bloody Dolly."

"Me father's sent ya money all these years and none of it spent on me. How dare ya say I've cost ya money. Without money from me dad ya wouldn't 'ave 'ad cash for stout every night."

Emma flew at her granddaughter, catching her at the side of her head with a swipe of her hand and knocking her across the room.

"I'm out of 'ere," screamed Dorothy. "And another thing. There'll be no more ten shillings coming from London every month. That's over."

Dolly couldn't believe Dorothy had the nerve to leave Emma and Tom and move in with her.

"Ya'll 'ave to sleep with me Dot," she said. "That's the only place for ya."

"It's all right Aunty Doll. I don't mind sharing a bed with ya."

Dorothy liked working on the pot bank. She felt grown up, especially when she picked up her pay packet on Friday after work. The first money she'd earned. She counted out the coins and gave Dolly eight shillings, keeping two for herself. Dolly cried when her niece counted the precious shillings into her hand. Now she could afford to buy stewing beef and make lobby, maybe some good tea, another towel, even cheese. She felt rich.

The three Cooper children still had to go to Gramma Bryans to be taken care of during the day, but their home life was improved with Dorothy as part of the household. They made it through each day, knowing there would be good food and a warm fire to go home to, and, more importantly, their mam and Dorothy to cuddle them.

Dorothy didn't regret her decision to stay in Longton. She assured her father, on her visits to London, that she was happy staying with Dolly.

As in Jubilee year, Edward insisted Dorothy be in London for King George VI's coronation. Coronation day was May 12, 1937 and the entire city of London was celebrating. It was an unexpected King who was being crowned. His brother, Edward, had abdicated the throne because he wanted to marry an American divorcee, Mrs. Simpson, which was not allowed. As head of the Church of England the monarch could not marry a divorcee. The younger brother, George, had not been raised as heir to the throne. He was withdrawn and shy and had a speech impediment—a most unlikely king.

Dorothy and Mrs. Arnold made their way to East Carriage Road, alongside Hyde Park, to watch the procession as it made its way from Westminster Abbey back to Buckingham Palace after the coronation. The King and Queen travelled in an open golden coach so that everybody could see them clearly. Dorothy didn't need a stool to stand on this time, and she jumped up and down as the carriage drove slowly past, waving madly at the royal couple dressed in their royal finery. She thought King George looked very much like his father—small!

"God save the king. God save the king!" shouted the crowds of people lining the street.

The Mews was, once again, turned into an outdoor dining room, with tables and chairs from the flats and houses brought out, and placed in a long line down the centre of the road. Union Jacks flew from every house and street lamp. The tables were laden with good food and drink. Everybody joined in the dancing and singing until the early hours of the morning. Dorothy danced until her feet were sore.

"Come on Father," she said, grabbing Edward's hand and pulling him from his chair. "Come and dance with me."

Edward had never danced in the street. In fact he had only left the confines of the flat a few moments before to greet his neighbours and drink the king's health. Now he was spinning around with his daughter, laughing and joining in the fun.

"Dorothy," he panted, "You'll have me singing next. Enough now, darling."

They both collapsed into their chairs, arms linked, enjoying just being together.

Edward had to admit to himself that, despite being disappointed Dorothy wasn't living with him, he was very proud of her and the decision she had made at such a young age—not choosing an easy life, but a much more difficult one. She was a brave girl with a great spirit.

LIVING WITH EDWARD

The year Dorothy was to live with Dolly and the children morphed into two, then three years. Somehow the time slipped by and it was never the right time to leave the needy family and move to London.

As often happens in life, the decision was made for Dorothy. She came home from a Saturday night out with the Marshall girls to find a man sitting at the kitchen table. Dolly introduced him as Joe McMurray. He worked at the same factory, she said. He was a small, thin man with a droopy moustache and he blinked his eyes all the time, as though he was trying to clear his vision. He smiled at Dorothy and whispered something she didn't catch. It was late and the children were supposedly in bed, but Dorothy caught sight of Albert peering around the door leading upstairs.

Joe McMurray became a frequent visitor. According to the local women he was trying to "Put his feet under the table," or "Set his cap at Dolly," both expressions meaning "courting." After Dorothy's trip to London one weekend, she found evidence of Joe's presence in the bed she shared with Dolly.

Her pillow had a greasy stain where his head had been and there was a definite smell of male body odour on the sheets.

The two boys treated him with suspicion. They stayed outside playing until dark, not wanting to be in Joe's company in the house. Dolly's little girl, Gladys, was jealous of the attention her mam was giving to the strange man— making him tea, even baking scones. She followed Dorothy around like a shadow when she was home, looking for the attention she was no longer getting from her mother.

After three years experience in gilding, Dorothy earned a good wage. Even after sharing expenses with Dolly, she still had a good allowance for herself. She bought smart clothes and make up and curled her hair in the latest style. Her frequent trips to London educated her on what the young women were wearing in the big city and Edward was always willing to take her on a shopping spree. The clothing he bought for her had not been taken to the pawn shop since Dorothy had moved out of Emma and Tom's house, so she had a wardrobe of fashionable outfits to choose from. The Marshall cousins had great fun borrowing clothes from Dorothy. On their nights out together, they all met in Aunt Sarah's parlour to get dressed and do each other's hair, with much laughing and giggling. Then off to the town hall in Longton for a night of dancing, where the young men stood around the ballroom daring each other to ask the beautiful girl with the dark hair for a dance.

As Joe moved in with Dolly, Dorothy moved out.

"Moving back 'ere?" Emma greeted her granddaughter with disdain. "I 'ear our Doll's got a fancy man. So, ya've lost ya place in the bed 'ave ya?"

"I'm just stayin' for a day or two," answered Dorothy, lugging her suitcase up the stairs. She had only brought a few necessary things with her, knowing the best clothing wouldn't be safe in her grandmother's house. The rest of her possessions were packed in a trunk she had borrowed from Aunt Mary-Ann, waiting at Dolly's house until she was ready to leave.

"I'm going to London to live with me father," announced Dorothy as she came back down the stairs. "I should 'ave gone three years ago when I left school. Now Dolly's settled and the children growing up, I'm leavin' for good."

"Don't bloody come back," said Tom from his chair in the corner. "Nothin' but trouble since ya were born. Bloody girls!" He puffed on his pipe, sending clouds of smoke into the small kitchen.

Three days later Dorothy was on the train to London, having used the chapel phone one last time to call her father to let him know. Edward was in his usual spot, under the clock, at Euston Station to meet her.

"This time is forever, darling," he said, hugging Dorothy close.

Mrs. Arnold was waiting at the flat. She didn't have to run a bath any more, or burn the clothes Dorothy wore, but she had prepared her room and bought some fresh lavender soap and crystals for her favourite girl. There was also a new "Dorothy handbag" sitting on the bed, made of soft brown leather—a gift from her father.

After all the years of travelling back and forth between Longton and London, Dorothy was finally in London to stay. She unpacked her trunk and suitcase for the last time, humming to herself and feeling the freedom she always felt when she was in the flat with her father in the next room. She set the old tin soldier on her bedside table, giving him a kiss on his worn head. She thought of giving him back to Edward, feeling she didn't really need the toy's inspiration of bravery now she had her father near, but maybe she would hold onto him for a while longer. A wise decision! How could she have foreseen what was ahead, and how she would need to hold the tiny toy again.

Dorothy was hired at the chemist shop in the High Street. She found the position purely by accident. She had been walking through the neighbourhood, on her way back from an errand for Mrs. Arnold, when suddenly her stomach had cramped with such force it doubled her over. She felt dizzy and nauseous and sat down on the steps of the chemist shop to rest. The chemist came out to see who was sitting on the steps and found Dorothy, ghostly white and in obvious distress.

"Oh, my stars!" Mr. Roland said. "Whatever is going on here?"

He helped Dorothy to her feet and took her into the shop.

"I'm all right," whispered Dorothy, who looked anything but "all right."

Mr. Roland gave her a drink of water and a pill to swallow.

"Get this into you. You'll soon feel better," he said kindly, guessing it was Dorothy's menstruation giving her some trouble. He'd seen it all before, many times.

Dorothy did soon feel better. That's when Mr. Roland asked about where she lived and how old she was and if she would like a job helping him out at the chemist shop.

It was the perfect job for her. Mr. Roland, the chemist, was a kind man with a good sense of humour, always telling jokes and playfully teasing Dorothy. There was a small radio in the shop, which played quietly all day, encouraging Mr. Roland to whistle and hum along to the latest tunes.

Mrs. Arnold was elated to have Dorothy living at the flat. On Dorothy's day off, the two of them would go to a museum. Mrs. Arnold loved museums and London had more than any city in the world. The Victoria and Albert Museum was Dorothy's favourite. It was such a grand building to begin with, and she loved the beautiful art displays from all over the world. It took many visits before they had completed the entire museum, then it was on to the next one. Mrs. Arnold also loved music and took Dorothy to an occasional opera or symphony concert.

"I will have to book an appointment to see you," laughed Edward. "You are always so busy. Mrs. Arnold has you hopping all over London, keeping her company. I hope you are not too bored, darling."

Dorothy laughed at the thought. "Never, father," she said. "I enjoy everything we do. But you always come first. You will never need an appointment."

Edward loved taking Dorothy out to dine. The Trocadero was his favourite restaurant. He taught Dorothy what the menu meant and how to order her food. She was adventurous, trying out the different dishes, so different from anything she had ever tasted. They enjoyed each other's company, sitting across the table from each other, sharing their thoughts about life. Dorothy telling her father all about her life in Longton, her kind great aunts, the Marshall cousins who were her best friends, the struggle of the working poor to make ends meet, the poverty she saw every day. Edward listened, hanging onto Dorothy's every word. In turn, he told her about his wife, Amy, and the house in Maidenhead.

"Does she know you have a daughter, father?" was Dorothy's question.

"Yes. I told her about you soon after you were born. She said I was never to speak of it again, and I never have. You must understand that we have a very different relationship than most married couples. To put it delicately, Amy prefers women, so the intimate part of our union has been non-existent. However, we have been married for a long time and are good companions for each other. I have enjoyed an independent life, free of the usual commitments of marriage. Except for weekends and vacations when Amy needed an escort, I have been master of my own life."

Edward paused as the waiter poured more wine into his glass.

"Your birth was my wildest dream come true, Dorothy," he continued. "I never imagined I would have a child. If your mother gave me nothing else, she gave birth to you and I am forever in her debt for that. The joy you have given me is beyond comparison to anything else."

Sometimes Edward took Dorothy with him in the taxi. The film studio Edward had a contract with booked the taxi to be in two screen shots in their latest movie. Edward had to have the taxi on the set by 5.00a.m. and asked Dorothy if she would like to see how a movie was made. What young woman would have refused such an offer, particularly when Edward told her the star of the movie was Laurence Olivier, the up and coming actor. They stayed all day watching the filming. It was the most boring day of Dorothy's life. Nothing happened for hours on end and everybody seemed to be sitting around drinking tea. The taxi scene was shot more than fifteen times. The same thing over and over. The taxi being driven down a street, that was it! Laurence Olivier wasn't even there. By the end of the day Dorothy fell asleep lying on a wooden bench with her head on her father's lap.

"Next time there's a film being made," she murmured as they made their way back home late in the evening, "Please don't ask me to go with you."

Dorothy wrote letters to her cousin, Marion Marshall, telling her all about London. She heard back from Marion about the family. Life didn't change much for any of them. Dorothy had no desire to go back to visit. She was happy to stay with Edward and immerse herself in her new life.

WAR

*M*r. Roland became more and more agitated with the rumours of war circulating London. He scoured the newspapers every morning. Listened to the radio news constantly.

"I don't like the sound of things, Dorothy," he said. "Mr. Churchill thinks this Hitler is a dangerous man. He thinks Germany is getting ready for war. I have a lot of faith in Mr. Churchill, even if the Prime Minister thinks he's just a warmonger."

Dorothy half listened to Mr. Roland's assessment of the political situation. She was more interested in displaying the new Max Factor products on the glass shelving in the tiny cosmetic department. The new shades of lipstick were so lovely, she thought she might buy one on Friday, out of her wages. It seemed everybody who came into the chemist shop talked to Mr. Roland about war. Dorothy guessed it was because most of them were old and could remember the last war.

"Father, do you think there will be a war with Germany?" Dorothy asked Edward as they sat down to dinner. "Mr. Roland talks of nothing else all day long."

"War with Germany?" Edward said. "No, darling. Germany is our ally now. The German people are wonderful, stable, well-educated people. The Great War was a huge mistake. They don't want war, especially not against Great Britain. Mr. Churchill is full of himself. Loves to hear himself talk. Don't you worry yourself about war. It will never happen."

In everything Dorothy trusted her father. He had never lied to her or given her unwise counsel. As the newspapers and radio continued to talk of war, she resolutely believed Edward was right and there would be no war with Germany. But the overwhelming evidence to the contrary was mounting daily. Joyce Jenkins, who lived in the flat above the chemist shop, showed Dorothy a letter from the government advising the family to prepare to send their two boys, aged ten and thirteen, out of London should England go to war. Tears rolled down Joyce's face at the thought of her boys being separated from her. Dorothy decided not to tell Edward about the letter, and pushed it into the back of her mind, hoping that if she ignored it, it wouldn't be true.

Two weeks after Dorothy's seventeenth birthday she joined Mrs. Arnold for breakfast, finding the housekeeper pouring over an official-looking paper.

"What do you think luv?" Mrs. Arnold said. "What a worry. We'll have to show your father as soon as he gets back from Maidenhead. He's not going to believe it."

Mrs. Arnold tried to look brave. Tried to convince herself and her young friend that they would all be safe, even if the worst happened. But her wrinkled old hand shook as she handed the paper over for Dorothy to read.

The paper informed the residents of 14 Chillworth Mews that they were to report to the local primary school on the following Saturday morning between eight o'clock and noon to be fitted for a gas mask.

"Why would we need a gas mask, Mrs. Arnold?" asked Dorothy.

"Because they think the Germans are going to gas us all," answered Mrs. Arnold. "If there's a war, they want to be prepared. Better to be safe than sorry."

Edward was not impressed with the official-looking paper and refused to go to the primary school to be fitted for a gas mask. However, he did encourage Mr. and Mrs. Arnold and Dorothy to go.

"It's all lies of course," Edward explained. "They're making a mountain out of a molehill. Gas masks! Whatever next? The government are whipping the population into a frenzy with this kind of stupidity."

He sighed as he looked at his two dear old friends and his precious daughter standing in a row in front of him across the dining room table.

"They've probably drawn up some kind of census to make sure everybody does their bidding, so by all means the three of you go down to the school on Saturday and be fitted for your masks. We don't want to break the rules do we?"

"Father, you will go too won't you?" asked Dorothy.

"No, Dorothy, I will not go," he said. "Now don't fuss, my dear. I will not wear a gas mask. There will be no gas!"

The three residents of 14 Chilworth Mews duly reported to the primary school on Saturday morning. There were cardboard boxes piled onto trestle-tables in the hall of the school. There was a long queue of people waiting to be fitted, and when Dorothy had given her name and address to one of the officials, she was directed to the box number for her size, where a young woman helped find the right fit. The mask had a window at the front and straps which went over her head and were adjusted to give a tight seal—very important, explained the young woman, so it wouldn't leak. Dorothy was also given several leaflets about the kinds of gas that may be used against them and how the gas would smell. The population would be warned of a gas emergency by the air-raid wardens, who would carry wooden rattles around the neighbourhood to warn everybody to put on their gas masks. They were instructed to carry the gas masks with them at all times once the war began.

Mr. Roland was whistling a merry tune when Dorothy arrived at the chemist shop on Monday morning. He smiled his beaming smile at her and gave her the good news.

"The Prime Minister has signed a peace agreement with Mr. Hitler, my dear," he gushed. "It's just been on the BBC news. So all the talk of war was for nothing. I knew it of course. Silly really, spending all that money on gas masks and such. Worrying all the people when there was no need. Now we can all relax again."

London was full of the news of the peace agreement with the Germans. Edward was smug and wore an "I told you so" expression for days.

Rumours of a pending war, however, continued in the city. Winston Churchill, branded as a warmonger by the opposition party, made speech after speech about the evil dictator ruling Germany. Hitler ordered the German army to invade Czechoslovakia. There were reports of Jews, Poles and Gypsies being arrested for no reason. Reports of Nazi Party members enforcing Hitler's new laws of oppression against the physically and mentally handicapped, homosexuals, non-whites, in fact anybody who was not a pure born Aryan.

Dorothy heard the daily update from Mr. Roland. At seventeen, she was much more interested in what show was playing in the west end and whether her father would take time away from his business to escort her. Or whether the handsome young man who came into the chemist shop almost every day, sometimes for toothpaste, sometimes for mint imperials, would have the courage to ask her out.

Christmas was coming, and the flat was dressed in the usual seasonal decor, with holly and mistletoe, garlands of red and white flowers and tiny sparkling lights around the picture rails. Mr. Arnold bought an aromatic fir tree for the living room, standing eight feet tall, and Mrs. Arnold and Dorothy dressed it up in red, blue and silver balls, tinsel and bells.

The flat was also bursting with festive food. Mrs. Arnold had baked up a storm with Dorothy as helper and they had both searched the street markets for the best fruit, nuts and cheese. The larder was filled to overflowing, only the chicken and beef needed to be bought on Christmas Eve.

London had never looked more festive. Every store, hotel, restaurant, office or bank had covered their buildings with lights, probably in opposition to the grave political situation in Europe.

As if it had been ordered, London was covered in a thick layer of snow on Christmas Day. Edward and Dorothy set off to walk to Hyde Park after breakfast, wrapped in their warmest clothes, Dorothy in her new fur-lined boots. The park was alive with activity. Children building snowmen and having snowball fights, their parents joining in, laughing as the snowballs hit them. The Serpentine River had a film of ice and there was a crowd gathering on its banks as father and daughter approached. About thirty men, dressed in swimming suits, were standing on the banks of the river, shouting encouragement to each other, patting each other on the back, laughing and shouting.

"Let's all go together on the count of three," yelled a tall skinny fellow, with his hand in the air. "Ready? One, two, three."

The men took off in one long line onto the thin ice, which immediately broke and plunged them into the icy cold water. There was much squealing and coughing, as they scrambled out of the water. Towels were thrown around their shoulders by laughing wives and girlfriends and they slid off through the snow in their bare feet to the pavilion to dry off, cheering and congratulating each other on their bravery.

"A good way to celebrate Christmas," laughed Edward. "Though I would prefer to sit in front of a warm fire with a glass of brandy myself."

The year ahead loomed like a ghost waiting in the dark. Many feared what the future held for England. Each week brought news of more atrocities from the Third Reich led by their Chancellor, Adolph Hitler. By the summer, nobody was in doubt that there would be a war. If England was to take a stand against Germany, who had threatened to take over Poland, then war would be a reality.

On September 3rd, 1939, Dorothy listened to the radio with Edward and Mr. and Mrs. Arnold and heard the prime minister, Neville Chamberlain, announce that Germany had indeed invaded Poland and that Britain was now at war with Germany.

It hit Edward like a bombshell. He sat with his head in his hands for several minutes after the broadcast.

"I never thought it would happen," he finally muttered. "The last war was supposed to be the war to end all wars."

Dorothy held his hand and kissed his cheek. She knew he had a great love for Germany and its people. He had spent much of his childhood there, while his father lectured at various universities. Now, for the second time in thirty years there was war between the two countries Edward loved.

What was that terrible noise?

"Air raid sirens," shouted Mr. Arnold. "Everybody grab your gas mask and make for the shelter—Piccadilly underground station for us."

"Father, quickly," said Dorothy, tugging at Edward's hand. "Come on. There's going to be an air raid. Bombs will be dropping on us."

"You go Dorothy. Don't worry, darling. Hitler isn't going to drop bombs on us the first day of the war. I will stay here until the all clear signal is given. I can have the kettle on and make everybody a cup of tea. How's that?"

Mrs. Arnold grabbed Dorothy's hand and they sped to the underground, joining the throngs of people pouring down the stairs. They all found a place on the station to sit down. It was unusually quiet. Families sitting together in groups, looking at each other. Everybody wondering what would happen. Each with their own thoughts and fears. Dorothy lit a cigarette and watched the smoke curling upwards, mingling with the smoke from dozens of other smokers. She listened intently for the sound of bombs, but it was so quiet and eerie that she felt the goosebumps rise on her arms. How long would they have to stay underground? Not very long, as it turned out. After fifteen minutes the all clear was sounded and the people in the underground quietly went back up the stairs and out into the London streets. No panic. No noise. They just followed what they'd been told to do.

Air raid sirens were sounded frequently during the first few weeks after war was declared. Dorothy became sick and tired of grabbing her gas mask and running to the shelter. There were no bombs, and the people began to ignore the sirens and stay in their warm homes.

Mr. Roland decided it was time to retire and closed the chemist shop. He had a sister living in Oxford who invited him to live with her and the old gentleman was only too eager to get out of London. His only regret was leaving Dorothy without a job.

Edward had agreed that his daughter could continue to live in London until the first bomb was dropped or Hitler invaded England, whichever came first. Then she was to go back to Longton, away from the danger. Her eighteenth birthday had come and gone and she was eligible for military service. She couldn't wait to join up and help in the war effort. Everybody said the war would be over by Christmas and she wanted to at least serve in some way for a few months before she missed her chance.

The army, air force and navy were looking for women with two qualifications; able to drive or type. Dorothy had neither skill, so was told a firm "No." Girls like her were encouraged to join the land army and move to the country to work on a farm. *No thanks*, thought Dorothy. She was scared of cows and horses and didn't fancy baling hay or mucking out stables.

As the young men and women were called into service, jobs became vacant and Dorothy went to work in the ladies dress department at Whitley's Department Store. The war didn't affect her life in any way. She wasn't short of male companionship, and dated several young men who were suddenly brave enough to ask her out, spurred on by the thought of being called up for duty at any minute. The beautiful girl in the ladies dress department was much sought after, and Dorothy enjoyed all the attention.

Edward was very protective and gave his daughter advise on how to handle over-enthusiastic young men. Dorothy couldn't help smiling at her father as he tried to explain the reaction a beautiful girl had on the hormones of young suitors. He stuttered and stumbled over his words, but managed to get the message across that they were all really only after one thing and would try all kinds of ungentlemanly guiles to fulfill their desires. Dorothy took note and was firm in stopping wandering hands and kisses that lingered too long.

Dunkirk. The name of the French town was on everybody's lips. The whole of Britain held it's breath as every available boat sailed across the English Channel to evacuate the remains of the British Expeditionary Force, fighting in France. No customers came into the shop and the sales assistants were all gathered around the radios in their departments as the first of the boats made their dangerous journey to rescue the stranded men. Germany had invaded France, Belgium and the Netherlands on May 10th and the troops from those countries, along with British troops, had been beaten back to the sea by the power of the Third Reich. Beginning on May 26th until June 4th, 1940 a constant fleet of fishing boats, recreational boats, anything that would float, rescued more than 380,000 men from the beaches of Dunkirk.

The German forces were unbeatable, it seemed.

The bombs began to drop on London in September, a week before Dorothy turned nineteen. The air raid sirens could no longer be ignored. Dorothy went to bed fully clothed and with her gas mask beside her bed, ready for the siren that would awake her with a jolt. Because of the blackout, it was difficult to navigate the way to the underground station. Mr. and Mrs. Arnold depended on Dorothy to help them find their way. Edward remained in his bed, confident a bomb would not fall on him, sleeping through it all.

Paddington underground station was cold and damp. The platforms were lined with people every night, trying to sleep. They carried pillows, blankets, food, and even chamber pots —the inadequate toilet facilities in the underground were unusable after the first few nights. The pots were shared between families, and emptied onto the track in the morning. The smell was stomach-turning at best! A permanent low fog of cigarette smoke, laced with the odour of urine and sweaty bodies, permeated the platforms. Dorothy took a silk scarf with her and dotted it with lavender perfume, so that she could sleep with the scarf covering her nose and mouth.

Mr. and Mrs. Arnold and Dorothy lived so close to the station that they always found a spot to bed down. People coming into the shelter after them often had to fight for a few square feet of space. When space on the platforms was full, people slept on the escalators or even on the tracks. The first morning train rattling the rails would send them all scrambling onto the platform, amid cries and yells from the cramped jumble of bodies.

After several nights of air raids, Edward told his daughter to pack up her bags and return to the midlands. She didn't want to leave him. She begged him to let her stay.

"It isn't safe anymore, my darling girl," Edward said, holding Dorothy close to his chest. "Heaven knows I don't want you to go back to your grandparents' house, but bombs are not falling on Longton, at least not yet. I promise, as soon as it is safe for you to come back to London, I will let you know."

Dorothy knew she didn't have a choice. She prayed her father would be safe, and that she would see him again. Leaning through the window of the train, Dorothy waved and smiled, until she lost sight of Edward in the smoke from the engine. She sank into the dusty seat with a heavy heart, as the train began its journey north.

CALL UP

The young people of Britain were on pins waiting for their call up papers. Those between the ages of eighteen and twenty-five were called into service first. Either to the military, the land army or munitions.

Dorothy was living in Longton once more, working at Crown Pottery as a gilder. She was used to slipping into her life with the Bryans after leaving her father's home in London. She'd done it since she was eleven years old. Only this time it was difficult, because she had lived in London for more than two years and she had never intended or imagined she would leave.

Emma was her usual inhospitable self, greeting her granddaughter with scorn and disgust.

"Ya back are ya?" she hurled at Dorothy. "Well, our Madge won't be 'appy, havin' to share a room with the likes of you again. Father fed up with ya was 'e? I 'ope 'e sent some bloody cash, 'cause we don't 'ave the money to feed ya."

"Nice being back," answered Dorothy. "Don't worry, I'll pay

my way, and more. You won't go short because of me." She didn't plan to stay long at her grandparent's house. The war would be over soon and she would be back in London to continue her real life.

The call up papers arrived in November, telling Dorothy to report for duty at the Swynnerton Munitions factory on the following Monday. She had to take the papers into Crown Pottery to have them stamped as proof they knew about her being called into service. She had no idea what to expect. The only instructions she was given was the train times and where to report when she arrived at the factory.

Bullets, bombs, shells. The ammunition of war.

Dorothy was thrust into the crazy world of munitions. One among thousands of young women working in shifts around the clock to produce the weapons that would combat the mighty force of the German Reich.

Swynnerton was a massive complex of factories, joined by trench-like walkways between the different buildings. It began by employing 5,000 workers, Dorothy being one of them. None of the girls with Dorothy were told much, only that everything was top secret. They were not to talk to anybody about where they worked or what they did at work. The rules and regulations were a mile long, mostly safety issues, but the young girls thought they were a bit of a lark, not to be taken too seriously. A big mistake. As things turned out, the rules had to be taken very seriously.

Dorothy hated shift work from the very beginning. Rotating every week, she never made the transition well, only becoming accustomed to the time change at the end of each week, when another shift cycle began. She hated getting up at 5:30a.m. to be at the train station in Longton to get the train for the seven o'clock shift. She hated the afternoon shift from 2.00p.m. until 10.00p.m., as there was no time to see her friends or the Marshall cousins, no time to go to the pictures or dancing. Dorothy slept in most mornings, trying to catch up on her sleep from the early mornings the week before. Nights were the worst, beginning at 10.00p.m. until 6.00a.m., which turned night into day and day into night. Her stomach churned from eating in the middle of the night. She was always tired because nobody slept properly during the daylight hours. There wasn't time to see both pictures at the Empire, and the town hall dances were only just getting going when she had to leave. Dorothy usually ended up sitting around at Aunt Sarah's listening to the radio, and having a beauty session with her cousins, washing and curling each others hair and putting on make up and nail varnish.

The routine of the day became second nature. Changing into uniforms as soon as they arrived at the factories, hanging their clothes on pegs. Removing hair pins and tying on turbans, being careful to tuck in every strand of hair, or it could get caught in the machinery, or turned a different colour from the chemicals. Lastly slipping their feet into rubber-soled shoes or boots, so that there was no chance of producing a spark from outdoor shoes.

Lasting friendships were formed between the girls on the same shift, in the same shop, filling the same munitions. Dorothy caught the train with Elsie Berry and Olive Turner and became firm friends with the two of them, along with Winnie Mellor and Alice Copestake, who were always waiting on the train with seats saved for the three of them.

"Our Eddie's on leave from the sappers," Dorothy announced one cold winter morning as they waited for the train on the bleak station platform. "He doesn't have a girl. Do ya want to come home with me after the shift, Elsie?"

Dorothy knew Olive was walking out with a young man who was a miner and exempt from the armed forces, but Elsie was single. She was tall and awkward, but so was Eddie. Dorothy thought they'd make a great pair. She was right, they hit if off right away and Dorothy congratulated herself on matchmaking.

Elsie was the serious one of the five friends, rarely seeing the funny side of anything, especially when it came to their work. She was a rule-follower and would continually lecture her four friends on what they should, or should not, be doing. After a night shift, Dorothy, Olive, Winnie and Alice would always fall asleep as soon as they found a seat on the train. Elsie would never sleep and would wake them up when the train came to their station. They relied on her completely. So when Elsie had two wisdom teeth removed and had to miss a shift, she wasn't with the girls to wake them up.

It was totally silent and dark when Dorothy awoke. Olive snored softly on the seat beside her. Winnie was sound asleep with her face pressed to the window and her mouth open. Alice's head rested on her chest as she slept.

"Wake up," Dorothy shouted. "Where are we?"

The three friends awoke with a start, blinking their eyes in the darkness and grasping each other's hands. They put the window down in the carriage to look outside. Where were they? Why was everything so quiet? There wasn't a sign of another train or station.

With no Elsie to wake them up they had slept through the entire drop off route and were on a railway siding somewhere north—miles away from their stations. They quickly realized that when a train isn't in a station, the carriages are a long, long way from the ground. They were stuck!

As daylight appeared slowly in the eastern sky, the four friends hung out of the window in hopes that they would see somebody to help them. It seemed like hours before a man appeared three tracks over, checking the train tracks with a long metal bar.

"Help, help, help," they chorused. "Over here, help."

The railway man looked up in surprise. Nobody was supposed to be on the siding train. He ran over to the girls, who told him what had happened. He thought it was very funny and the girls could hear him laughing as he went to find a ladder to rescue them.

"I'm not surprised," Elsie said when they explained what had happened. "I'd better not miss another shift. You four need somebody to look after ya."

The only time Elsie relented her rule-keeping was when Winnie lost her pass. Elsie's shift had been switched for a month and she was on days when her friends were on nights. Dorothy persuaded Elsie to lend Winnie her pass to get onto Swynnerton, so that Winnie could go to the office and apply for a new one once she was on the grounds. None of them really thought it through.

On their tea break Dorothy went to the office with Winnie to apply for a new pass.

"How did you get into the factory?" asked the woman behind the desk.

"I borrowed me friend's pass," said Winnie innocently.

"That's an offence," the woman barked.

"Sorry," Winnie whispered.

"Stay here, both of you," were the next instructions from the woman.

She went into another office and used the telephone. Five minutes later two military police officers came into the office and marched Winnie and Dorothy into a room with no windows at the end of the corridor.

"We'll be late for our shift. We're only on tea break," Dorothy explained.

"You won't be going back to your shift," said the M.P. Officer. "We'll inform your department."

The interrogation was long and detailed, with the officers asking questions about their home life, their friends, where they were born, did they speak another language, had they been outside Staffordshire in the past six months. On and on. A report was added to their personal files and a strong reprimand was given. The two girls were both shaken up by the whole experience, especially when the police officer's final statement was, "You could have both been shot as spies."

Elsie was mortified that she had agreed to something illegal. She was called to the section head's office the next day, where a reprimand note was put in her file. She felt like a criminal.

The rules were not to be broken, and they now knew the consequences of breaking them.

The worst, most dreaded job the bomb girls did could be summed up in two words: Yellow powder!

Not all ammunition was filled with yellow powder, but

enough of it was. Dorothy, like all the girls, dreaded moving to the yellow powder shop. They were filling shells for tanks and anti-tank guns. The yellow powder ate through clothing and turned skin a horrible yellow colour, even with all the precautions they took. Huge vats of Max Factor cream and powder were provided, in the hopes that a thick layer of the expensive cream, with powder over it, would protect the skin on the face. Dorothy lathered her face in the perfumed cream, but it never worked. Within three days her skin was yellow and her dark hair had a funny red glow to it. An exemption from working in the yellow powder could be obtained if you were pregnant, getting married, or if your boyfriend was coming on leave. The yellow effect would take days to wear off, so that by the time skin was back to normal, it was time to go back into the shell shop again.

The work in every department was tedious and boring. Accidents happened when people were distracted or tired. Dorothy caught her finger in a bullet machine one shift. It could have taken her finger off—she was lucky it just split her finger and ripped off the nail. Every day there was news of an accident somewhere in the vast facility. A young woman had accidentally left a bobby pin in her hair and it had caused a spark. The whole shop was blown up. None of the girls ever knew how many were killed. They all tried to pretend it would never happen to them.

LONGTON STATION

The intense bombing of London had lasted for fifty-six days after Dorothy had left in September of 1940. Night raids continued until the following May, destroying much of London and leaving more than a million people homeless and over twenty thousand dead. Newspapers were full of pictures of the blitz on London and the stories of the heroes and victims, the brave people who lived with the daily threat of bombs and death. Most children had been evacuated out of London and billeted with families all over the country. Every day, when Dorothy saw the newspaper, or listened to the radio, she worried about her father. So far, the bombs had missed Edward's flat, even though there had been a couple of very close calls, with half the street destroyed in one raid. Edward still slept in his own bed, and refused to go to a shelter. He wrote to his daughter every week, giving her his version of the war, underplaying the danger, telling her how resilient the people were, despite their hardships. Urging her to stay where she was, out of danger.

London wasn't the only city being bombed. All the port cities were targets for the Luftwaffe: Liverpool, Hull, Bristol, Southampton. The industrial cities of Manchester, Sheffield, Birmingham and Coventry were smashed into rubble, leaving a swath of death, injury and destruction across England.

In May of 1941 Germany's focus moved to attack Russia. Although there were still sporadic bombing raids over England, after two months of quiet and infrequent attacks, Edward agreed that Dorothy could visit London occasionally.

Dorothy stood with her back to the wall, just outside the ticket office, keeping out of the way of all the thousands of heavy-booted feet. She was determined to continue her trips to London on the rare weekends when she wasn't working. This was the second such trip since Edward had given his permission and she was full of excitement at the prospect of being in London again.

Longton station was full of troops, all heading to London, going back off leave. Uniforms were everywhere, and friendly banter echoed between the soldiers, sailors and airmen as they waited for their trains. Mingled with the vast sea of young men were their families seeing them off, clinging to their sons, brothers, husbands or boyfriends while they could.

As Dorothy waited, she watched all the young men with their families. They were all her own age, between eighteen and twenty-four years old. She thought the sailors looked the most handsome. They always seemed to be laughing and having a good time, not like the soldiers, all dressed in itchy khaki uniforms. They always looked uncomfortable and stood up too straight, as though there was an officer around every corner. There were a only a few young men in air force uniforms on the station—those lucky enough to be given a few days leave. A small group of uniformed women stood chatting and sharing cigarettes. Dorothy envied them and wished she had made it into one of the services, but she hadn't been educated enough to get a posting. The military were looking for secretaries and drivers.

As she waited, a tiny lady, with her skirt down past her ankles and her hair drawn back in a bun at the nape of her neck, came out of the ticket office. A tall soldier took her arm as she almost tripped on the step.

"Watch yourself, Ma," he said. "Wouldn't want ya 'urting yourself before I catch the train."

She smiled up at her son, her eyes shining with love for him as she settled herself beside Dorothy, with her back to the same wall.

"Are ya all by yourself, duck?" she asked Dorothy.

"Yes, I'm waiting for the London train," Dorothy replied.

"Oh, good 'eavens, you're not going to London on your own, are ya, duck? The troop train isn't a place for a young woman all by 'erself, and you're not in uniform either."

"Don't worry about me," Dorothy told her. "I'm used to travelling on me own. Me father lives in London and I visit 'im when I'm not working."

Dorothy smiled at the small, kindly lady. It was nice of her to be worried.

"Well, duck, that just doesn't sit well with me," she continued.

"Me son 'ere will keep ya company and make sure ya're safe, won't ya Fred?"

For the first time Dorothy looked at the tall son. He was in the uniform of the Welsh Guards, more impressive than the general infantry, because they wore their caps so low on their forehead that it looked like they were always at attention. He blushed a deep red when Dorothy looked at him and didn't meet her eyes. His mother poked at his arm to get him to answer her.

"Ma," he finally said in a quiet, deep voice, "she probably doesn't want me 'angin' around 'er all the way to London. She says she's used to travellin' on 'er own." He blushed again, trying to avoid looking at Dorothy.

"Oh, our Fred, it would be nice to 'ave company on that long journey. It would stop any unwanted attention from other soldiers. I can't imagine being on me own on a train full of troops. Now, you stay with this young lady, like I've said." She pushed out her chin in a determined way and turned to smile at Dorothy. "Don't you worry now, duck, Fred will keep you company on the train."

Dorothy murmured a quiet "Thanks," but didn't think the son would follow through on his mother's plan, he looked so uncomfortable.

Kisses, hugs and tears blanketed the platform as the train chugged into sight, black smoke preceding the engine into the drafty station. Dorothy elbowed her way through the people saying their goodbyes and hopped into the nearest carriage. She wanted a seat and had to be quick on her feet to secure one. Tossing her bag onto the rack above her head, she plopped down into a window seat, letting out a sigh of relief. Fred plopped down next to her, balancing his kit bag on the floor between his knees.

"Ya needn't stay with me ya know," Dorothy said. "Ya've probably got mates on the train you want to be with."

"No, that's fine. Me ma was countin' on me keepin' you company, and that's what I'll do."

Did he blush every time he spoke? Dorothy wondered. *He hasn't even looked at me yet, and if he would just take off that cap, I could see what he looked like. He has a big nose, like his mam.*

The train was bursting with people. Standing room only, with very little room for everybody's feet between the people who were lucky enough to be in a seat.

Fred stole a couple of glances at his companion, feeling more than a little uncomfortable at his mother's interference. He could feel the heat rising in his face and wished he wasn't so shy. She was really beautiful!

I'm never going to make it through this journey, sitting next to her, thought Fred. *She's a looker, all right, and I'm just going to keep on blushing every time I look at her. I have to say something to her. I can't sit here for hours and not talk to her. She probably thinks I'm a real dope doing what me ma tells me. I'm sure she can see me sweating. Or smell me sweating—even worse. This uniform is so thick and hot and itchy. At least I can take me 'at off now we are on the train.*

Dorothy watched as her companion took off his peaked hat and put it on top of his kit bag. Now she could see his fair almost auburn hair and deep forehead, his kind blue eyes. She liked what she saw.

"So, ya stay with your dad, do ya?" Fred finally managed. "Where does 'e live, then?"

"He lives in a flat near Paddington Station. I love it there and wished I could live there, but my father thinks it's too dangerous. He doesn't even like me visiting on the weekends."

"I don't blame 'im. The Gerries 'ave been bombin' the 'eck out of London just about every night since last September, but the RAF 'ave fought back every step of the way. Brave lads those flyers! 'ave ya been goin' to London since the war started?"

"I was living with me father until the bombing started, then 'e sent me to Staffordshire to live with me grandparents. I didn't want to leave, but me father insisted, with a promise that I could visit when 'e thought it was safe. I was called up to Swynnerton munitions factory, so I only go to London when I'm not working. I didn't go at all while the Battle of Britain was on. Father said it was very bad in London, with whole neighbourhoods wiped out. 'E will never go to the shelter and 'as been very lucky so far, though I worry about 'im constantly."

Dorothy found it easy to talk to this quiet young man. She could see his eyes now, they were pale blue, with fair lashes. He had strong hands with long fingers, and a lovely smile. He shared his cigarettes with her, his fingers touching hers as he offered her the lit match.

Despite his blushing and discomfort, Fred had never talked to a stranger like he talked to Dorothy. The war changed people that way. He may not see her again, so why not enjoy her company while he could. Now he looked at her directly, meeting her eyes, which were dark brown and almond shaped. She had creamy skin and beautiful lips, painted a deep red, her lustrous dark hair was curled into a pageboy style. She was slender and dressed in a modern fashion, not like Fred's mother, who believed ankles should not be seen. In fact most of the women in the family and at the Chapel they all attended dressed the same way. No ankles, let alone knees, and no make up and definitely no smoking. It was also a Mission Chapel, where everybody signed a pledge that they would never drink alcohol. Very straight-laced and proper.

Maybe that's why Fred was drawn to the girl on the train. She was just about opposite to all the women he knew in his life. He smiled to himself as he imagined what his ma would think if she knew his companion smoked, and showed her knees when she sat down.

Halfway to London, Fred took a brown bag out of his kit bag and shared the food his mother had made for him. Cheese sandwiches, with homemade pickle, sugar and butter tarts and a bottle of milk. Dorothy laughed as she took half the food offered. She never brought food along for the journey, probably because there was never any food to bring from Emma's kitchen. The food from Fred's ma's kitchen was delicious.

I wonder if he knows how lucky he is? Dorothy thought.

The four-hour journey seemed over too soon for the young couple crushed into the corner of the hot, crowded troop train. Fred was stationed at Codford Barracks, close to Salisbury Plains, and Dorothy was off to the flat near Paddington Station. As the train started to slow down, Fred rummaged in his kit bag for a pencil and found half an envelope. He asked Dorothy to write down her address, so he could stay in touch. He couldn't believe he was brave enough to ask her, but that was what the war did, made people brave. Dorothy scribbled down her address in Longton, 27 Edward Street, and handed it back.

"You don't 'ave to stay in touch ya know," she said. "But you can if ya like. Well, it must be 'ard being a soldier and away from 'ome. If it would 'elp you feel better, it's alright to drop me a line."

Now, she was the one blushing, and she never blushed. Young men didn't affect her. She wasn't really interested in them, except for dance partners at the town hall.

Fred crammed the half envelope and pencil back into his kit bag and got to his feet as the train stopped. Euston Station was a sea of troops moving, like a tide, towards the exit doors. Fred took Dorothy's arm as they were swept along with the crowd. Once through the exit doors, they looked breathlessly at each other and laughed.

"It was a pleasure," said Fred.

"I enjoyed it too."

"I'll write then."

"I should give you me father's address too," offered Dorothy.

She found an old receipt in her handbag and borrowed Fred's pencil.

"Thanks," he said shyly. "By the way, I'm Fred." He laughed as he held out his hand.

"I'm Dorothy," she said as she took the offered hand.

"Pleased to meet you," they both said together, and burst out laughing. It had been a good day and they parted and went their separate ways, both hoping they would meet again some time.

WALKING OUT

"*T*here's a soldier at the door," announced Albert, the eldest of Dolly's children. He had been sharing a chip butty with his grandfather, Tom, before he had answered the door.

"A soldier? At our door?" Emma lifted her bulky body off the horse-hair sofa to see for herself.

"Who are ya looking for, lad?" she asked the tall guardsmen standing outside the door in the rain.

"Is this where Dorothy lives?" he asked.

"Some of the time, she does," answered Emma with sarcasm. "Some of the time she's off in London. What do ya want with the likes of 'er?"

Fred didn't answer, but asked another question. "Is she at home now?"

"No, she's at Swynnerton bomb factory doin' the evening shift. She's never mentioned she knows a soldier."

"Please tell her I called and that I have a three day pass. I'm staying with me mam and dad in Normacot. I'll call again tomorra, earlier."

"Well I never," Emma said to herself, ambling back to the sofa and swigging on her stout. "A soldier asking for Dot. A bloody guardsman as well."

Dorothy slept late the next day, after an exhausting evening shift and a walk home in the rain, leaving her sodden and cold. Emma couldn't wait to tell her about the visitor.

"A bloody soldier came 'ere looking for ya yesterday. Said he knew ya. I don't want any soddin' soldiers 'anging about the 'ouse. Ya never said ya knew a soldier. Ya'll fall on your bloody arse ya will, like ya mother before ya."

"Was 'e tall and thin? Was 'e in the Welsh Guards? Did 'e say 'e'd be back?"

"Well, well, we are bloody interested all of a sudden, aren't we?" Emma snapped. "Said 'e was coming back today."

"What time?" asked Dorothy.

"'Ow do I know. Earlier, 'e said. Said 'e was staying with 'is mam and dad in Normacot. Ya'd better watch yourself my girl. Them soldiers only 'ave one thing on their mind, especially when they're only on a three-day pass, like 'im."

Dorothy flew upstairs to change into a nice frock and put curlers in her hair. If Fred came back today to see her, she didn't want to look a mess. She'd written him three letters since meeting him on the train to London, and he'd written four, which she'd managed to grab from the postman before Emma could see them.

Fred had been bowled over by his meeting with Dorothy on

the London train. She was so beautiful. So different from any girl he had seen before. He went over the journey he had shared with her dozens of times in his mind. Seeing her dark hair and eyes, her red lips, her slim but curvy figure, her knees when she crossed her legs. He had fallen in love. He was convinced he would never meet another girl he loved as much as he did Dorothy. She filled his dreams and his daylight hours, causing his mates to make fun of him and want to know "Who's the girl, Fred?" "Who did you dream about last night?" "Sarg will be after you if you don't stop daydreaming about your girl."

Dorothy had struggled with her feelings for Fred. She had been so determined she would leave The Potteries and live in London. She had never wanted to fall for somebody who worked in the pottery industry. Fred was a master potter, working for Josiah Wedgwood & Sons in Etruria. He had trained as an ornamentor, skillfully placing white figurines onto the Jasper ware, for which Wedgwood was renowned all over the world. After the war his job would be waiting for him and he would spend his life working in the industry. Yet she had thought of little else since she had met him. He was like nobody she had ever met, with his quiet manner and his caring attention.

Fred knocked at the worn, wet door, keeping his fingers crossed that Dorothy would be at home. His stomach was a knot of butterflies. He felt sick. He wanted to run away. Yet he stood his ground as footsteps came closer on the other side of the door. He held his breath.

There she was! More beautiful than he remembered, smiling down at him across the red step.

They stood staring at each other for a small eternity, neither knowing how to begin a conversation.

"Ya came then?" Dorothy managed at last.

"Yes," a strangled whisper from Fred as his face turned the usual bright red.

More silence.

"I wondered if ya'd like to go to the pictures?" Fred bravely asked.

"I can't. I'm on evenings at the factory. I have to be on the train by six."

"Oh!"

"But I can come out now for a bit if ya like? We could walk down to Longton Park now the rain's stopped," Dorothy suggested.

"Yes, that would be so nice."

"Wait 'ere then. I'll just grab me coat."

Dorothy didn't want him to come into the house. She didn't want to give Emma a chance to talk to him again.

Walking beside the tall soldier, Dorothy felt protected and somehow comfortable. He didn't talk as they walked, but halfway to the park, he bravely grasped her hand. She had long thin fingers and beautiful nails, polished a shiny red. Dorothy was proud of her hands, and whenever she wasn't working would paint her nails and rub Ponds vanishing cream into her fingers. Fred's hand was large and strong and once again, Dorothy had the feeling of security.

They sauntered around the park, sitting on benches whenever they needed a break, telling each other about their lives since they last met.

Fred made Dorothy laugh with his stories of training for war with no guns and no tanks. The British had no weapons to equip their army—factories building armaments for the war effort were working around the clock, but it took time to manufacture the weapons of war.

"We 'ad to run around Salisbury Plains in tank formation— five to a tank, pretending we were fighting the Germans. I'm a tank gunner, so I'm always first into the tank (if we actually 'ad one). The gunner sits down in the belly of the tank to fire the gun. We also pretended we 'ad rifles, and were all issued with wooden sticks. The Sergeant drilled us for hours, as we pretended to fix bayonets or "charge" the enemy. There were days and days of spirit-breaking chores, like whitewashing coal, and paintin' the buildings of the barracks over and over again. Some of them 'ave already gone home, broken by the futility and repetition of meaningless training. Several of the lads shot themselves through the foot with a borrowed gun from the guards on the gate. Many a night I 'eard lads of eighteen, or twenty cryin' in the night for their mams. I believe if Hitler 'ad come across the channel after Dunkirk, 'e could have taken England in a couple of days. We 'ad no guns, no ammunition, no tanks. Nothin'! Everythin' the army 'ad was left in France. We couldn't 'ave stopped 'im. I can't 'elp wonderin' why Germany didn't invade." Fred pondered.

Dorothy told Fred all about Swynnerton and her best friends. Telling him about the visit of King George VI and Queen Elizabeth, when the entire factory was "poshed up" for the royals.

"We were all shocked when we got to work and there were flowers in tubs placed outside the canteen. There were table-cloths covering the worn wooden tables, and there were china cups and saucers instead of tin mugs. We were allowed to line the route to see the King and Queen and were all given flags to wave. I was shocked to see how little King George VI and Queen Elizabeth were. I remember seein' the King's father in London when I was a young girl, and I was surprised to see 'ow small 'e was—for a king! The King and Queen 'ad to wear rubber shoes durin' their tour, which made them look smaller than ever. I bet the King was only about five foot six inches tall. The Queen maybe five foot— she was tiny! We all had a great day though. Of course, the next day we were back to wooden tables and tin mugs and no flowers. Pretty funny!"

As they walked back to Edward Street, hand in hand, Fred tried to pluck up the courage to ask Dorothy if she would be his girl. He wanted a picture of her to take with him. He wanted to see her on every leave. He was enraptured with her and couldn't bare to think of her seeing another man.

"Dorothy, I would be 'onoured if ya would be me girl," he said, blushing deeply as he turned to face her at the top of Edward Street.

Dorothy almost laughed. He was a funny sort of a fellow. Always so polite and quietly spoken. She wasn't at all sure she wanted to be "his girl" exclusively.

What about the dances at the town hall? What about all the other service men, sailors included, who look so smart in their uniforms? What about the young men in London I've had dates with off and on? (Some with plenty of money).What about tying myself to a potter? Do I really want to?

"I'll think about it," she finally said, knowing by the look on his face that he was disappointed in her answer.

"Maybe when ya come on your next leave, I could tell ya? And I'll keep writing to ya."

Although it wasn't the answer he wanted, Fred nodded in agreement. She wasn't breaking the friendship off, anyway. She was still going to write.

"I 'ave a five day leave due, but it won't be for three months," he added. "But I'll write and tell ya when I'm coming 'ome next time."

Three months was a long time for any young woman. Dorothy kept writing to Fred, but also going to dances and to the pictures with different young men. She made the most of the scarce evenings off and joined her Marshall cousins at Aunt Sarah's to get ready for an evening out. Stan Marshall became an expert at drawing a "seam line" up the back of his sister's and Dorothy's legs to mimic them wearing nylon stockings. Nylons were too expensive, and also on ration, so the girls browned their legs with tanning lotion and Sam drew the lines. The Marshall cousins and Dorothy shared lipstick and nail polish. They curled each other's hair into the latest pageboy style. They shared Evening in Paris perfume, dabbing a small amount behind their ears and on their wrists.

There was never a shortage of partners at the Town Hall dances. French troops were stationed nearby at the Trentham Estate, awaiting their summons to join the fight for their country's freedom. They poured into Longton on dance nights, only too willing to partner the local girls and maybe sweep them off their feet with their French accents and romantic reputation.

Emma decried everything Dorothy did, bombarding her with constant criticism and insults. Dorothy shut her ears to it all, and became harder and tougher with each passing day.

"Why can't ya be more like our Madge?" Emma whined. "She

stays at 'ome every night. She doesn't doll 'erself up and wear bloody lipstick. Ya get it from that soddin' mother of yours. Ya'll end up in the same mess, mark my bloody words."

Madge wasn't part of the good-time-girls, as they called themselves, preferring to be miserable. She was seeing a strange, silent man named Herbert, who sat in the parlour with her night after night. Dorothy never saw the point of their relationship, and felt like shaking Madge to wake up and have some fun. Herbert was dull as dishwater. He never smiled. He never talked. What was the point? Emma was delighted with her girl, Madge, when she told the family she was getting married.

"To Herbert?" gasped Dorothy, as they stood in the kitchen drinking tea. "Why would you marry 'im? 'e never speaks. Ya can't possibly think ya'll be 'appy, our Madge."

"Some of us aren't worried about bein' 'appy," Madge replied, glowering at Dorothy over the rim of her mug. "Some of us get married because it's bloody expected. It's a good thing to be married. Not like some—Gertrude, ya mam, for instance."

Madge smirked at her young niece. Only two years separated them, yet they were worlds apart. Any opportunity to get a dig in, Madge would do it, egged on and encouraged by her mother, Emma.

"That's right, our Madge," Emma retorted. "A married woman 'as respect. 'Er little 'uns aren't bastards, like some."

"Shut up," yelled Dorothy. "You both never cease with your insults. I wouldn't marry 'erbert if 'e was the last man alive. Bloody boring lump of lard, 'e is."

"What makes ya think anybody would ever ask you. A bastard! Most men are picky when it comes to choosing a good wife." Madge flung the final insult as Dorothy headed through the door, heading for Aunt Sarah's house to tell them the news.

They'd all have a good laugh about Madge and her lump of lard!

As with most family fights, it all blew over quickly, and Dorothy and the Marshall girls all ended up at Madge's wedding, some as bridesmaids, wishing her well on her wedding day. Weddings during the war always had a cloud hanging over them, as most of the men were in the military and waiting for the call to fight. Marriage was a temporary institution, two people joined for an unknown amount of time. Everybody celebrated wildly while they could.

Fred's letters were light hearted and funny. He was careful not to scare Dorothy away with any declaration of how he felt about her. His next leave was marked on the wall in Dorothy's bedroom and she was relieved to see she wasn't working in the yellow powder. Her skin would be almost back to normal by the time she saw Fred again. She was ready with her answer.

On his next leave they went to the pictures to see How Green Was My Valley at the Empire Cinema in Longton. Dorothy cried through the entire picture, leaving Fred's handkerchief a sodden mess. When Fred slipped his arm around Dorothy's shoulder during the film, she didn't pulled away. He could feel the warmth of her skin beneath his hand, making his heart beat faster and the blood rush to his face. He had somehow made it through the past three months of training —at least the battalion had been issued with a real tank, which they all took turns training in. He hoped he would go back after his leave with a picture of his girl and a promise from her.

"The answer is yes," said Dorothy on their walk home. "I've thought about being your girl since I saw ya last time, and the answer is yes."

Fred stopped walking. He turned his girl towards him by her shoulders and right in the middle of the street he kissed her very gently on her lips. It was like a bolt of lightning. His legs weakened and he pulled her into a hug to steady himself. Had there ever been a happier man? Dorothy was "his girl." Even if he was called into action after this leave, he would have her kisses to take with him, her picture in his pocket, the memory of her arms around him. He was the luckiest man alive!

Dorothy snuggled closely to her soldier. Of all the dates she had been on, this was the man she felt a connection with. Yet he was so opposite to her in many ways. He was quiet and shy, he didn't swear or get angry, he was gentle and kind, he loved his parents and his brother and sister. Most of all he looked at her with such adoration that Dorothy felt deep down inside that he would love her forever.

By the end of the five-day pass, Fred had Dorothy's picture in his pocket, along with the memory of many kisses, leaving the taste of her lipstick he never wanted to wash away.

"I'll count the days until the next pass," he told Dorothy as they stood in each other's arms on Longton Station waiting for the troop train to take Fred back to London. "I'll write every day. I've been thinking about 'ow to let you know if our regiment 'as been deployed. My letters will all begin "Dearest Dorothy," but if we are on the move and sent abroad my letter will begin "My Darling Dorothy", that's 'ow you'll know I'm not in England any more. It won't get past the censors if I tell ya where we are."

"Don't even talk about it," Dorothy sighed, "Maybe the war will be over soon, even before you 'ave to go and fight. Germany 'aven't invaded us yet. I think they're afraid to attack Britain."

Dorothy stuck out her stubborn chin and gazed up at her tall guardsman, willing him to agree so that she didn't feel so scared for him. He simply nodded and smiled, knowing that the massing of the British armed forces in the south of England was intended for only one thing. They would cross the English Channel and fight the Germans, it was only a matter of when.

Despite the rainy morning and the smoke-clouded town, Dorothy wore her white coat, bought on her last trip to London, and an especially beautiful dark red hat. She wanted to make an impression on Fred he could not forget. A memory to take with him, wherever he was headed. Everything about Dorothy had the desired effect on the guardsman. He could barely tear himself away from her and left it until the last minute to jump onto the train. As the train drew out of Longton station, Fred leaned through the open window, his eyes fixed on his beautiful girl. Through the train smoke Dorothy waved and blew kisses until the train disappeared.

Goodbyes were always hard, especially when it might be forever. The women on the station turned away with tears, images of their husbands, fathers, sons, brothers and boyfriends disappearing through the smoke. Dorothy stood there alone, until every trace of smoke from the train engine had dissipated. She suddenly felt cold and alone. She finally turned and followed the other women down the metal steps, off the station and back to Edward Street.

QUESTION AND ANSWER

"Permission for exemption from yellow powder," Dorothy said as she handed the duly completed form to the sour-looking staffer at the central office. The middle-aged woman glowered at Dorothy over her glasses as she saw the reason given as "boyfriend on leave."

She took the form and stamped it at the top and bottom, tearing it along the perforated line and giving the bottom half back to Dorothy.

"Half the bomb shop seems to have boyfriends coming on leave. Pity for the poor bloody soldiers—they'll be fighting with no bullets or bombs."

"It's not our fault the bloody chemicals make us look a mess," retorted Dorothy. "You should get off your fat arse and try filling bullets and bombs all day with yellow powder. Then you can talk, you old bat."

Dorothy turned on her heel and marched out of the office. Winnie was waiting outside and linked arms with her friend as they headed to work their eight-hour shift.

"Ya shouldn't 'ave said that to her, Dot," Winnie said. "She could have ya up on charges ya know."

"She won't though," Dorothy answered. "She shouldn't go on about us 'aving time off for our fella's leaves. None of 'er business."

By the time Fred arrived on leave, Dorothy's skin was almost back to normal. With a bit of rouge and red lipstick, it was hardly noticeable. It had been three months since they'd last seen each other. An eternity for both of them.

Since the attack on Pearl Harbour in December of 1941, the whole of the British armed forces had been on high alert. Now the Americans were part of the war, equipment came flooding into Britain. The merchant navy and its American counterpart formed a constant convoy, crossing the Atlantic Ocean—a sitting target for the German Uboats that stalked the allied supply ships from the depths of the sea, sinking 3500 merchant ships and 175 warships during World War II.

At the Codford barracks of the Welsh Guards, where Fred was stationed, there were daily updates on the war effort. Daily reminders to be ready at a moment's notice for the invasion of France. The guards who remained in Fred's battalion were the ones brave enough and stable enough to survive the basic training—the ones who hadn't survived were found desk jobs, or work with the land army producing food. The soldiers now had real rifles with bayonets and real tanks. They spent their days polishing those tanks until they shone, inside and out. They still had to whitewash the coal, paint the buildings over and over again, and do hours of drills in all weather. They were up at dawn, running with full packs for miles. Fred had never been so thin. Even though the mess food was plentiful, he was always hungry. Three square meals a day is what the army served. There were no snacks or after-dinner treats.

Dorothy was thin too, from not having enough to eat and working long, arduous shifts. Rationing was a nightmare for the working people. Everything was rationed! Coupons were needed to purchase most food, clothing, furniture and household items. As food was a necessity, that's where it hit the hardest. There were never enough coupons to buy the necessary food. Corned beef from Argentina was a stand by, cooked into hash with the other plentiful foods—potatoes and cabbage. Milk, cheese, butter, eggs, fruit, meat, chicken, bread, flour, and sugar all became luxury items. There were few, if any, overweight people in Britain, most were skeletal —like Dorothy.

Picking up a girl from her house when you were "walking out," the name used for "dating," was the gentlemanly thing to do. Dorothy hated being picked up at her grandmother's house. It seemed to cast a pall on the meeting. It was always dark, dirty, moist, smelly and inhospitable. She was always ready to go the minute the knock came on the door so Fred didn't have to come into the house.

Friday at 7:00 p.m., the knock came. Dorothy, dressed in a new pale blue blouse and a flared grey skirt, grabbed her coat and bag and ran to the door. She had curled her hair and applied her favourite Max Factor lipstick, and had dabbed a little of her Evening in Paris perfume behind her ears. She was all ready to wow her soldier.

Fred had been home to drop off his kit bag and greet his family. His mother, May, had a fine dinner prepared, sausage and mash, after saving the ration coupons for a whole month for enough sausage for the four of them. Seeing his family was wonderful, but there was only one person on Fred's mind. In fact, she had been on his mind every day since he had left twelve weeks ago. He was obsessed with Dorothy!

"Well then, I'm off to meet my girl," Fred announced after finishing up the last of the sausages. "Don't wait up, I may be late."

"When are we goin' to meet 'er?" asked May. "Seems pretty serious to me."

"You've met 'er, Ma," replied Fred. "At Longton Station that day you were seeing me off. You told me to keep 'er company. Don't you remember?"

"Oh, our Fred," laughed his mother. "As if I remember a young woman I only met for a couple of minutes. We'd like to meet 'er. Bring 'er round on Sunday for tea."

The mile between the Podmore house in Normacot and the Bryan house in Longton was covered in record time, as Fred half walked, half ran the distance. He was panting and red in the face by the time he knocked on the door, his stomach flipped over, his heart pounded in his ears. The door flew open immediately and there she was. So beautiful! Every time he saw her she was lovelier than he remembered. He didn't move, or speak, stunned by her very presence. Dorothy stepped down and closed the door behind her. She stood very close to him and gazed up into his soft grey eyes.

"Hello," she said.

Still no words would come, only the blush which kept up its intensity.

She stood on tiptoe and placed a ruby red kiss on his lips, staining his lips slightly with the same colour.

"Dorothy."

The kiss was deeper and longer as Fred held the back of her head in his large hand and pressed his lips into hers, not caring that the lipstick would smudge with the pressure of the kiss. There was no doubt in his mind that he wanted to spend the rest of his life tasting those kisses. His five-day passes were small islands of surreality in a world absorbed with war.

The back two rows of the Empire Theatre were cuddle seats. Seats for two with no arm between, like a small love seat. The ushers saved them for young couples, knowing the young men were more than likely on leave for a few short days, and they had little intention of watching the pictures. Cuddling and kissing was the expected occupation in the lover's seats, and Fred and Dorothy took advantage of the situation. While Humphrey Bogart did his best on the big screen, the young couple held each other, sitting so close that their legs touched from ankle to hip, their fingers intertwined, their lips caressing ears, cheeks, necks. Almost too much for Fred to bear!

After the movie they went to the Dunrobin Pub for a drink. They laughed and giggled trying to find their way from the theatre to the pub in the blackout. All over Britain every source of light was covered with a black-out curtain. From a farm in the middle of nowhere, to villages, towns and cities, not a chink of light could be shown. No light that the German planes could spot from the air. Every window of every house had black-out curtains covering them. No street lights were lit. No flashlights were used. This was the law from 1939 to 1945. Dorothy kept her left hand out to the side so that she could feel the buildings and keep them on course. Everybody tended to walk to the right, with no guideline. Dorothy had been lost several times, finding herself in the wrong street, having counted the turns incorrectly. The pub was warm and bright, welcoming them in from the darkness. A small table in an alcove gave them some privacy away from the crowd near the bar, and Fred brought over his pint of beer and Dorothy's gin and orange, his eyes never leaving hers.

"Mam's asked ya for tea on Sunday," he said, as he lit Dorothy's cigarette. "Will ya come?"

"All right. I'd like that," Dorothy answered. "Who'll be there?"

"Just me, Ma and Dad and me younger sister, Margaret. I'll come and get ya though, at about four o'clock. Ma goes to chapel at six, so she likes an early tea on Sundays."

After their drinks, they stepped out into the darkness again, which seemed more black than ever after the bright pub. Fred took Dorothy's hand and pulled her into the entry beside the pub, opening his army great coat to shield her from the cold and so that there were less layers of clothing between them. As they snuggled closer, Fred saw an older man stagger into the entry. He'd obviously had too much beer and was looking for a place to relieve himself. The entry was convenient.

"Just stay still and put your head inside my coat," Fred instructed, not wanting Dorothy to witness even the shadow of the old man and what he was about to do.

Dorothy put her head inside the warm coat. She could hear the shuffle of feet close by. Then she heard water splashing. Then she felt the stream of warm water hitting her leg and filling up her new suede shoes. She didn't dare move, because Fred would have been so embarrassed, so she just stood there letting the pee fill up and overflow her shoe, thinking it would never stop. She walked all the way home with her shoe squelching with each step. She burnt her shoes in the kitchen fire before she went to bed.

May made a special effort with Sunday tea. She'd asked her sister, Daisy, for her cheese coupons and begged Mr. Grimsby, the grocer, for an extra loaf. The cheese sandwiches had very thinly sliced tomato, as well as a smear of best butter. Tinned peaches, saved for a special treat, were opened and the top of the milk skimmed to produce a few spoonfuls of cream for the peaches. May had baked six jam tarts with the rationed flour, which sat on her very best flowered china dish in the middle of the table.

Dorothy wanted to look her best, and wore a rose pink dress with a flared skirt and buttons down the front. She ran over to Marshall's house, where Sam drew a line down the back of her legs, then she slipped on her high-heeled shoes, applied her lipstick, ran a final brush through her hair and was ready to go.

As she walked with Fred up the hill towards Normacot, Dorothy wished she had not worn her high heels. They looked so fashionable, but they pinched her toes and rubbed her heels, making her grimace with each step by the time they reached Bell Avenue. "Grin and bear it," she told herself, smiling up at Fred as he opened the front door for her.

May and George Podmore welcomed their son's girlfriend warmly. She towered over both of them, making her wonder how Fred had grown to such a height when his parents were so tiny. Fred's sister, Margaret, came in from the kitchen to say "hello." She was the same size as her mother.

The small house was immaculately clean. The table set with a pure white cloth and rose-patterned china. The carpets beneath their feet were layered to protect the main carpet underneath. Dorothy counted at least three layers of carpet on top of the linoleum-covered floor. May and Margaret scurried back and forth between the kitchen and living room, making tea and serving food. Fred sat beside Dorothy, his face aglow with a constant blush as he watched his family's reaction to the girl he wanted to marry.

His father, George, was a quiet man. He glanced at Dorothy out of the corner of his eye, not wanting to appear too inquisitive or make her uncomfortable.

She's a real looker! I can see why our Fred's taken a fancy to 'er. Ma's not goin' to like the short skirt, or the lipstick though. Obviously not a chapel girl. I 'ope our Fred's not setting 'imself up for 'eartbreak with this one. I 'ardly dare look at the front of 'er dress— seems a bit too low. Lovely lookin' girl though.

May's thoughts flew through her head as she noticed everything about their young guest. She checked off her disapproval in point form. *Dress too short. Neckline too low. 'igh 'eels. Lines on 'er legs. Lipstick. Curled 'air. Crosses 'er legs—I could see 'er knees. Smokes. Cocky attitude—thinks she's somebody. Our Fred should be with that nice girl from chapel. Maureen Corbett, that's the one. A 'umble girl, who knows 'er place and goes to Chapel every Sunday. This one's only goin' to bring our Fred grief. I should never 'ave told 'im to keep 'er company on that troop train. She's from Neck End—common as muck.*

"I think that went very well," Fred said, as he walked Dorothy home after tea. "I think they really liked ya."

Dorothy's thoughts were different. She had seen the way May looked at her, frowning as she stared at Dorothy's high heels and short skirt, a quiet cough when she lit a cigarette, a glance over her teacup at the lipstick on the cheese sandwich Dorothy was eating. May was old-fashioned to the extreme.

Black skirt, two inches above her ankles, a flowered blouse with long sleeves, fastened up to the neck, with a brooch at the throat, her hair gathered into a bun at the back of her neck, small wire-rimmed glasses, no sign of make up. Her tiny feet were enclosed in black lace-up shoes with a small, sensible heel. A Bible sat on the sideboard, along with two Christian Awake magazines. No, Dorothy thought, she didn't think she'd made a good impression at all.

"I should come in and meet your family when I pick ya up tomorra," Fred suggested.

"They're very different than your ma and dad, Fred. Me grandad and grandma drink and swear and the 'ouse is never clean. I don't know if I want ya to meet them."

Emma forced a smile when her granddaughter led her young soldier into the kitchen the next day. Fred shook Tom's hand first, the old man struggled to his feet to accept the hand-shake, doing his best to stand tall and attempt a smile. Then Fred turned to Emma, taking her hand gently and smiling at her.

"I'm very pleased to meet you, Mrs. Bryan," he said.

"Well, we're pleased to meet you too, young man," said Emma, wishing she had put on a clean apron and suddenly aware of the bottle of stout on the table in front of her.

"Sit and 'av a cuppa," Emma offered. "Our Eddie's in the sappers ya know. Nice to see a young man in uniform, I say."

"We're not stayin'," Dorothy said. "We're off to the pictures. It's Fred's last night on leave."

Dorothy dragged Fred by the hand, through the parlour and out the front door, not wanting to stay a moment longer than necessary.

"I'm back on night shift tonight, so we'll miss the end of the picture and I won't be able to see ya off tomorra at the station. Let's go to Aunt Lena's instead of the pictures. She'll let us sit in 'er parlour and won't disturb us."

They hurried through the darkened streets to Aunt Lena's house and settled in the front parlour. Aunt Lena even let them build a little fire, so they were cozy.

"Dorothy, I can't begin to tell you 'ow I feel about ya," began Fred, feeling the familiar warmth flushing his face. "I want to marry ya. I want to be with ya for as long as we 'ave. I don't know 'ow long the war will last. We all expected it to be over in a few months and now it's been over two years. But I want ya with me every second I'm on leave, and when it's over and I come 'ome for good, I want you waiting for me."

Dorothy didn't answer immediately. Their courting days could be counted on two hands. They barely knew each other. She wanted to go back to London when the war was over, not stay in The Potteries. She wrestled with the decision she had to make. If she said "yes," she would seal her fate and never go to live in London. If she said "no," this wonderful man, who wanted to marry her, would be lost forever. Maybe they would only be together for a few days, or weeks, or months. The future was so uncertain but she wanted to share that uncertain future with Fred.

"I want to be married to ya Fred," she said, kissing his warm lips. "I want to be married to ya soon, so that you can take the memories of our wedding with you wherever ya go. I want us to sleep in the same bed and wake up beside each other every day. I only want you and nobody else."

Tears filled Fred's eyes. Dorothy had never seen a man cry before. He didn't even brush them away, but let them spill down his cheeks. He was so overwhelmed, he could only wrap his arms around her and hold her close. He only released his hold on her to tip her face towards him, gently lifting her chin with his index finger.

"Dorothy. Darling Dorothy," he whispered, sealing her lips inside his own. The kiss lingered, leaving them both breathless.

"No matter what lies ahead for us, I'll always love you. My precious, beautiful girl." Fred rained kisses on Dorothy's face. "I am the 'appiest man alive."

Dorothy threw back her head and laughed from sheer joy. She felt light and dizzy and full of happiness. This quiet, shy, gentle soldier made her feel so full of love for him that she thought she would burst.

"My Fred! How 'appy you make me," she said. "I feel like there's just the two of us in the whole world. Just you and me."

As they walked back to Edward Street, Fred was thoughtful. He was considering what should happen next.

"Can you come down to London one weekend soon?" Fred asked. "I'd like to speak to your father and ask 'is permission. That's the right thing to do. I could get an evening pass and come to your father's flat."

"I can probably get a weekend next time there's a shift change. We'll 'ave to plan ahead, so I can let ya know. I 'aven't been able to get away very often, but I can phone me father on the Chapel phone once arrangements are fixed, so 'e knows when to expect me.

"Let's get married soon then," Fred whispered. "On my next leave."

PERMISSION

*D*orothy told everybody about Fred's proposal. The Marshall girls were delighted and offered their help with preparations for the wedding. Marion Marshall offered the use of her wedding dress, and Gladys said Dorothy could use her white shoes, because they were the same shoe size. Emma just said "Ya won't get your own way with 'im, little miss muck. That young man'll be the boss of you."

Dorothy had to wait for six weeks before the timing was right for her to get away for the weekend. She had written to Fred, giving him the dates and the telephone number at the flat, in the hopes that he could get an evening pass and meet Edward.

There were changes at her father's residence. Edward had handed over the taxi business to his long-time driver John Goodwin. Amy's investment had been paid back to her, with interest, years ago. The taxis were still housed below the flat and Edward had an arrangement with John that he would have priority when he needed a ride, in exchange for free garage space. John hired another driver and continued the taxi business throughout the war years, spending many nights volunteering his taxis to transport injured Londoners to the hospital.

Mr. Arnold had died suddenly on a cold February night in 1941 as he hurried to the air raid shelter. Mrs. Arnold thought he had tripped in the blackout, but when she went to help him to his feet, he didn't respond. He lay there on the wet pavement, not moving, not breathing. People on their way to the shelter stopped to help, calling an air raid warden over, who quickly sent for an ambulance. It was all over so quickly. A heart attack, the doctor said. Mrs. Arnold believed it was the war—never sleeping in their own bed, trying to sleep on the cold concrete floor of the underground at Paddington station. Never knowing if they would be alive at the end of the night, or take a direct hit and be blown into a million pieces. Never knowing if the flat in Chilworth Mews would be there when they returned after a sleepless night, worrying that Edward would be gone, blown away by a German bomb.

Mrs. Arnold went to live with her sister in Surrey. Edward was sorry to see her go, but understood she needed to be in a safe place, away from the hell of the capital city. Maybe it was time he moved to Maidenhead to live with Amy until it was safe. But Edward had never chosen the "safe" way, and he didn't want to live in boring Maidenhead. It was enough that he was there almost every weekend. If London was to crumble, then he would crumble with it. Until then, he would stay where he was and find another housekeeper.

The distinguished elderly gentleman, standing beneath the clock on Euston station waved his hand as his daughter hurried towards him. Edward's breath caught in his throat as he grasped Dorothy's hand and kissed her cheek. Oh, how he had missed her! As he drove her through the London streets, Dorothy was aghast at the vast spaces where houses, shops, and banks used to stand. She barely recognized Chilworth Mews. Half the street was missing. Barney Millword's house was gone and so was Mrs. Jenkin's flat, two doors away from Edward. The rubble and mess was all cleared away and it seemed the homes had disappeared into thin air—as though they had never been there.

It was strange not to be greeted by Mrs. Arnold. Edward introduced Dorothy to Mrs. Taylor, the new housekeeper, who had lived in one of the first neighbourhoods to be bombed. She was a widow with two grown sons, both in the army. When she lost her home and all her possessions she had registered with the Salvation Army, who found her a place to stay, gave her emergency provisions, and helped her look for a job. She was delighted to be working for Edward and living in the comfortable flat, with her own bedroom and bathroom. Dorothy liked her immediately.

After a light supper, Dorothy went to sit beside her father in the living room.

"I've met a young man," she began, her accent slipping into the familiar London dialect. "He's in the Welsh Guards, stationed at Codford. I want you to meet him. He has the phone number and will call tomorrow to let me know if he can get an evening pass."

"Well now," Edward said. "Is this a serious affair? You've never wanted me to meet any of your other young fellows. You had better tell me all about him."

Dorothy's eyes shone as she described meeting Fred on Longton station, writing to him, going out with him when he was on leave. How he was an ornamentor at Josiah Wedgwood & Sons before the war, which was a highly skilled job. Everything she knew about Fred she passed on to her father, except that Fred had proposed to her. She had agreed with Fred that Edward's permission should be sought first.

Edward poured himself a scotch and looked down at his daughter.

"Dorothy, how involved are you with this soldier?"

"He's not like anybody I've every met. He makes me feel wonderful. I think I love him. Even though I haven't known him for long."

"Don't you see, darling, that it's the war pushing you into these feelings? A young soldier, waiting to be deployed. Waiting to fight. Of course you think you love him. Who wouldn't? How many days have you actually spent with him? Probably about ten or twelve leave days! Dorothy, think straight. Your home is here with me when the war is over, not in the Potteries. Look at the life you would be giving up."

"I know it's hard for you to understand, Father," Dorothy said. "But the war has changed everything. Look at London now—broken and fallen. The people who have lost their homes, scattered into the countryside. The children all gone. How will London ever be rebuilt? I feel like this war will last forever. Now the Americans are here and the whole country is full of troops and war equipment, I know Fred will be sent to France to fight. He may not survive! I want him to at least know I will be here waiting for him to come home."

"Listen to yourself. It's exactly as I've just said. Your feelings for this soldier are all centred on the war and whether or not he will survive. Don't make this decision lightly, Dorothy. It may be a "forever" decision. You may be stuck in Longton for the rest of your life. You could marry well. Think of the young men who have wined and dined you here in London. Did you not like any of them?"

Edward poured himself another scotch. He knew how stubborn and determined his daughter was, especially when she was opposed.

Well into his seventies, Edward had imagined life with his daughter, watching her enjoy London society, meeting interesting, affluent young men. One day, make a decision to marry well, choosing a partner who could offer her all of life's luxuries. He wanted Dorothy to have the life her mother, Gertrude, had dreamed of.

"I liked some of the young men I dated here in London, Father," Dorothy replied. "This is different. Fred is different. I feel so happy when I'm with him. He's nothing like me, but it works somehow. Wait until you meet him, Father, you will know what I mean."

After their conversation, Dorothy headed to bed. She would sleep in her own bed tonight and couldn't wait for the soft sheets and pillows to envelop her in comfort.

London was on high alert still, but the air raids were infrequent now and the sirens only sounded when the spotters on the south coast saw the planes heading for London. Mrs. Taylor said it was almost worse than the blitz, when they had been bombed every night. Now they never knew when the bombs would fall, lulling the population into a sense of security for days, then another raid. Many people couldn't sleep, even in their own beds, knowing they may have to run to the shelters in the middle of the night. Some chose to go to the shelters to sleep anyway, rather than be disturbed from their sleep.

That night, no sirens sounded and Dorothy slept, although restlessly.

Mrs. Taylor answered the phone in the hall while Dorothy and Edward were eating breakfast.

"It's for you, Dorothy," she called.

Fred wasn't used to making phone calls. As soon as he heard Dorothy say "hello," he shouted into the mouthpiece so loud that Edward could hear him from the dining room.

"I can come today," Fred yelled. "See you at six o'clock. I have the address."

The phone slammed down in Dorothy's ear before she could answer him.

The day passed slowly. Dorothy helped Mrs. Taylor bake chicken pies and Edward spent most of the day at his club, contemplating the visitor due at six o'clock. By the time Fred rang the doorbell, the table was set for the evening meal and the three inhabitants of the flat were all tense from waiting. The doorbell made them all jump. Dorothy ran to open it.

If Dorothy was nervous, it was nothing compared to how Fred felt. He had only had a short time to get ready. His day had been filled with drills, barracks inspection, a five-mile run in full kit, a lecture on the horrors of contracting VD, plus two hours of unloading and stacking fuel cans. He barely had time for a shower, which he badly needed after his day of exertion. His uniform was brushed and pressed, his boots shone like glass, his cap sat straight on his head, the peak following the slope of his nose.

"Come in," Dorothy greeted him. "I hope you're hungry. There's chicken pie for tea. Father and Mrs. Taylor are anxious to meet you. Come on into the living room."

It was like stepping into a different world for Fred. The rooms were large and airy, the furnishings lush, the carpet soft under his army boots. It was very "posh" by anybody's standards. This is where Dorothy lived when she came to London!

"I'm pleased you could come, Fred," Edward said, shaking hands with the young soldier. "Make yourself comfortable and I'll pour you a drink. Scotch? Beer? A Sherry?"

"A beer, thanks," replied Fred. The older man was taller and distinguished. He made Fred feel like a country bumpkin—awkward and inferior. He was so sure of himself when he asked Dorothy to marry him back at home, but now he saw where she lived in London and who her father was, he was filled with doubt. He wasn't good enough for her! She could marry anybody she chose!

Mrs. Taylor said "hello" to Dorothy's young man, then excused herself to finish preparing the meal. Dorothy followed Mrs. Taylor, winking at Fred on her way through to the kitchen. Fred felt sick.

"Well now, young man," began Edward. "When are the Welsh Guards going to put the Germans in their place?"

"I'm not at liberty to talk about it, Sir," answered Fred, aware of his thick midland accent in comparison with Edward's King's English tongue. "But when we are deployed we will be very well prepared. We will win this war I believe."

"Good job," Edward added. "That's the spirit. I was in Gallipoli in 1915—dreadful war! We were lucky to get out alive. Something one never forgets."

The two men fell silent. Two soldiers from two different wars, fighting for the same country, for the same reasons.

Edward didn't know this young soldier at all. He seemed honest and forthright. He held himself well, tall and straight, and looked Edward in the eye despite his obvious nervousness.

"Sir," Fred said into the silence. "I, I, I came today to ask your permission to marry Dorothy." There, he had said it. He gulped in air and tried to steady his breathing and his racing heart. "I loved 'er from the first moment I saw 'er. I will do everything in my power to take care of 'er and make 'er 'appy. I know we are at war and the future is unknown, but even in these uncertain times love is our 'ope. It's the one thing we can cling to, when everything else around us doesn't make sense."

It was a big speech for Fred. It had taken all his courage to speak so frankly about his feelings for Dorothy. He stood looking at Edward expectantly, waiting for the older man's reaction and praying, silently, for his blessing. Fred's forehead beaded with sweat as he waited for an answer. Although, without Edward's permission, the wedding would go ahead anyway, he knew how much it meant to Dorothy to know her father approved of the match.

"You must know I had other hopes regarding Dorothy's future," Edward said. "I also doubt you have known each other long enough to make such a commitment. The war pushes people into an accelerated life, particularly when two young people are separated for months at a time, fanning the flame with letters, feeling the loneliness. I understand that, I do."

"This isn't infatuation, sir," Fred said. "I truly love Dorothy, and will until the day I die. She is everything to me and I want to assure you I will always take care of 'er."

"I don't doubt your intentions. Only that you haven't really thought this through. You will be married in the middle of a war. A war that may last for months or even years. Where will Dorothy live while you are with the army? Where will you live if or when the war ends and you go home? Have you given your future together any thought?"

Dejected, Fred walked over to the window, looking out onto the street below, watching the rain bounce off the pavement. They had talked about her staying with his parents in Normacot after the wedding, but Dorothy didn't feel comfortable with that arrangement. She didn't really know Fred's family well enough. She said she didn't mind staying with Emma and Tom just until the war ended. She would plan to be in London when Fred had leave, so that they could stay with her father. There didn't seem to be much point in planning beyond the end of the war—whenever that would be.

"Come over here, my boy," Edward said gently. "I can't bear the thought of standing in the way of happiness for my girl. If this is what she wants, then you have my blessing. I'm an old man and it's your time now. Marry her! Be happy! I wish you both well."

Edward grasped Fred's hand in both his hands. Fred was so overcome, he just nodded and smiled.

"Let's tell Dorothy," Edward said.

Mrs. Taylor's chicken pie had never tasted so good, washed down with a bottle of chardonnay and many toasts to the happy couple. As Dorothy kissed her Welsh Guardsman goodbye at the door, she thought how very lucky she was to have found such a wonderful man.

WEDDING

*A*rranging a wedding during war time was a bit like shooting at a moving target with a bent arrow. So many factors came into play that would not be normally there during peacetime. *Would the groom be at the wedding or somewhere overseas? Would the groom's leave dates suddenly change? Who would give the bride away? Would the chosen brides- maids be able to get their war work shifts changed to attend the wedding? Where would the wedding take place? What would happen after the wedding?*

Dorothy studied Fred's leave dates for the upcoming months and compared them with her Swynnerton shift schedule. September was the only option! September 12th, 1942.

All systems were go as the Marshall girls, along with Dorothy's Swynnerton friends, planned the wedding details. Marion Marshall's wedding dress was cleaned and pressed and Gladys' white shoes were polished like new, ready for the bride. Three bridesmaid dresses were borrowed from Winnie's sister, who was married before the war started. Real nylons, and a girdle courtesy of the four Swynnerton friends were bought. A photographer was paid for by Aunt Mary-Ann and flowers for the bride were promised from the Marshall cousins. Dorothy planned to pay for her own veil, but it meant a fight with her grandmother, Emma. Dorothy had won the day and refused to hand over her entire wage, which was a break with tradition in the Potteries, where wage envelopes were handed over unopened to the woman of the house, until you left home.

"Ya nothin' but a piece of shit," Emma shouted. "All ya life y've been nothin' but a drag on me and everybody else in this bloody 'ouse. Now ya want 'alf the money for yaself. Selfish bloody cat! After all I've done for ya."

Dorothy ignored the tirade, knowing Emma would calm down eventually. She threw half of her wages onto the table and ran upstairs to her bedroom. She would have enough money to buy the beautiful veil she had seen in Bratt and Dykes Department Store in Hanley. She didn't care if Emma didn't speak to her for months—it would be worth it.

Who would give the bride away? Not her father. He didn't need reminding of the town in which his daughter had been raised. Apart from Dolly and Fred, Dorothy was the only person who had met Edward. Turning up for the wedding would raise questions for his daughter he chose to protect her from. Not her grandfather, Tom. He would be the last person Dorothy would choose to walk her down the aisle. The next closest relative she had was Eddie. There was the added complication that he was also in the army. How could his leave possibly coincide with Fred's? Fortunately, Eddie's Royal Engineers Regiment was more lax with its leave times than the guards regiments, and he was stationed near Coventry, relatively close by. A special three-day leave was tentatively granted, if the regiment was still in England. Eddie was delighted to be asked to give away his niece. He was forever grateful to her for matching him up with Elsie, whom he intended to marry one day, maybe after the war ended.

The last time Fred and Dorothy met before the wedding was in June of 1942. They spent three days together in London at the flat in Chillworth Mews, properly chaperoned by Mrs. Taylor, who looked after them very well. Fred used Edward's room, as Edward had gone to Maidenhead for a few days to attend an important function with Amy. The young couple poured over their plans for September 12th, which was two days before Dorothy turned twenty-one. Fred still couldn't believe they were getting married. He prayed the British would not invade in the next few months. He prayed he would marry Dorothy as planned.

May tried her best to put on a brave face when Fred wrote and told his family he was to be married in September. He was just a boy! Only twenty-two! What did he know about girls? What did he know about life? Marrying such a girl, from Neck End. Not the girl May would have chosen for her son. He was obviously swept off his feet by her looks and glamour. Well that kind of looks and glamour didn't last forever. What then? He would soon tire of her.

"What do you think about this wedding, George?" May asked her husband as he sat smoking his pipe beside the fireplace. "Did you ever think our Fred would marry somebody like this Dorothy from Neck End?"

"She seemed like a nice girl to me," George said. "It's the boy's choice, mother. Fred's a soldier after all. 'E wants to get married before 'e's sent abroad to fight."

May shook her head and called her daughter into the living room.

"Get the writing paper, our Margaret," her mother instructed. "Write a letter to our Fred for me. Say we're 'appy for 'im (though I'm not) and tell 'm we're all looking forward to the wedding."

Margaret wrote slowly and carefully, adding her own good wishes at the end of the short sentence her mother had dictated.

"I 'ad a letter from Dorothy," said Margaret. "Asking me to be a bridesmaid. I'm so 'appy she's asked me. I 'ave to go to 'er Aunt Sarah's 'ouse this Saturday to 'ave the dress fitted. I never thought I'd be a bridesmaid."

"Silly girl," murmured her mother. "She asks ya to be a bridesmaid and ya think she's wonderful I suppose."

Margaret looked at her mother, but didn't say anything. She was happy for her big brother and thought Dorothy was the loveliest girl she'd ever seen. Margaret was short and stocky and had inherited the Podmore family's big nose and ears. She secretly hoped that one day a young man would ask her to marry him, but for now she was delighted about the upcoming wedding.

The train from London seemed to take twice as long as usual as Fred made his way home on September 11th. He walked the mile from the station in Longton up the hill to Normacot to stay with his family overnight. It would be the last night at number five Bell Avenue as a single man. Despite her reservations, May greeted her son with a hug and some tears and fussed over him, making him tea and toast. George looked at his tall son, so handsome in his guard uniform. He looked so young. Yet old enough to fight for his country, so old enough to be married.

"Come on, our Fred," said George. "Put your best foot

forward. I'll take ya over to the Cinderhill pub for a pint on your last night as a bachelor."

"Great idea, Dad," said Fred. "A pint would go down a treat tonight."

"I can't believe the two of ya are goin' to the pub," May gasped. "George, ya've broken the temperance enough times I know, but our Fred 'asn't, 'ave ya Fred?"

"I'm afraid I 'ave, Ma," laughed Fred. "Many times. Sorry to shock ya, but a pint of beer isn't the end of the world. Don't fret now. I won't go to 'ell because of it."

May sat at the table and put her apron over her head. The temperance chapel she belonged to would disown her son, like they'd disowned her husband after the Great War. George had taken the rum ration issued by the army to the soldiers in the trenches and on his return to chapel, he had been called in front of the congregation and asked the question:

"Did you take the rum ration, George?"

"Yes, I did," was George's reply.

"Then you've broken the pledge of abstention from alcohol and are no longer welcome in this church," Mr. Barker, the elder, pronounced.

From that day, George Podmore had never set foot inside the chapel.

Father and son walked past Newhall Mission Chapel, May's chapel, and crossed the recreation ground to the pub in Cinderhill. To Fred's surprise, some of his mates from before the war were there waiting to celebrate with him. George had passed the word around to his pals in the pub that Fred was getting married, and that any boys on leave were welcome to come for a drink the night before the wedding. Bill Copestake was Fred's best man, so already had leave for the weekend. He greeted his friend warmly and pulled him into the middle of a group of young men all in different uniforms. The beer flowed as George paid the tab for the group of young soldiers. Soon they were singing the popular war-time songs, as Bill played the old honky-tonk piano in the bar.

By the time George and Fred rolled home, it was much later than expected and they had drunk considerably more than one beer. May was not amused and glared at her husband as he came through the door, supported by his son's arm.

"Well, mother," George slurred. "What a night we've 'ad! A night to be remembered! Fred's mates were there, well the fellas who could get leave, and they gave 'im a right good send off."

"George Podmore, I'm ashamed of you. Letting the lad drink goodness knows 'ow much beer the night before 'is wedding. E'll still smell like a brewery tomorra. I suppose you both want a sandwich and some tea now?"

"Thanks, Ma," Fred said, trying not to laugh at the sight of his indignant little mother. "A sandwich and tea would be great."

May bustled into the kitchen, muttering under her breath. What was a good Christian woman to do? Make the sandwiches and tea, that's what. She cut thick slices of bread from the loaf, buttered it sparsely and filled the sandwich with raw onion and thinly sliced tinned corned beef. Fred came into the kitchen to carry the two big mugs of tea with milk and sugar. He smiled happily at his parents as he ate his sandwich and drank his tea.

This was the home he had grown up in. He had been loved and nurtured his whole life. He had never heard a swear word or a criticism—only encouragement. There had always been enough food, despite the rationing. George was a platemaker at John Tams & Sons Ltd., and had made a decent wage, although he'd paid for it dearly—his hands were now stuck in the position of the plates he made. Apart from his two beers at the pub on Friday nights, the money was all spent on the family's needs. It had helped that Harry, ten years Fred's senior, had started to work at the coal mine in Florence when he was fourteen. The money he earned became part of the family income, making life easier for the younger two children.

Fred was a good footballer and Harry had bought him his first pair of real football boots. He played for the school team and for the city schoolboys team. He was also a very good swimmer and trained with an elite swimming club, the membership also paid for by Harry. At thirteen, Fred had been made to choose his sport, as his swimming coach said the two sports were working different muscles. Fred chose football, although he remained a strong swimmer.

Munching on his sandwich, Fred's eyes brimmed with tears as he thought of the love that these precious people had poured into him over the years. Tomorrow was his wedding day and he didn't know how to express to them, or thank them, for all they had given him.

"Ma, Dad," he choked, the beer making him more senti- mental than normal. "I love ya both so much. You are the best parents a man could 'ave. I want ya to know I appreciate everything ya've done for me."

Both parents were moved to tears and both walked over and put their arms around their tall son who sat at the table, covering his upturned face with their kisses. It was such a perfect ending to Fred's last night as a single man.

The next morning, Aunt Sarah's house was bursting at the seams with girls getting ready for the wedding. Uncle Felix and the boys in the family had walked over to Aunt Dolly's house to get out of the way. All the girls had been to the baths early. They had used lavender soap and talcum powder, brought from London by Dorothy. Giggles and laughter came from the parlour as the bride and her three brides-maids, helped by the other cousins and friends, primped and powdered. They helped each other with hairstyles and make up and last minute details like a small seam in the wedding dress that needed fixing.

"Something old. Something new. Something borrowed. Something blue."

That was the bride's "good luck" motto. Dorothy had them all in place. She wore a blue garter around her thigh, a new pair of pearl earrings (well fake pearl), a borrowed lace hand-kerchief from Aunt Mary-Ann, and hidden in the stems of the bouquet was the Prussian Captain—Edward's repre-sentative!

Uncle Felix tapped at the door to the parlour.

"Are you ready, girls?" he asked. "The taxi will be 'ere soon and the rest of you, who are walking, need to start out right away."

Uncle Felix had paid for the taxi to take Dorothy, Eddie and the three bridesmaids to the church, but the other members of the family, who were able, would walk to St. James Church, located halfway between Longton and Normacot. Mr. Gunn, the barber on the high street, had offered to drive Felix, Sarah, Tom and Emma and he arrived just as the parade of family and friends set out on foot.

St. James the Less Anglican Church was dedicated in 1763 and was an imposing building, with a tall clock tower dominating the smoky skyline. Dorothy felt very small as she took Eddie's arm and began the slow walk down the long red-carpeted isle to where Fred stood like a statue. Fred visibly shook as he watched his bride coming toward him. He thought he might pass out, but kept his eyes fixed on Dorothy, whose face was a blur behind the wedding veil. As Eddie lifted the long veil and moved it to the back of the bride's head, letting it fall to reach the hem of her dress, Dorothy smiled up at her groom, giving him the confidence he needed.

Neither of them remembered much about the ceremony, only that they repeated the vows the vicar recited in a monotone voice, Fred slipped the utility nine-carat gold ring on Dorothy's finger, and they walked out of the church, down that long aisle and into the sunshine, as man and wife. Home-made confetti reigned down on them as their friends and family shouted good wishes. The photographer snapped a picture of them standing in the church doorway, and the taxi whisked them away to Fred's house in Bell Avenue and waited while they changed their clothes to take them to Longton Station. Eddie had taken Dorothy's suitcase to the house the day before, so that all would be ready for her after the wedding ceremony.

The train was full of troops as usual. The carriage smelled of cigarettes. Up in the corner by the window sat the young couple, confetti still clinging to their hair, oblivious of the rest of the passengers. They were on their way to London for four days together.

HONEYMOON

*T*he flat had been made ready for the newlyweds. Edward had instructed Mrs. Taylor to buy new silk sheets for Dorothy's double bed, with new eiderdown and matching drapes. A man's small armoire had been placed by the side of the bay window, along with a man's valet stand to hold Fred's trousers, jackets, shoes etc. (Fred had no idea what it was when he first saw it). Mrs. Taylor had stocked the pantry with good food, as rationing in London didn't seem to be much of a problem, and left several prepared dishes in the ice box, before leaving to stay with her aunt in Surrey for five days. Edward had vacated the flat too, moving down to Maidenhead while the young couple were on honeymoon. He left a note to say he would be back for Fred's last night of leave to take them to dinner. Tucked inside the envelope was twenty pounds "spending money" for their London stay.

What bliss! To be together for four days with nobody around to disturb them. Too exhausted to think of anything but sleep after their journey, there was no wedding night romance. They curled up beside each other, warm and safe, and fell into a deep dreamless sleep. Fred awoke first the next day, dazed at finding himself in a strange room, then instantly aware of the warm, soft body beside him. Also aware that he wore only pyjama bottoms and she wore only a silk nightgown. His heart pounded, his body responded uncontrollably, making him leap out of bed and run for the bathroom to get himself under control. He had no experience with girls. He'd only heard the other soldiers bragging about their conquests, fumbling about in the dark, up against an entry wall, or in a haystack in the country. Why hadn't he learned more about what to do? Why hadn't he read something about it? He was embarrassed and uncomfortable, as the control he sought seemed to evade him whenever he thought about going back into the bedroom to his wife.

After several minutes, he tiptoed back to the bedroom to find Dorothy propped up on the pillows. She smiled at him and patted the bed beside her. They had to learn together, like most newly married couples, how their bodies worked. Making love was uncomfortable and embarrassing for both of them. They spent hours holding each other, breathing in each other's presence, feeling the beat of each other's hearts. Fred became less and less shy, loving his young wife more and more each day. Dorothy glowed in the adoration of her new husband. It was a new beginning. Life was starting over. For Dorothy the loneliness was over, forever. Even when Fred went back to the army after his leave, she knew she would feel connected to him, no matter where he was in the world.

Edward's generous gift made it possible for Dorothy to show Fred around London in style. They saw two West End variety shows, filled with song and comedy that helped the audience forget, for a couple of hours, the reality of war. Most of the tourist attractions were closed, but Dorothy asked John Goodwin to drive them out to Hampton Court Palace, where they wandered around the extensive gardens, lost themselves in the high-hedged maze and ate lunch at a small hotel nearby. Everywhere they went Fred was greeting by other servicemen as Taffy, the nick name for the Welsh Guards.

"Shall I call you Taffy?" laughed Dorothy. "It suits you very well."

"No, you can not," answered Fred, laughing too. "Some of me mates call me Rick though, 'cause me full name is Frederick, but I'll always want you to call me Fred."

Living in a bubble couldn't last forever, and the days together came to an end all too soon.

Edward arrived at the flat, looking robust and healthy after his four days in the country. He enjoyed walking and riding still and had made the most of his time in Maidenhead, enjoying the river and canal walks and riding in the Windsor park lands. He ran up the stairs anxious to greet his newly married daughter and her husband.

"Congratulations!" he greeted the two young people. "Many congratulations! How was the wedding? Tell me all about it. Have you had a wonderful time here in London? Did Mrs. Taylor leave provisions for you?"

They hardly had time to answer before Edward was whirling through to his bedroom to get changed.

"We have reservations at the Trocadero for dinner. Dress beautifully Dorothy. It's a celebration dinner after all."

John picked them up in the taxi promptly at 7.30p.m. Edward dressed in dinner jacket and bow tie, Dorothy in one of her "London" dresses she saved for such occasions, Fred in uniform—the khaki serge uniform with the peaked cap of the Welsh Guards. All three snatched up their gas masks hanging on hooks beside the door as they left.

The people of London had become accustomed to the city being blacked out for the past three years, and made their way around the familiar streets almost as though they were still lit. Piccadilly Circus felt quite eerie in the dark. The statue of Eros looked like a dark ghost standing on one leg in the centre of the busy square, bow in hand, under the shelter of a black tarpaulin.

The Trocadero was buzzing with diners. Edward was greeted warmly by the maitre d' and shown to a table for three in a quiet corner of the room. Fred followed Dorothy, trying not to stare at the generals, colonels and admirals, in dress uniform, seated at the tables with their wives and families. His uniform felt suddenly more scratchy and drab. His father-in-law put him at his ease, patting him on the shoulder and ordering drinks, as though he was dining with his best friend. Fred didn't understand the menu; dishes he had never heard of were listed in French on the gilt-edged document handed to him by a waiter wearing white gloves and a white towel over his arm.

"Let me help you with that," Edward offered, leaning over and pointing out the different dishes to Dorothy and Fred. "Dorothy usually tells me to go ahead and order for her, but I wouldn't presume to guess what food you would enjoy, Fred. There is really everything on the menu you could possibly imagine: fish, beef, lamb, pork or duck for the entrées with vegetables of your choice. I could recommend the cream of asparagus soup, or maybe the prawn cocktail, or smoked salmon for starters. I'll order some hors d'oeuvres for us all to try while we're waiting for our food. Fred looked at his wife for help and they both chose the smoked salmon and beef steak with potatoes au gratin. Edward smiled at their unity in selecting the same food and ordered himself prawn cocktail and the venison with mushrooms and green onions.

Edward ordered a bottle of champagne and lifted his glass to toast the bride and groom. Fred had never tasted champagne and sneezed as it tickled his nose on the way down. Three small dishes, accompanied by a tray of warm dinner rolls, were served for them to enjoy while waiting for their starters. Bacon-wrapped scallops, chicken skewers with coconut sauce and mushroom pate on tiny toasted baguettes. Fred hardly knew where to start with the food, which looked like it was made for fairies, not people. Everything seemed so small. Edward was bigger and taller than Fred, yet he looked completely at ease using the small fork to serve himself with the small portions of foreign-looking food. Fred followed his example, but felt his hands had suddenly become twice their size as he tried to maneuver the hors d'oeuvres. Dorothy laughed at his efforts, relishing her favourite bacon wrapped scallops which her father always ordered for her.

The meal was a wonder to Fred with foods he had never seen or tasted before. He wondered why there was all this posh stuff in London when back home they were living on tinned corned beef, cabbage and potatoes. The rationing was so severe that each family was allocated two ounces of cheese each week, one orange for each child under twelve, a tiny amount of sugar and tea. On and on! The working people in the north were managing on next to nothing while here, in a London restaurant, there was every luxury you could imagine. He felt ashamed that he was eating so well when most of the country was undernourished.

The final course of the meal was dessert and Fred just said

"I'll 'ave what you're 'avin'" to his father-in-law. The ice cream came in a long-stemmed silver goblet, reaching almost to Fred's nose. The spoon was almost as long as the stem on the goblet, with a tiny bowl at the end of it. Edward elegantly scooped up a small amount of the ice cream and rolled his eyes with pleasure as he popped it into his mouth.

"Ah! That is delicious!" he exclaimed. "The perfect ending to such a meal."

Dorothy wished she could have captured a picture of Fred trying to eat the ice cream before him. She almost choked on her chocolate mouse, he looked so funny. Fred wasn't amused and blushed his way through the "stupid" dessert, wishing he hadn't come.

As they waited in the foyer of the restaurant for John to pick them up, one of the staff hurried forward to brush off Edward's jacket. Turning to Fred, he brushed off the khaki soldier's uniform jacket as though it was the best dinner jacket in the world. He winked at Fred as he brushed his shoulder pads.

"Thanks mate," was all the staff member said. It meant the world to Fred and he walked out of the Trocadero restaurant feeling a foot taller, his mood suddenly changed. Who cared if the place had been full of senior officers. Who cared if the food was French and posh. He was there with his beautiful wife and the man at the door had thanked him for being a soldier.

THE FALL

The rain poured down as Fred packed his kit bag. The newlyweds had returned to his parent's home in Bell Avenue that afternoon and would spend the night there before going their separate ways. Fred would return to his unit in Codford, and Dorothy would pick up her old life, living with her grandparents in Edward Street and working at the munitions factory. Their four days of bliss were over. Reality faced them.

The canvas kit bag was heavy as Fred dragged it to the top of the stairs. Dorothy was in the kitchen downstairs making tea and toast for them. May and George were already in bed and Margaret was reading a book beside the fireplace in the living room. There was nothing breakable in the bag, so Fred picked it up and threw it down the stairs. In an instant, before he could think, his left foot somehow pivoted under him and he lost his balance.

The noise reverberated throughout the house.

Dorothy froze, the kettle poised over the teapot.

Margaret dropped her book and ran to the small front hallway.

George and May awoke, not realizing what had disturbed them.

Fred lay at the bottom of the stairs in a crumpled heap, not moving.

Margaret screamed as she saw her brother lying on the floor, bringing Dorothy racing from the kitchen, her face white with horror. She knelt beside her young husband, lifting his head onto her lap. The blood oozed from the back of his head. His eyelids fluttered but he didn't open his eyes.

"Fred, talk to me," Dorothy begged. "Say something. Let me know you're all right. Please, Fred, please." Then in a whisper, "Don't die!"

George and May appeared at the top of the stairs to look down at the scene in disbelief.

"Our Margaret," said George, his voice low and steady. "Run to the telephone box outside the post office and call an ambulance. Do it quickly. Take the coins from the tin by my chair."

Margaret grabbed the whole tin, not stopping to count the coins and took off through the front door.

Fred's mother brought towels from the bathroom and helped Dorothy mop up the blood pooling around her onto the floor. Fred's face was deathly pale, but he was still breathing. The two women sobbed as they stroked the hair and face and hands of their beloved Fred, willing him to respond. Willing him to live. May bowed her head and prayed out loud to her Lord to save her son. As Dorothy adjusted his head on her cramped knees, she noticed the blood was now changing to what looked like pieces of liver coming out of the damaged skull.

He's going to die! Look at all the blood. He can't possibly lose this much blood and still be alive. We only had four days together. Help us God, please help us. Make the bleeding stop. Get the ambulance here quickly. I won't let him die like this. If I hold onto him, I know he will be all right.

The sirens acknowledged the arrival of the ambulance and soon the small hallway was cramped with people.

"Move out of the way, duck," one of the ambulance men told Dorothy. "Let us do our job now. 'e's in good 'ands. We'll work faster if we 'ave the room."

Dorothy and May, both covered in blood, moved into the living room, where George had mugs of tea waiting for the two of them. His hands shook as he handed the drinks to the two women.

Fred's sister arrived back from the telephone box, only to set out again to ask Mr. Warrilow from Lower Spring Road to bring his car around to follow the ambulance to the hospital. He was only too happy to help and was up and dressed in a few minutes.

Fred was on a stretcher and into the ambulance quickly. It was imperative that he received medical attention at the hospital as soon as possible. The ambulance men could do no more for him.

George and May were still in their nightwear, Dorothy was covered in blood. She ran upstairs and hurriedly changed her clothes, before running down again to grab her handbag and jump into Mr. Warrilow's car waiting in the avenue. Margaret jumped in beside her, calling to her parents that they would get word to them as soon as they could. The elderly couple clung onto each other, tears flowing freely. How could their world have turned so upside down in such a few minutes. All their fears of their son being in the war and being killed or injured in action, and such an accident had happened right here in their own house.

Somehow, miraculously some would say, Fred survived the fall. He fractured his skull, but the doctors at the North Staffordshire Royal Infirmary told Dorothy it was good he had bled so badly; it probably saved his life. Dorothy sat beside his bed in the emergency room overnight, holding his hand, whispering into his ear, as the nurses and doctors did their work. At six o'clock in the morning Fred opened his eyes and smiled at his wife, which, the doctors agreed, was a very good thing. At ten o'clock Fred asked for a drink of water and said he had one heck of a headache.

The only thing Dorothy could think was: "He's alive and he's not going to die."

Fred was in the hospital for two weeks, until the doctors were sure healing of the skull bone had begun to take place. He was sent to the military convalescent hospital at Trentham Park for a further four weeks before he was pronounced fit for duty.

Dorothy lived with her grandparents once more, but was able to visit Fred regularly around her shift work at Swynnerton. They were both keenly aware that Fred had escaped death by a hair. They walked hand in hand around the beautiful acreage which surrounded the temporary war hospital, basking in each other's company. They stopped when they were sure they were alone to exchange warm kisses and press their bodies together, remembering the few short days of their honeymoon, which seemed so long ago.

"Knocked you off ya feet did she, Taffy?" joked Fred's buddies when he reported for duty. "Must have been quite the honeymoon."

Fred laughed good-naturedly. Thankfully his battalion had not been deployed into the North African campaign, where the war was raging. They were still training, keeping the tanks oiled and ready. Keeping themselves fit and healthy. Waiting and watching the war month after month. Listening to Mr. Churchill make speeches. Hearing the news of Uboats sinking merchant marine ships in the Atlantic.

The time dragged on for Dorothy, working in munitions, living with Emma and Tom, writing to Fred every day, counting the days until his next leave. She moved to live with Fred's parents while he was on leave, but felt uncomfortable staying there on her own. They were very nice to her, but she hardly knew them. She would soon have her own bedroom in her grandparents house, as Madge was getting married.

Madge and Herbert married at the registrar's office with a handful of people in attendance. Madge wore a blue two-piece suit and wouldn't let Dorothy do her hair or apply even a tinge of lipstick. Herbert had flat feet and a heart murmur, so was exempt from the army. He worked at Paragon China factory in the kilns, responsible for building the fires to "fire" the china.

Longton had the highest number of bottle-neck kilns in the six towns that made up the City of Stoke-on-Trent, with as many as fourteen ovens in one street. When all the kilns were firing, the smoke was so thick in the town that you couldn't see for more than a few feet. The sunniest day would seem like sunset, with the sun casting an orange glow through the mire. On rainy, cloudy days it was dark as night with the rain turning the smoke and soot into black slime on the buildings and pavements.

Emma asked the landlord to let her know if any houses became vacant nearby, and a month before Madge's wedding a small terraced house, tucked in behind a pot bank at the top of Mercy Street, was vacated after the old man who had lived there was found dead in his bed. The landlord had the bits of furniture moved out of the shabby rooms, but did nothing else to make it habitable. It was beyond dirty, the grime of years clung to the walls, floors and ceilings. Herbert went to work, with the help of two of the Marshall boys who were on leave, scrubbing and whitewashing the walls and ceilings. They ripped up all the linoleum, caked in years of greasy dirt, and relaid mismatched pieces of new linoleum. It looked like a patchwork quilt, but it was clean and smelled better.

Herbert and Madge had been frugal. They had never spent money on anything while they were walking out. Herbert had saved enough to buy a few pieces of furniture allowed by the government for couples getting married. The utility bedroom suite was their pride and joy. Madge had been saving ration coupons and buying household items for over three years, so they began their married life with most of the necessities—small compensation for the narrow, tiny house living in the shadow of the bottle-neck kiln.

Leave days for Fred meant a trip to London, where Dorothy was waiting at the flat. There was nowhere in Longton for them to be together and Edward always went to Maidenhead when they were in London, giving them their privacy. Each leave was like another honeymoon—a few precious days together, ending with "Goodbye." Both of them wondering if it was the last "Goodbye."

The German army was bogged down in Russia, the brutally cold winter taking its toll on the ill-equipped troops. More than a million Soviet soldiers were killed and over a million civilians lost their lives in the battle for Stalingrad. Against all odds, Germany was forced to retreat. The second attempt to take the city, led by Germany's famed Sixth Army, ended in a Soviet victory and the newspapers called it a turning point for the war in Europe.

War raged on and on in the Pacific against the Japanese and in Russia, North Africa and Europe against the Germans. The whole world was involved in the conflict in some way. The United States were manufacturing tanks, weapons and ships as quickly as they could be built. The convoys of ships were like a constantly moving caterpillar across the Atlantic Ocean, prime targets for the German Submarines. There were almost daily reports of another ship being lost. The troops and civilians, crammed onto the small island of Great Britain, read their newspapers and listened to their radios, following the war reports as confusion and conflict clashed across the world.

As the allied forces made headway, pushing back the enemy in North Africa, bombing Rome and Naples, Hamburg and Berlin, the mass of troops crammed onto the small island of Britain strained at the leash to cross the English Channel to begin the liberation of Europe.

Fred's second battalion of the Welsh Guards were part of the Armoured Division trained as specialists in tank warfare. They had been on high alert for more than a year now and the men's nerves were frayed from the waiting. Living every day for months thinking *Is this the day we go?* was more than some of the soldiers could bear. On short evening passes on a Friday or Saturday night they would go in groups to the nearest town and drink themselves into oblivion, usually being escorted back to barracks by the military police. Punishment for such misdemeanours was light—whitewash more coal, or peel more potatoes. The officers knew the men under their supervision were stretched to their limit. The call to deploy couldn't come soon enough.

DARLING DOROTHY

*S*ix weeks after Fred's leave at the beginning of October, 1943, Dorothy filled in the paperwork at the factory office to be excluded from yellow powder. Reason given: suspected pregnancy.

Dorothy had missed her period and the stringent rules of the Swynnerton munitions factory were to apply for exemption from yellow powder if pregnancy was suspected.

She didn't want anybody to know, but her best friends questioned her immediately when the next powder shift came and Dorothy wasn't on the shift.

"Why are you exempt, Dot?" asked Winnie, with Olive listening in. "Fred had his leave last month, so it can't be because he's coming on leave again so soon. The only other reason is health. Or, are you in the family way?"

"Don't tell anybody else," Dorothy said, her eyes giving her condition away before she spoke. "I want to make sure first. I've only just missed—a couple of weeks, that's all. It could be something else. No use goin' to the doctors before three months. Promise ya won't say anything to Elsie. She'll tell our Eddie and 'e'll tell Emma. I don't want them to know until I've told Fred."

After missing another period, Dorothy went to see Doctor Elizabeth Livingstone. She confirmed the pregnancy and gave the expectant mother information on how to eat well, if that was possible with the rationing. There were forms to fill out, which Dr. Livingstone signed, applying for extra ration coupons for milk, orange juice and a few ounces of extra meat. The doctor also advised Dorothy to book a midwife for the birth and gave her the names of three women who lived in the area. Dorothy glanced at the list and noticed there was a telephone number beside each name.

"Do not let that grandmother of yours talk you into having the old woman from Mercy Street help with the birth. We have trained midwives available now, who are better qualified to attend you. This is your first baby. It can be a long and sometimes difficult labour. The midwife will recognize any problems and call me if necessary," Dr. Livingstone cautioned Dorothy.

Christmas leave for the majority of the armed forces was a crazy time to be travelling. Fred made his way from Pickering, North Yorkshire, where his battalion had relocated in October of 1943, and joined the thousands of troops on the move. Changing trains three times, he finally reached his destination, slung his kit bag over his shoulder and hurried to his parent's house, where Dorothy would be waiting. He had told her not to try to meet him at the station because he had no idea when the train would arrive, but to pack her suitcase and go to Bell Avenue on Friday December 24th and wait for him there.

Swynnerton factory was just about empty. With all the military not yet deployed coming home on leave, just about every girl working there had applied for a few days off.

As Dorothy sat with May and George Podmore, waiting for Fred to arrive, they listened to the six o'clock news on the radio. The war hadn't stopped because it was Christmas Eve. There was a national radio address by President Roosevelt announcing that U.S. General Dwight D. Eisenhower would command the Allied invasion of continental Europe during the coming year.

"About time," muttered George on hearing the news. "Don't know what's taken 'em this long."

"Does that mean Fred will have to fight?" asked May.

"That's what 'e's been trainin' for," replied George. "For more than four years may I add."

But we're having a baby, Dorothy wanted to say. *All this time waiting and waiting and now we're having a baby they're planning an invasion. Sometime this year? When? Our baby may never have a father!*

Dorothy gave her head a shake and gulped down the lump in her throat. The flutter of fear at the top of her stomach, however, did not go away, as she listened to the rest of the news. American destroyer USS Leary and British destroyer Hurricane were both torpedoed and sunk in the Atlantic by German submarines. For the wives and families of those brave sailors, the war of waiting was over.

The evening dragged on. May served tea and more tea. At least the house had a lav just outside the kitchen door, off a small porch which was open to the elements on one side but had a roof and a tiled floor. The lav also had a chain flush, so was very modern compared with the outhouse in Edward Street. Handy, after all that tea!

At last they heard heavy footsteps running up the path to the front door and Fred burst in, the cold sleet driving into the hallway behind him. He threw down his kitbag and picked up Dorothy, swung her around and kissed her on the lips, producing blushes from his mother. May's turn next; her tall son picked her up while she squealed and laughed at the same time, then he grabbed his father's two hands and shook them both at the same time. Breathless, Fred looked at the three people he loved most in the world. He was so happy to be home. He went back to put his arms around his wife and held her close. She smelled wonderful as he buried his face into her soft dark hair. He could hardly wait to get closer to her.

George was happy to have his son home. They kept up the tradition of going to the pub in Cinderhill for a pint on Christmas Eve. When they arrived home, Dorothy made cheese and onion sandwiches for them, followed by mince pies. Dorothy followed Mrs. Taylor's recipe for flakey, melt-in-the-mouth pastry, which both men declared was the best they'd ever tasted.

Fred cuddled into Dorothy as they lay together in the feather bed, pulling the blankets over their heads against the frigid cold of the unheated bedroom. Fred's parents were in the next room, just a thin wall separating them, making the young couple conscious of every squeak and creek the bed made as they made love. Dorothy waited until they were lying peacefully in each other's arms before she whispered her secret.

"Fred, I have exciting news. I'm having a baby!"

"What?" Fred shouted, forcing his wife to cover his lips with her hand. "How do you know?"

"I've been to the doctors, and anyway, I know because of other things, like missing my period."

The young soldier stared at his wife in the dim light from the gas lamp in the street. He could just see her dark eyes looking up at him. He let his tears fall onto her upturned face, as the thought of a baby, their baby, growing inside her overpowered him.

"We shouldn't have done what we just did," he finally said. "It's probably hurt the baby."

"Don't be silly. Of course it hasn't hurt the baby. Don't worry, everything is fine," Dorothy assured him.

The following morning they told Fred's family about the baby.

"What a Christmas present, eh Ma?" George laughed. "Good on ya, Fred."

He shook his son's hand, beaming at the thought of becoming a grandfather again. May blushed a deep red, not quite knowing what to say, and certainly not able to look at her son. Her son was going to be a father. Well, well, well!

After a hearty breakfast of a whole month's egg ration saved for the occasion, and an exchange of small gifts, Dorothy and Fred left for London, to spend Christmas with Edward.

The flat was dressed in all the Christmas finery, with a tree in the living room and garlands of streamers above each window. There were the usual bowls of fruit, nuts and chocolates laid out on the dining room sideboard, as though rationing was non-existent. A Christmas dinner was waiting for them when they arrived, prepared by Mrs. Taylor who joined them for the meal. Roast chicken, potatoes, stuffing, carrots, green beans and a rich gravy, followed by plum pudding and rum sauce.

As they were finishing dinner, the young couple told Edward their news.

Edward had waited a lifetime to have his own child. He was fifty-two years of age when Dorothy was born; a child he never thought he would have. Now he was to have a grand-child. He jumped up from his chair and gently pulled his daughter to her feet, embracing her in his arms, the emotion showing on his face.

"Darling girl," he said. "You have no idea how happy this news makes me. A grandchild! Becoming a father was almost more than I could imagine, but this is beyond anything I had ever dreamed."

Edward turned and took Fred's hands in his.

"Congratulations my boy. You are about half the age I was when I became a father. Congratulations!"

Mrs. Taylor made more coffee and they sat around for the rest of the evening enjoying each other's company and listening to the songs from the hit musical Show Boat on Edward's gramophone. Fred loved the song Old Man River, and the following evening Edward surprised them with tickets to the musical in the west end. The theatre was full of soldiers, sailors and airmen from Britain and America, but Fred knew he was the happiest among them all. He had the prettiest wife and he had a baby on the way.

All too soon the weekend was over and they were travelling back to the midlands. Fred to pack his kit bag once more and left for Yorkshire and Dorothy returned to Emma and Tom's house in Longton. It was a routine that they had fallen into. It was life!

Spring wore into the summer. The entire country was waiting on a daily basis for news of the impending invasion.

The letter lay on the table in the kitchen waiting for Dorothy. There was nothing unusual about it. A letter came most days from Guardsman Podmore. It was June 5th, 1944, a quiet Monday afternoon, and Dorothy had been at Aunt Mary-Ann's knitting baby clothes. Aunty Mary-Ann was an accomplished knitter and had patterns and needles galore. Dorothy learned quickly under her great aunt's supervision and had made several knitted jackets and a beautiful shawl in a feather and fan pattern. Everything she made was in white, suitable for a boy or girl, and the expectant mother had begged ration coupons from everybody to get enough wool for her projects.

Dorothy tore open the envelope, smiling at the SWALK on the back, the code for " Sealed With A Loving Kiss." She threw her coat onto the sofa as she flipped open the envelope and took out the single sheet of paper. Her face paled and her hand went to her throat as she read the opening of the letter.

"Darling Dorothy," it read. Not "My Dearest Dorothy," like all the other letters. The war had begun for Fred. The coded message told his young wife that his unit had been deployed.

She sat down with a thud on the sofa on top of her coat, reading the beginning of the letter over and over. The sensor would have blacked out any mention of war activity, so Fred had been careful to keep the note light and chatty, how training was going, Friday night at the pub playing dominoes with the lads, non-stop rain over the moors. The important words were all in the greeting "Darling Dorothy."

The baby was due in less than four weeks. Fred's leave was already booked—five days compassionate leave to begin when the baby was born, approximately July 3rd, 1944. The two words at the beginning of the letter told Dorothy that he wouldn't be there for his leave. He wouldn't see his baby. He would be somewhere across the English Channel fighting the Germans.

"What's up with ya?" Emma questioned, seeing the change in her granddaughter. "Bad news, is it?"

"Fred's battalion's been deployed. He's going abroad to fight."

"Well, that's why 'e's in the army," piped up Tom, puffing on his pipe and trying not to look at Dorothy. "It 'ad to 'appen. Mr. Churchill knows what 'e's doin'. 'E'll send them bloody Gerries packin' when our lads get over there."

It was more words than Tom had uttered together for a long time. He was proud of the soldiers going to fight. He was proud of young Fred who would be one of the first over there. His eyes glittered in the firelight as he imagined the troops leaving England and sailing across the Channel in a mighty force.

"I'm going out," Dorothy said, grabbing her coat. "I have to tell Fred's mam and dad about the letter."

It took Dorothy thirty minutes to walk up the hill to Normacot to take the news to Fred's family. She was heavy with the baby and she walked slowly, going over what she would say when she arrived at the house in Bell Avenue. The words weren't needed. One look at her face and George knew.

"When did you 'ear?" George said quietly.

"Today. I came straight 'ere," Dorothy replied, her face crumpling into tears.

"What's it all about?" asked May, looking from George to Dorothy in confusion.

"It's Fred," explained Dorothy through her tears. "'E's gone abroad with 'is unit."

"Abroad?" May questioned. "What does that mean?"

"Ma," explained her husband. "It means 'e's going to fight. Abroad means to another country. Not England. Over the channel—probably into France."

"France?" May said, still confused by it all. "I don't think 'e'll like that much. They eat very funny stuff over there, I 'eard."

Then as it dawned on her that her son would be in the middle of the war, fighting the Germans. She sat down at the table and covered her head with her apron. The three of them sat in silence, each with their own thoughts of what the news meant to them.

The following day, June 6th 1944, the radio began repeating the same message over and over. It was D-Day and the invasion had begun. Thousands of allied troops, transported by over four thousand ships, had landed on the French coast, supported by RAF attacks and parachute regiments. King George VI addressed the nation asking for the people to pray for the men going into battle. Every military unit stationed all over Britain moved south towards the English Channel as more and more troops followed the initial 156,000 who landed on D-Day.

BABY

The 2nd Battalion of the Welsh Guards, Fred's regiment, was among the troops moving south in June of 1944. The small country roads of England were jammed with tanks and armoured vehicles slowly crawling their way towards the English Channel. Fred's legs and back ached from being crammed into the bottom of the tank in the gunner's seat. He was ordered to spend several hours a day in that seat to accustom himself to the claustrophobic and cramped conditions. The rest of the time, when the tank was on the move, he tried to be up top with his head out in the fresh air, watching the English countryside glide by at a speed slower than a walking pace.

Fred thought of Dorothy constantly, because he knew what this big move south meant. Their baby was due very soon and he would not be there. His heart ached at the thought of it. He didn't share his feelings with his mates. They were all in the same boat. All had wives and some had children. The camaraderie between the soldiers living in such close quarters with each other for such a long time, was a bond closer than a brother. These five tank mates were Fred's second family—the men he had trained with, showered with, slept with, eaten with for four years. They told jokes, played cards and dominoes, drank beer and sang songs together. These were the men who would lay down their lives for each other if needed.

Thoughts of Dorothy and the baby filled Fred's waking hours as the English Channel loomed in front of him. The tank regiment was lined up along the quay waiting to load onto a ship. They had been there for two days, waiting. The Channel was notoriously rough water and the crossing to France for the young guardsmen was no different. The water was choppy, the waves broke high on the bow of the ship, pitching the ship up and down with each wave. Many of the soldiers were lined up along the railings on each side of the ship retching into the sea, Fred among them. It was June 18th and they were on their way to France.

The work of clearing the beach and pushing back the Germans had fallen to those first soldiers at the beginning of June.

Nothing could have prepared the troops on board the ship for what greeted them on the shores of France. Wide sandy beaches full of tanks and armoured vehicles, the previous tracks of numerous other disembarkations criss-crossed the beaches. It looked chaotic. It seemed to take hours to offload all the tanks onto the beach. The men were not at their best; many had been sick during the crossing, they were all tired from days of waiting, sleeping in tents on camp cots fully clothed. They were grateful that they were not welcomed by the German army firing on them from the pill boxes in the sand dunes.

Fred's regiment made its way to Bayeux, a small town about

four miles from the coast. It was the first French town to be liberated after D-Day. The regiment, along with other tank regiments, set up camp in the fields outside the town and waited for orders. The weather was warm, so sleeping outside wasn't any great hardship, except for mosquitoes which seemed to enjoy the blood of the young Englishmen immensely. Fred, who was fair skinned, was particularly bothered by the pesky insects and after two days he was covered in itchy bites. Water was available from a pump house at the end of the lane. Latrines were dug in a separate field behind a hedge, with soldiers on "water duty" bringing water in buckets for hand washing. Each tank designated a soldier to collect an empty gas can full of water every day for cleaning up—every soldier had to shave every day, as well as use the small amount of water for an occasional strip wash. They laughed and joked about the Germans attacking while they were stripped naked, lathered in soap. At least if they were captured they would smell nice and be clean shaven.

On June 29th, 1944, the warm, sunny weather in Longton was replaced by a dark, cloudy sky. Rain threatened but didn't start. It was Thursday and Emma had been to Aunt Lena's for the afternoon. Dorothy's back ached and she had the beginnings of a headache. She had spent the day with Aunt Sarah, making scones. With her large family, Aunt Sarah had enough coupons to buy flour to bake a few scones once in a while. Dorothy mixed the small ration of butter with lard to make it go further. They would spread it onto the scones while they were still warm—what a treat!

Everything was ready for the baby. She would have moved to Fred's parents to have the baby if he'd been coming on leave, but didn't feel right about being there without him. Mrs. Plant, who was widowed and lived on her own, loaned Dorothy a single bed, and the Marshall boys set it up in the front parlour of Emma's house. The midwife, Janet Brannigan, had been notified of the baby's due date. The tiny clothes had been washed and lay in a clean cardboard box under the single bed, along with a blanket and all the necessary equipment on the midwife's list. The Marshall girls had scrubbed and cleaned the parlour at Emma's house until it shone. It was probably cleaner than it had ever been.

As Dorothy ate her warm scone, she suddenly felt nauseous and put the scone down.

"What's up?" asked Aunt Sarah anxiously, seeing the change on Dorothy's face.

"I'm not feeling so well," explained her niece. "Maybe just the cloudy day. And I have such a back ache."

"Well now, I'll get ya a glass of water," fussed Aunt Sarah. "Ya just sit there and take deep breaths."

By the time Dorothy had made her way across the street to Emma's house, she was feeling worse. She decided to sleep in the single bed in the parlour instead of climbing the stairs. The bed was all made ready and she sunk onto the mattress, happy to be off her feet. She felt better when she was lying down. She slept fitfully, waking many times with the pain in her back. On Friday morning, when she went up the yard to use the lav, there was no doubt what the back pain was. She was in labour. The signs the midwife had told her to look for were evident. Her baby was on its way.

The midwife sent for Dr. Livingstone on Friday night. Dorothy had laboured all day and was reaching exhaustion. The back labour was painful and the labour wasn't progressing. The doctor sympathized with Dorothy, but said all was well apart from the position of the baby, which was causing the back labour.

"It's unfortunate, but the baby will take its time, Dorothy," the doctor said. "Everything is as it should be. You will deliver the baby eventually. Try to sleep a little between contractions."

Dorothy put her head under the bed sheet and cried quietly. The pain was much worse than anybody had described. The midwife left, promising to return in a couple of hours. Dolly and the Marshall girls popped in and out, bringing Dorothy warm scones and making tea—neither of which she could keep down. Sips of water moistened her mouth and wet cloths on her forehead gave some relief. The heat was oppressive. Dorothy couldn't find a comfortable position to lie in the narrow bed. She tried sitting on the side of the bed, then kneeling beside it. She tried standing with her arms outstretched clutching the mantle over the fireplace. Nothing eased the pain.

"Just keep Emma away from me," Dorothy said, glaring at Marion Marshall through frightened eyes. "She's been in 'ere enough times to scowl at me, calling me a 'bloody cry baby.' Please, Marion, get 'er out of the 'ouse if ya're me friend."

Dorothy doubled over as a surge of pain racked her thin body.

Marion did as she was bid and persuaded her Aunt Emma to spend some time at Sarah's house, bribing her with the promise of freshly baked soda bread and strawberry jam.

In the silence of the dim, steamy room, Dorothy thrashed and moaned through each contraction. She reached under the bed for her small "London" case. Lifting the lid, she rummaged through silk underwear, high-heeled shoes, make-up and jewellery bags, hand cream and perfume. Her fingers finally touched on the small metal statue. Symbol of bravery! Maybe it would help her now. As the next wave of pain engulfed her, Dorothy squeezed the Prussian Captain with all her might, leaving the imprint of him in the palm of her hand.

The thunderstorm began in the early hours of Saturday morning, as though it sympathized with the young mother's birth pangs, by banging and crashing, shaking the small house with its fervour. During the worst of the storm, at six o'clock in the morning, the midwife guided a small head out of the birth canal, then gently supported the tiny body as it slid into the world. A tiny baby girl with black hair and a loud scream was born in the same room as her grandmother, Gertrude. The big difference being that her father wasn't there to see her. He was somewhere in France.

July 1st, 1944 dawned hot and humid, and the soldiers of the expeditionary force crawled out of their tents, stretching and yawning to face the day. The commander of the 2nd Battalion of the Welsh Guards was a famous film star, Anthony Bushell. None of the regular soldiers had ever met him. He gave the orders to the NCOs and they passed the orders down the line. There was no need for the commanding officer to meet or talk to a regular soldier, unless there was a severe breach in discipline or some other very important reason.

"Guardsman Podmore, report to the CO immediately," yelled the sergeant major from his tent entrance.

Fred was playing football with his mates in front of the tents when he heard the order. He put his jacket on, grabbed his hat, checked his boots for mud and hurried to the CO's tent.

"Come in, Guardsman," said Anthony Bushell. "There's a telegram for you."

FRED JULY 1ST A DAUGHTER BOTH WELL
DOROTHY

The CO took two glasses from the desk drawer, and reached for a bottle of scotch. He poured the scotch into the glasses and handed one of them to Fred, who took it in a daze.

"Congratulations Guardsman," said Commander Bushell. "A baby girl. Well done!"

He clinked Fred's glass and drank the scotch. Fred hadn't moved. The CO coughed and pointed a finger at the glass in Fred's hand. Fred poured the scotch down his throat, feeling the burning as it went down and feeling reality return.

"Thank you, Sir," he managed to say. Then, saluting and turning on his heel he walked out of the tent, the telegram clutched in his hand.

He didn't go back to his mates right away. He needed time to read the telegram again and absorb the few words it contained. A girl! A baby girl! He walked to the far side of the field and sat under the hedge, staring at the precious piece of paper and thinking about Dorothy. He prayed he would see his baby one day. That he wouldn't be killed. He begged God for compassion, even though he knew thousands had already died and thousands would yet die. He asked for protection from his God so that he would see his baby one day.

BLIGHTY

*N*ormandy was one giant battle field as the British pushed forward. Resistance from the German army was strong as they battled for the small towns of northern France. The German Tiger tanks were feared and respected by all. Bigger and more powerful than the Sherman and Cromwell tanks of the Guards regiments. Losses on both sides were heavy and the countryside was soon littered with burned-out tanks, armoured cars and broken bodies.

The telegram from Dorothy was folded neatly and carried in Fred's inside pocket next to his heart. As the noise of battle surrounded him, he thought about his wife and baby. In the belly of the Cromwell tank, crammed into the gunner's seat, firing shells at the enemy as ordered, he wondered at the futility of it all. Young men killing young men. The future of every country in jeopardy with the loss of a generation of young men. Orders were followed without question as they fought on through each small town. Four years training did that! No questions, no thoughts of your own. Just follow orders.

A long-awaited letter from Dorothy somehow made it to Fred. The envelope looked like it had been through its own battle. Covered in splatters of mud, one corner torn, the writing smudged. There was a small bulge in the envelope and Fred could see that it had been opened and resealed. He tore it open and read the single page from his wife. She had named their baby Ann. He liked it! From Dorothy's description he imagined how she looked, and brushed away a tear and tried to swallow the lump in his throat. The soft bulge in the envelope was a slipper—the first one worn by his baby girl. Fred gazed at the tiny white satin slipper, amazed at how tiny it was. He put it with the telegram, next to his heart.

As they neared the Belgian border, the German soldiers were putting up less and less of a fight, many surrendering without firing a shot. The Welsh First Infantry Battalion, now joined with the Second Tank Regiment, took two hundred prisoners in one morning. On September 1st, Fred's tank was among the first to enter Belgium, leading a reconnaissance group down the narrow country lane into the first small town in Belgium.

The Germans had fled and the people of Belgium were waiting. They streamed out of their houses, cheering and crying. They threw flowers and flags onto the tank. They were ecstatically happy. After four years of German occupation, the British were liberating them. They were free. Fred and his mates waved and smiled from the top of the tank. They sent a rider back to the CO to say there was no resistance and slowly made their way onto the next town.

The 2nd Battalion of the Welsh Guards had the honour to be the first allied troops to enter Brussels. On September 3rd, at

7 o'clock in the morning, the first tank entered the outskirts of the great capital city. The people were waiting, running out of their homes, some still in their nightwear. The streets were ablaze with flags and soon the tanks were covered in flowers. The people of Brussels cried and laughed and sang as they handed the soldiers fruit and cakes. Bottles of wine, beer and even champagne, hidden for years beneath floorboards and in attics, were gratefully handed to the soldiers. It was time to celebrate and celebrate they did.

As Fred's tank came to a halt and parked in a side street for the night, a woman approached the five young men and asked if they would like to go to her house for something to eat, and to clean up. She had bread, cheese and a thick soup waiting. The soldiers hadn't had a warm meal for weeks. They ate the soup with relish, feeling it warm their cold, tired bodies. The bathroom was put at their disposal, which was a luxury to men who hadn't seen a bathroom since June. Being used to sharing whatever facilities they could find, they had no inhibitions about sharing the bathroom. The kind lady who owned the house had left soap, towels, shaving brushes and razors for them to use. They rotated around the small room—one on the toilet, one in the bath, one having a shave, until all five were clean and shaved. The warm bath water soaked away the grime of months living rough, although, by the time the fifth soldier used the water, it didn't look clean any more. The shave, with warm water and soap that smelled of pine trees, made them all feel like new men.

They couldn't thank the kind lady enough. She smiled and wept and thanked them for freeing her country.

"My husband, he would have been proud to have you in his home," she said. "He never accepted the occupation and died two years ago because it made him so sad."

One by one the five soldiers hugged and kissed their benefactor.

By nightfall it seemed the whole city was involved in the party as they danced in the streets, finding more and more bottles to share. A band came from somewhere, and played in the square in the city centre until the early hours of the morning.

The soldiers slept under the tanks or on the wide boulevards for a few hours, contentedly filled with food and wine and the joy of the day.

Then the fighting began again. Orders were received to push towards Nijmegen to secure the bridge. Days turned into weeks as the tanks fought their way further into German occupied territory, the battles becoming more and more intense. The Battle of the Bulge they called it, and it seemed there were days when the soldiers didn't sleep or eat.

Sleeping in a field, the tank parked on the other side of the hedge in the lane, the dawn crept over the ice-crusted ground to wake the soldiers. Fred couldn't believe how cold he was. He had barely slept. He couldn't feel his hands and feet. Even with his thick army blanket wrapped around him, he shivered as the cold penetrated through to his thin body. Enough! He stood up and jumped up and down, flapping his arms to get his circulation moving.

"Guardsman," shouted the Sergeant Major, coming into the field and seeing Fred awake. "Take this note up the line to the CO. Quick as you can."

"Yes, Sir."

Fred took the note from the sergeant and jogged off up the

line to deliver it. As soon as he had placed the note in the hands of the CO's adjutant, the shelling began. A line of German Tiger tanks were on the other side of the next field firing shells onto them. They had the distance right and the shells were hitting their targets. Fred raced back down the line to get to his tank, orders to engage the enemy being shouted as he ran.

He could see his tank, but there was no way he was going to make it into the gunners seat. He always had to be first into the tank to get into its belly before the other four took their places. He saw his mates jumping into the tank. He would have to take another position and one of his mates would fire the gun. They were all trained to do each other's jobs just in case. Fred reached the tank and jumped up to get inside as quickly as he could—the other four were all inside. He opened the hatch to enter the tank, but didn't make it.

BOOM! Fred's ears popped. His head filled with the noise of the shell. Everything went black. Pain! Pain in his right knee. He was being dragged, or carried by somebody. The noise was deafening as shells landed around them. Somebody was leaning over him and telling him to lie still in a distant voice. Fred realized he wasn't dead and opened his eyes to see his sergeant leaning over him.

"Stay where you are. A medic will find you," the sergeant said.

There was nothing Fred could do except lie still. The sergeant had dragged him into a field, where he lay listening to the terrible sounds of war. The pain in his leg tore into him. He looked down to see his right knee a mass of blood. The right leg of his pants had been blown away, along with his right boot. The blood pooled under his knee, spreading out on the ground below and soaking into the earth. He didn't dare move. What had happened? Where were his mates? Was his tank still firing on the enemy? Would he get out of this alive?

When the noise finally stopped, the silence was deafening. Fred felt like his head was full of cotton wool. Maybe he was deaf! Then he heard the sounds of people moving on the other side of the hedge. Not knowing if they were British or German, Fred kept quiet. He could see smoke above the hedge and smell burning rubber and sulphur. The Tiger tanks had caught them unprepared. Fred doubted it was his regiment he could hear.

"Anybody out there," rang out a voice into the field.

Fred couldn't believe what he was hearing. He tried to raise himself on one elbow, but collapsed back to the ground.

"Over here," he forced himself to shout back.

The medic splinted and wrapped Fred's leg and said he'd call for a stretcher.

"What happened to my tank?"

"Don't know, mate," said the medic. "It's chaos on the road. Lots of injuries, so it might be a while before they get to you. I do know the CO got some infantry blokes behind the German tanks and knocked them about enough for them to take off. Good on him, right?"

Fred waited a long time for a stretcher. He thought they'd forgotten him. The sky darkened and the cold increased as he lay shivering on the wet earth. He took out the telegram, now worn and stained, and read about his baby girl, imagining her so tiny and beautiful. She seemed very far away.

"This one's lost a lot of blood," said the stretcher bearer, waking Fred.

As they carried him out of the field into the lane, Fred saw what was left of his tank. It had taken a direct hit. He had been thrown clear because he hadn't made it inside. He didn't have to ask what had happened to his four best friends. There would have been nothing left of them. They had been blown to pieces. The young men he had shared his life with for four years. They were gone. Fred closed his eyes as they carried him to the field ambulance. The explosion of grief too overwhelming, he was sobbing quietly as he slipped into unconsciousness.

The field hospital doctor told Fred he had shattered his knee cap and lost a lot of blood. His leg was stitched and dressed and he was sent to the ward to recover. The large tent where Fred was taken was full of soldiers on cots, but rather than a depressed atmosphere, Fred found camaraderie among the injured soldiers. They were the soldiers who were not injured badly enough to be evacuated home. They were all expected to heal and go back into service. They played cards during the day and listened to the radio, cheering when they heard of battles won.

The field hospital medical and orderly staff did their best to celebrate Christmas with the injured soldiers in their care. They formed a choir and sang Christmas carols. They stuck dead tree branches into a barrel in each tent and the soldiers decorated them with paper chains. The cooks even managed to produce canned chicken, mixed with rice for Christmas dinner. Anything to diminish the sadness of being separated from loved ones at such a time.

Fred wept into his pillow late on Christmas Eve. He held Ann's little satin slipper in his hand and squeezed his eyes shut, imagining Dorothy holding their baby. He could hear other stifled sobs coming from other army cots in the hospital tent. It was a longing for home they couldn't share with each other.

"You're for Blighty," the orderly told Fred two days after Christmas. "Germans have launched a big counter attack and our boys are losing ground. They're worried the field hospital may have to be moved back. We can only keep the chaps with minor injuries, who can be back in the war in a few days."

Fred's injury had a long recovery time. He was on his way home, along with hundreds of others who would convalesce in England. He hadn't been able to get a letter to Dorothy for weeks. There had been no postal service while the battalion was on the move. He couldn't let her know he was heading home.

The agonizing trip from the field hospital in the back of Red Cross lorries was slow and painful. The wait on the docks lined with hundreds of injured soldiers was interminable, with flies and mosquitoes swarming around the sweltering young men. The Channel crossing added to the suffering, with waves tossing them up and down. The only place to throw up from a stretcher was on the deck, which was soon awash with more than sea spray. Some didn't survive the journey. Fred never took his hand off the precious little slipper in his pocket, and prayed he would soon be warm, dry and safe.

IS THAT ALL

*D*orothy doted on her baby. Her confinement had been difficult and her recovery long, but it was worth it when she looked at her baby. Her perfectly formed round head, covered with a soft down of black hair. Her dark eyes, her cherry lips, her perfect round cheeks. The midwife had guessed she weighed about six pounds. She was healthy and strong despite her size.

After receiving a letter almost every day from Fred, there had only been a few since June. The letters had been full of questions about baby Ann and full of love for Dorothy. Sometimes he had inadvertently disclosed some taboo information and Dorothy opened the letter to find lines blacked out. She wrote back diligently, sharing everything about their little daughter, even sending Fred the first shoe Ann wore. The letters, although infrequent, were a lifeline between the young couple.

May and George wanted Dorothy to move in with them once the baby was born. Dorothy desperately wanted to get away from Longton, so she packed up Ann's pram and balanced a suitcase on top and walked up the hill to Bell Avenue.

Emma was happy to see them go. She didn't want any more babies in the house.

"Off ya go then, Miss Muck," she hurled at Dorothy as she was packing her bags. "Off to live in a posh 'ouse with a bloody indoor lav and 'ot water. See 'ow they like 'earing that babbie crying all bloody night. Ya've lived off us long enough, Miss."

May had the upstairs bedroom all ready and waiting. She had borrowed a cot from her sister, Daisy, and had it set up for baby Ann. Margaret was happy to sleep in the box room on a single bed. George couldn't stop smiling as Dorothy asked him to hold the baby while she unpacked her things. His eyes misted as he looked down at the perfect little face. Fred's baby! Maybe the only part of his son he would have to hold onto.

Visiting her father had been off limits again for Dorothy. Germany had launched their flying bombs, called doodle-bugs, at London in retaliation for D-Day. As many as one hundred of the dreaded silent bombs fell in one day over London, making it extremely dangerous. As the allies began to make inroads into the occupied territory, the attacks became less frequent and, by October of 1944, had dwindled to practically nothing. Dorothy's first visit to see her father with Ann was in November.

Edward arranged for John Goodwin to pick Dorothy up at Euston Station and bring her to the flat. He anxiously paced the floor, calling on Mrs. Taylor every few minutes to make sure the kettle was boiled and all was ready for his daughter's arrival. Her light step on the stairs sent him hurrying towards the door.

"Darling girl," he greeted her. "Come in. I've been waiting all day."

Edward itched with anticipation at the bundle in Dorothy's arms. Fast asleep, Ann was handed to her grandfather. He pulled the blanket away from her face and gazed in wonder at the baby. She looked like Dorothy as a baby. His face crumpled into tears as his memory took him back twenty-three years to the most important day of his life. This day was probably the next most important day. A granddaughter!

"What do you think of her, Father?" asked Dorothy, coming around to the side of him and linking her arm through his. "Isn't she beautiful?"

"She is indeed. I am the happiest man alive at this moment."

Ann was one spoiled baby. Her grandfather had to buy her everything. The best pram, the best cradle, the best clothes. For Dorothy, a lovely rocking chair in her bedroom with a footstool for nursing the baby, new coat and hat, new boots. Dorothy was back to her "other" world. Their days were spent walking in Hyde Park, eating Mrs. Taylor's delicious food, talking and resting and listening to music. Edward insisted on taking Dorothy out to dinner, and Mrs. Taylor happily babysat. They stayed for two weeks, but Dorothy was anxious to get back to the Potteries in case there was a letter from Fred. She promised her father that she would come back for Christmas, and he reluctantly kissed her goodbye.

Two letters from Fred were waiting for her. They were both quite old, both dated in August, but she was happy to just see his handwriting and hear his voice speaking through the words he wrote. The weeks flew by with Ann growing and changing. As promised, Dorothy went to London for Christmas, to the delight of her father, who loved having his daughter near. This year in particular was extra special with a baby in the middle of their lives. Ann loved the lights on the Christmas tree. She loved Edward and delighted in him bouncing her on his knee and singing to her. Her smiles were all for him, and he adored her. Dorothy had such a rest when she was at the flat. Mrs. Taylor looked after all the cooking and cleaning and shopping. The young mother had only her baby to care for and her father to keep company. The worry of the war was always with her, but they heard every day news of allied victories and Dorothy was sure Fred would soon be home.

After Christmas, January dragged on, cold and bleak. Dorothy and Ann were back in Bell Avenue, not venturing out unless the rain stopped long enough for a walk to the shops on the high street. No letter had arrived since before Christmas, which made Dorothy nervous. Every day she watched for the post man and saw him walk past number five. Where was Fred? What was happening? Was he safe?

A telegram arrived in the middle of January. It was addressed to Mrs. Dorothy Podmore and was from the war office. With trembling hands, Dorothy read the telegram out loud to Fred's waiting parents.

GUARDSMAN FRED PODMORE IN MANCHESTER ROYAL INFIRMARY STOP

"Oh, my God!" whispered Dorothy, handing the telegram to George. "He's been injured. I must go at once."

May sat at the table, putting her apron over her head, which was her usual pose when something bad happened.

Dorothy organized everything quickly. She had enough

money for the train fare to Manchester. It wasn't far from Longton. Fred's cousin, Emmy, had a telephone and got in touch with a bed and breakfast close to the hospital in Manchester and booked Dorothy in for a week. Margaret said she would go with her sister-in-law to help look after Ann; George gave his daughter her train fare and money towards the accommodation. By the afternoon they were on their way. Dorothy packed Ann's pram with all the things the baby would need and the pram was put into the guard's van at the back of the train.

By four o'clock the two young women had found their lodgings and Dorothy, having fed Ann, left her with Margaret and set out for the Manchester Royal Infirmary, not knowing what she would find.

As she walked through the main door of the hospital, all Dorothy saw was men with their eyes bandaged. *Oh no! He's blind! It's a blind hospital. He'll never be able to see our baby. He'll never be able to go back to work. He'll need help for the rest of his life.* The thoughts raced through her head as she made her way to the information kiosk and gave them her husband's full name.

As she made her way through the corridors of the vast hospital, Dorothy passed wards filled with wounded soldiers, spilling into the corridors on stretchers or cots. She thought she might faint at the sight and smell of the wounded surrounding her. Terrible injuries. Men with no legs, no arms, heads bandaged, ghastly pale faces, burn victims covered in purple stained cloths.

She reached ward 42B at last and scanned the rows of beds for her husband.

"Can I help you?" the nurse sitting at the desk just inside the ward asked.

"Guardsman Podmore."

"Bed number eighteen. It's on the right," the nurse instructed.

Dorothy's legs were weak and wobbly as she neared bed number eighteen. The curtains were drawn around the bed next to it, so that she couldn't see who occupied the bed until she was past the curtains.

It was Fred!

He was sitting in bed reading a newspaper.

"Fred," Dorothy called to him, making him drop the newspaper with a jolt. "Tell me what's wrong."

Fred dropped the newspaper and tried to get out of bed, almost falling on the floor in the process. He propped himself up with his good leg and engulfed Dorothy with his arms, burying his face in her hair and trying not to cry.

"Tell me what's wrong," Dorothy repeated.

"It's me leg. I've shattered me knee cap,"

"Is that all!" exclaimed Dorothy, a look of relief washing over her face.

"Is that all?" echoed Fred.

"I'm so sorry," she whispered into his ear, laying her head on his shoulder. "I had imagined every kind of terrible injury as I walked through the hospital. I'm sorry you're injured. I'm just happy you're not blind."

She lifted her face to his and kissed him gently on his lips. Fred almost toppled over again. Having Dorothy in his arms was something he had been imagining for months, and he clung onto her, showering her with kisses. The soldiers in the ward hooted and whistled at the passionate display, but shy Fred just kept right on kissing Dorothy.

They had so much to say to each other. So much time to make up. Yet it was enough to be close.

"Where's the baby?" Fred asked, once the initial shock of his wife turning up so unexpectedly had subsided.

"She's with your sister, Margaret, at the lodgings we're staying at. Margaret came with me so that she could watch Ann while I visited you. Babies aren't allowed in the hospital."

"But I can come outside in a wheelchair to see her. Can you bring her tomorrow? I'll ask the nurse if I can get a wheelchair for an hour in the afternoon. They're in high demand around here, as you may imagine, but the nurse on duty tomorrow likes me and I think she'll cooperate."

It was all set up for the following afternoon. Dorothy and Margaret wheeled the pram around to the hospital at three o'clock. Ann was dressed in a cozy pale pink pram suit, knitted by Aunt Mary-Ann, and sat propped up on a pink pillow.

Margaret stayed with Ann, while Dorothy went to the ward to collect Fred.

A nurse wheeled Fred outside, bundled in blankets and found a quiet spot along the street from the main door for the quick visit. Margaret wheeled the pram beside the wheelchair and gave her brother a kiss on his cheek as she brought the baby alongside. Her brother's eyes were only on his baby. Eyes that overflowed with tears as he saw her for the first time, sitting there looking so beautiful with a gummy smile and shining dark eyes.

Dorothy lifted her little daughter out of the pram and handed her to Fred, whose arms had escaped from the blankets to hold her. Ann looked up at the strange man. Her face crumpled into tears and she began to howl. Fred tried to soothe her, but she became more upset, looking around at her mother for rescue. Dorothy took her and hugged her close, stopping the crying instantly.

"Don't worry, Fred," Dorothy said. "She makes strange with anybody she doesn't know. She'll get used to you. She doesn't know you're her dad."

Ann peeked at the stranger from the protection of her mother's shoulder. She even let the stranger touch her fingers. Fred couldn't believe he was a father. He stared and stared at the miracle in front of him. She looked like Dorothy. He thought his heart would burst with love for both of them. He stroked her tiny fingers and tried to make her smile, but she just glowered back at him and hid her face again.

It was enough. Fred had met his daughter.

The wheelchair wasn't available for the rest of the week, but Fred treasured the memory of that first meeting and every time he closed his eyes it was Ann's face he saw. Dorothy was there every day to visit, holding his hand and dreaming about life after the war. Fred was assessed and told he would be moving into a convalescent home soon. By the time Dorothy's week in Manchester was over, Fred had learned of his transfer to Trentham. So close to home! He would stay there until he was completely healed, before rejoining his regiment. He was being moved the following week and the young couple were ecstatically happy.

VICTORY

Trentham Park was a maze of tents. Wounded soldiers filled every available space in the designated area for convalescence. The park covered many acres and was covered in trees and shrubs. Walkways ran in every direction like rivers across a delta, giving the soldiers pathways to explore and fresh air to breath. Only a few miles from the city of Stoke-on-Trent, where the black smoke of the kilns never stopped filling the sky with their pollution, Trentham Park was an oasis.

There was about twelve inches of space between the cots in the tent where Fred was housed. He was used to living in close quarters after almost five years in the army. He was grateful he was still alive and that he had a clean cot to sleep in, food to fill his belly and his wife and baby only four miles away. His knee improved every day and he could manage with two sticks instead of crutches. His open wounds had healed well and it was just a matter of waiting for the bones in his knee cap to knit together.

More damaging was the emotional distress of the last day of

battle, when Fred's four best friends had been killed. They were closer than brothers. They had spent years together, living, eating and sleeping a few feet from each other. He dreamt about them, he thought about them. He had days when that's all he thought about. Why had he not been killed along with them? If he hadn't have taken the message to the CO, he would have been killed. The faces of his friends haunted him day and night, the crash of the shell hitting the tank crashed into his dreams, waking him with a jolt, his body covered in sweat and his heart racing.

Most of the young men around Fred were going through the same ordeal. Night time was not for the faint-hearted in their tent. Screams and shouts and men sobbing were regular sounds during the dark hours. They all had their demons to deal with, demons they couldn't talk about. The days were better, filled with walks around the park, playing cards, watching movies in the hall, listening to music on the radio. Fred even learned to sew—he made a green felt horse for Ann, complete with saddle, mane and tail. He named him flicker.

Dorothy left Ann with Gramma May when she went to visit Fred. Ann could drink from a bottle, so Dorothy had time to catch the bus to Longton, then Trentham, and didn't have to rush back to feed Ann. Children under twelve weren't allowed on the grounds and Fred wasn't allowed out, so he never saw his baby girl. The young couple had no privacy, but walked hand in hand around the tents under the trees. They snatched a quick kiss or two when they thought nobody was looking, but invariably there were soldiers around who would whistle and whoop at the sight of the kiss, causing Fred to blush and Dorothy to laugh.

Within a few weeks, Fred no longer needed two canes and

was reassessed and received orders to report to Knights-bridge Barracks in London.

This was the greatest news for Dorothy. She could move in with Edward and live in the flat while Fred was in London. He would have regular leaves, even weekends or days. She would be able to see him all the time. He would get to know Ann.

It was almost spring and the news from the war on all fronts was positive. The allies had crossed the Rhine and were in Germany. The allies had pushed back the Japanese and were liberating island after island in the Pacific. Maybe Fred wouldn't have to go back into action after all.

Edward was delighted to have his daughter staying with him once more. Any opportunity he had to give her and his granddaughter a home was grasped. Mrs. Taylor had been busy once more preparing the flat for Dorothy and Ann, brushing down the pram and crib and washing all the blankets and pillows. London in the spring, with no bombs falling! Spring blossoms in Hyde Park. Green grass and bud-laden trees. Ducks and swans to feed on the Serpentine Lake. The people of London, friendly and cocky as ever, enjoying the promise of rebuilding their city, of welcoming their children home, of seeing their young men return. The tide had turned and the allies were gaining ground.

The quartermaster's store was Fred's new assignment. It was like falling into Aladdin's cave. The massive warehouse was full, floor to ceiling, with every imaginable product used by the army.

"Anything you want, Dot," Fred said, as he greeted his wife at the door of the barracks. "I'm not kiddin.' This placed is filled to the rafters with stuff."

Dorothy laughed. They had been in London for only a week and Fred hadn't had a leave yet, but she had visited him twice at the barracks, where he had been able to get away for a quick smoke outside.

"Soap flakes for Ann's clothes would be nice," Dorothy said. "Coupons only cover the harsh washing powder. Baby's skin is all red from washing with it."

"No problem. There's a ton of that stuff around here. I'll fill ya a bag right away."

"Won't somebody see ya?" asked Dorothy, worried he would get into trouble.

"Nah! The sergeant won't care anyway. Wait 'ere, I'll be right back."

Fred disappeared into the building and returned five minutes later with a full brown bag. The visit was over and Dorothy hurried back to the flat to rewash Ann's clothes in the soft, mild soap flakes.

As the weeks went by, Ann gradually lost her fear of the strange soldier who stepped in and out of her life at odd times. Fred could pick her up and play with her, although she pulled all kinds of funny faces at the feel of his itchy uniform jacket. He was sure that no man had ever loved his daughter as much as he loved his. He lay on his stomach on the carpet, building blocks into towers for her to knock down. He read to her, he fed her mashed potatoes, he even helped bathe her —too nervous of dropping her to do it by himself. When she was sleeping, he sat beside her crib watching her breathe. She fascinated him. He adored her.

The spring not only brought warmer weather, but a growing anticipation that victory was imminent. The Germans were surrendering on every front and the allies were moving towards Berlin. The news of Hitler's suicide on April 30th flooded Britain like a giant sigh of relief. Dorothy and Mrs. Taylor ran out into the street, leaving Ann with Edward. There weren't many homes left standing in Chillworth Mews, but the two women ran to the end of the street to be with other Londoners who had heard the news. They hugged complete strangers. They laughed and cried together. They linked arms and made long lines of joyous people, kicking up their legs, exuberant in their celebrations.

Dorothy and Mrs. Taylor ran back to the flat. Edward had poured three glasses of champagne, which he handed to his daughter and his housekeeper, smiling broadly.

"A toast," Edward said. "To England. To our brave soldiers who have defeated the enemy. To victory."

They drank champagne, laughed and cried again. Ann, sensing something very important was going on, laughed and flapped her arms up and down. If this was a party, she wanted to be part of it. Dorothy wished Fred was there with them. She would go to the barracks tomorrow. Hitler was dead and the whole world celebrated.

The Germans signed the surrender on May 7th and the whole world went crazy. London had never seen such a celebration. Overnight the city was covered in flags and buntings, hanging from every building. All the shops closed. All the offices closed. Nobody went to work. Fred had instant leave and fought his way across London to get to his wife, people stopping him every few steps to hug and kiss him and hang flags around his neck. He arrived at the flat quite a sight, with flags draped over his shoulders and lipstick marks covering his face. He picked Dorothy up and held her tight.

"It's over, Dot," he choked. "It's over! V-E Day! Did ya ever think we'd see it? Did ya ever think the war would be over? But it is!"

He bent to scoop up Ann from the carpet and kiss her all over her face, making her giggle and scrunch up her face. Another party!

Edward shook his son-in-law's hand firmly, then grasped his shoulders, looking into the younger man's eyes. Edward had been through this feeling before, almost thirty years ago when the first war ended, and knew what Fred was feeling. The eyes of the old man said it all, he didn't have to speak.

"Let's go down to Trafalgar Square, Fred," Dorothy said. "Mr. Churchill's giving a speech at three o'clock. I'd love to hear him."

"You two young people go out there and enjoy victory day. Ann will be fine with me," Mrs. Taylor said. "The crowds will be crazy. It's no place for a baby."

The crowds were crazy. Thousands and thousands of people dancing, singing, waving flags, kissing anybody in a military uniform. When Mr. Churchill began his radio address in Trafalgar Square, the crowd stood in complete silence, hanging onto every word. This was the man who had got them through the war. The man who would never let them give up. The man who had promised them victory. Yet it had come at such a price. The people standing in the crowd had all made a sacrifice, and as they stood listening to the words of victory, there were tears of sorrow on many faces. For the husbands, wives, brothers, sisters, sons and daughters who wouldn't be coming home. For the families and homes shattered by the bombs. For the six years of hardship and worry.

The silence lasted for several minutes after the speech had

ended. People from every walk of life standing together remembering their own war stories, frozen for those few minutes in a time warp.

Then the silence was broken and the singing and shouting commenced.

"The royals are out on the balcony at Buckingham Palace," somebody shouted.

The crowd began to move towards the palace like a great river. Dorothy and Fred moved with them, caught up in the sheer emotion of the day.

The King and Queen came out onto the balcony eight times on that day, waving and smiling at the masses of people in front of the palace and along the Mall. Mr. Churchill joined them and so did Princess Elizabeth and Princess Margaret. Dorothy and Fred joined in as the crowds sang "God Save The King" and "Rule Britannia" followed by every wartime song ever written. After the third round of "We'll Meet Again," Dorothy and Fred headed to Chillworth Mews. What a day it had been.

The war was over!

Fred reported for duty as usual at Kensington Barracks the next day. His head felt like it was filled with lead. He had hardly slept. He had kept Edward company, sitting in the living room, drinking whiskey, listening to the merry-making still going on in the streets, until the early hours of the morning. When he finally crept into the bed beside Dorothy, he cuddled up closely to her—neither of them slept. After making love to his wife, Fred lay watching Ann's chest rise and fall. He knew he was blessed. He had escaped a certain death by being thrown clear of the tank as it took a direct hit from the Tiger tank. He had prayed God would keep him safe, and He had. Yet he couldn't bring himself to thank God. God hadn't protected his friends. God had stood by and watched millions die. News of extermination camps, liberated by the allied troops, had been reported almost daily as the liberation armies moved deeper and deeper into Europe's occupied countries. The horrors of those camps could only be imagined. Where had God been? Where had God gone?

Nobody expected England to be back to normal immediately. It took many months to organize the military and civilian chaos. Untangling the numerous threads of wartime life was a mammoth task. It had been six years since anybody in Britain had lived a normal life. That life was gone, and the best they could do was begin again, one step at a time.

WAITING

*A*nn learned to walk in London. She held Dorothy's one finger and walked around the statue of Peter Pan in Hyde Park. Ann loved the statue, particularly the small bunny on the base by Peter's feet. She stroked it and cooed to it and kissed it. She knew where the statue was and once they entered the park, she would point and squeal in its direction until she could see it, then her face would light up with happiness. There he was! Peter Pan! Her first steps on her own were from Dorothy to the rabbit. On days when they didn't go to Hyde Park, Ann was definitely out of sorts. She would go to the window of the flat and point outside, looking at Dorothy with a frown. Edward couldn't stand it, and had Ann dressed and in her pushchair heading for the park, despite rain or wind, before Dorothy could intervene. In all weathers Edward and Ann went to visit Peter Pan.

Much of London had been destroyed during the blitz in 1940. Over one million homes were blown apart, leaving hundreds of thousands of civilians dead or injured. Vast areas of the city had become wastelands. Churches and landmarks, which had existed for millennia, had been reduced to rubble. The task of rebuilding seemed insurmountable! The Londoners, resilient as ever, made the best of what they had. If they had lost their homes, other families in nearby areas made room for them. Temporary schools and hospitals were set up in patched-up buildings. The children, evacuated to the country six years before, returned to their families. For many of the younger children, moving away from their adopted families was traumatic—they hardly remembered the families they were born into. Thousands of children had spent the past six years in small towns or villages, close to the countryside. Now they were plunged into big city life, where dust and concrete surrounded them. It would take years to build new homes, schools and hospitals, but until they were built, the people of London found ways of adapting to the new reality.

Life looked completely different than it had been before the war. In every part of Britain people tried to put their lives together, despite the tragedies they had endured. Many of their loved ones would not be returning home. Women who had lived alone for six years of war now had to be strong and determined to move forward into the future, for the sake of themselves and their families.

"Father," began Dorothy one day after breakfast. "You know we have to move back to The Potteries when Fred is demobbed don't you?"

"I know," replied Edward.

"He's a potter. He has to go back to work at the Wedgwood factory. He can't do his job anywhere else," persisted Dorothy.

"I realize that, Dorothy," her father said. "I gather you are not looking forward to leaving London?"

"It's not just that. I'm confused about how I feel. I want Fred to be out of the army and free to get on with his life, and I knew when I married him that, after the war, we could only live in one part of England. But I love it here, living with you. Yet I know it's not reality. It's not my home, it's yours. Fred and I have to move on and make a life for ourselves, in our own place. Life is so easy living here with Mrs. Taylor to look after us and no money worries, but it's not REAL, is it? It has to come to an end. I'm not sure I'll be able to make the switch and be happy in the Potteries, even with Fred beside me."

Edward took his daughter's hand and held her eyes with his. He steadied his emotions so that she wouldn't see how upset he was at the thought of losing her. It seemed he had spent his life saying goodbye to Dorothy, and now that he was an old man, the pattern continued. Maybe it would be the last goodbye. He squeezed Dorothy's hand, nodding his head and reassuring her as he always had.

"You are a strong girl, darling," he said. "You have spent your life moving between London and Longton and coped very well. Selfishly I want you to stay with me, of course. But, as you say, it's not reality. You will go back with Fred and make your own life, build your own home, your own family. I will be forever grateful for the time you've spent with me here, but I must let you go. In fact I must encourage you to look ahead to a life you must begin with your husband and your child."

Everything Edward said made perfect sense, but the knot in Dorothy's stomach stayed a knot as she thought about a new beginning. How would they start? Living with May and

George in Bell Avenue again? Returning to Edward Street to live at Emma and Tom's house was not an option as far as Dorothy was concerned.

The months inched by, slow as molasses. Fred was still stationed at Kensington Barracks, working at the quarter-master's store. England was flooded with troops as they began to arrive home from all over the world, many injured in body and mind. The Atlantic became an armada of ships as the American soldiers were transported home.

The Japanese had not surrendered, although the allies had secured most of the occupied lands and islands in the Pacific. On August 6th the Americans dropped an atomic bomb on the Japanese citiy of Hiroshima, and on August 9th on Nagasaki, causing devastation beyond imagination. Japan surrendered on August 15th. The war that had cost so many lives was finally over. Everybody was going home.

Dorothy had a letter from Fred's sister, Margaret, at the end of August. She was getting married in October and wanted Dorothy and Ann to be at the wedding. Fred applied for five days leave so that he could be there too and they travelled together on the train back to Longton. How many times had they made this same journey? The smell of the train would always remind them of the war, when the trains were packed with cigarette-smoking troops and kit bags. They sat in comparative luxury, each having a seat to themselves and room for their feet and bags, while the train chugged north. Ann fell asleep, bored after the first fun five minutes of looking through the window, and lulled by the sound of the train's movement. Dorothy put her head on Fred's shoulder and sighed as she watched the bombed-out buildings from the train. It seemed the remnants of war would be with them for a long time.

The tiny house at five Bell Avenue was cramped with six people living there. The double bed in the second bedroom was pushed up against the wall to make room for Ann's cot. With only about a one-foot space between bed and cot, Dorothy could lie in bed next to Fred and hold Ann's hand through the cot railings. The only place for the small wardrobe was in front of the window, making the room dark day and night. May had placed a small table beside the wardrobe to provide a surface for some of Ann's things. There was a light bulb in the middle of the ceiling. The miracle of electricity had been installed into the houses on Bell Avenue. There was still no heat upstairs; the only heat came from the coal fire in the living room downstairs. The hot water boiler, behind the fire, provided enough hot water for a shallow six-inch bath, but in the summer, when there was no coal fire, there was no hot water. The fire was lit usually once a week so that everybody could have a bath that night. May and George didn't like the bath. They were unaccustomed to taking off all their clothes and getting into a tub of water. May was probably the cleanest woman who ever lived and banned the family from the kitchen every morning for fifteen minutes while she boiled the kettle for hot water and strip washed from top to bottom. George only bathed occasionally, although living with May, he was nagged into taking a bath more frequently than most of the men of his age, who only bathed on special occasions, some as little as once a year. So different from life in London, where the constant hot water and central heating provided a life of comparative luxury.

Margaret's young man, Bob, was quiet and friendly. He had served in North Africa and was discharged with shell shock. As a result, he spoke with a stutter and suffered with stomach ulcers. He worked in the slip house, dipping the china before it was fired in the coal ovens, at the same factory as George. He was also a volunteer in the home guard three nights a week, walking the streets watching for anything suspicious, but mostly reminding people about the blackout if he saw a chink of light coming through the black out curtains. Bob was a foot taller than Margaret and was her hero. Her dream of a young man loving her one day had indeed come true.

The wedding was at St. James' Church, where Fred and Dorothy had been married. Afterwards they walked to Newhall Mission Chapel, where the chapel ladies had made sandwiches and cakes. Margaret was radiant in a dress borrowed from her cousin and Dorothy's veil. A young man had asked her to marry him. Bob suited her perfectly, although Fred's mother whispered her fears to Dorothy the morning of the wedding.

"I'm worried about our Margaret," she confided. "Bob's such a big man, and our Margaret's so tiny."

"What can you mean?" Dorothy asked her mother-in-law, trying not to smile.

"Well, you know. The wedding night. Men only want one thing on their wedding night, and as I said, he's a big man. Poor Margaret!"

Dorothy couldn't answer. She turned away so that May couldn't see her stifled laugh.

Bob and Margaret rented a tiny house just outside Longton, in Ashwood. It was up a steep hill from the town, so tended not to harbour as much smoke. It was an old terraced house, and had gas lights and no hot water. The toilet was outside across the yard and shared with the next-door neighbours. The newlyweds were happy to have their own home and generous family members gave them bits and pieces to begin their life together. Bob had a double bed at home, so he moved it to the house, along with his wardrobe and chest of drawers. Aunt Daisy, May's sister, gave them a small armchair, which was a bit threadbare. Mrs. Barker, from the chapel, gave them another armchair from her parlour. They bought a utility table and two chairs themselves and had enough coupons left to buy some pots and pans for the kitchen. An old gas stove had been left behind by the previous owner. It was a beginning.

After the wedding, Dorothy, Fred and Ann returned to London, and life settled into a routine once more—a waiting routine. Slowly, very slowly, the men and women who had fought for six years began to be demobilized. Released from their military service and returned to their former lives. Out in the streets of London young men started to reappear in civilian clothing. An odd sight at first. So unusual it made people stop and stare, not knowing why, then realizing what was different—they had only seen young men wearing uniforms for the past six years.

The Welsh Guards were not one of the first regiments to be demobbed. Fred had his ear to the ground daily, waiting and listening for any news. He had been taking inventory of the stores it seemed for months. Shipping out quantities of products to military barracks all over the country, until there was only a skeleton supply left. Surely it couldn't be long now before they were sent home. But it was long. Christmas came and went, with the usual wonderful atmosphere at Chillworth Mews. Ann was the centre of attention, old enough to rip open her own presents and say "thank you."

The shine of spending Christmas with Edward in London

was overshadowed by the longing Dorothy and Fred had to be on their own. To move forward with their lives.

In January of 1946 Dorothy received a letter from Margaret, who still wrote on behalf of her parents, telling her that number seven Bell Avenue was to become vacant. Mrs. Carmichael had lived there with her three young girls since the houses were built, but her husband had been killed in action and she was giving up the house. She was moving to Manchester to live with her sister. May had asked the rent man if they had another tenant and he'd said they hadn't as yet. Dorothy was to write immediately if she was interested in the house.

Interested in the house? Was it a joke? Of course she was interested in the house!

Dorothy didn't even wait to ask Fred; who knows when she would next see him. She scribbled her reply and left Ann with Mrs. Taylor to run to the post office, praying the house hadn't been rented by the time they received it.

Every day Dorothy watched for the mail man. Why was it taking so many days to answer her letter? She should have heard something by now. There was the postman, coming around the corner. *Please stop at the flat. Please bring the letter I'm waiting for. Please let it be good news.*

There it was! The letter lay on the carpet below the letter slot, along with other mail. It was Margaret's handwriting and Dorothy snatched it up, opening it as she hurried into the living room. If they wanted the house, they had to sign a rental agreement by Friday. That was two days away. It seemed impossible! They would require Fred's signature, not hers. How could Fred possibly get leave to go up to Stoke-on-Trent at such short notice. Dorothy called the emergency number Fred had given her, which connected her with Kensington Barracks. She left a message for Guardsman Podmore to phone her as soon as possible, and he was on the phone an hour later, thinking there was an emergency with Ann or Edward. When Dorothy explained about the two letters, he said he'd do what he could and let her know.

Fred's sergeant was like most sergeants in the British army, gruff and a stickler for rules. He didn't bend easily to any request from the guardsmen under him. Fred didn't fancy his chances of getting leave for something like signing a rental agreement on a house. Particularly when the regiment was still on active service duty and no mention of demobilization had occurred. Sergeant Thomas frowned as he listened to the plea from Fred. His fingers tapped on the desk as the frown turned to a scowl. Special leave was given for important things like a death in the family or birth of a baby or wedding, not for signing a rental agreement. Fred's heart sank as he saw the obvious signs of a rejection written all over the sergeant's face.

"It's just that we don't have a place to live when I'm demobbed, Sir," explained Fred, willing to give it one last try. "My wife and baby have been living in London to be near me, but we have to go back to the Potteries because of my work. I'm a master potter by trade, Sir. I know everybody's in the same boat, trying to pick up the thread of their lives, but this would give us such a good start. I doubt we'll get a better chance than this, Sir."

Then he waited, feeling the tension creeping into his neck and shoulders. There was nothing else to say. Sergeant Thomas held Fred's fate in his hands and he knew it. He kept tapping his fingers, holding the request for leave in front of his face while he read it again.

"Because I'm a soft hearted old bugger, I'm granting your leave, guardsman. Be back in barracks promptly on Monday morning."

"Thank you, Sergeant," Fred said. He saluted, did an about-turn and marched quickly out of the room before the sergeant could change his mind.

"Dorothy," yelled Fred, bounding up the stairs to the flat two at a time. "I got the leave. I can go home and sign the rental agreement."

He burst through the door to find his wife in the kitchen with Mrs. Taylor, flour on the end of her nose, baking biscuits. She hadn't heard a word he'd said, so he repeated everything breathlessly.

Bags were packed and they were at Euston Station once more to make the trip north, this time to make concrete plans for their future together. Ann, sensing the excitement, didn't nap this time, but bounced up and down on the dusty seat, sending puffs of dust into the air with each bounce. She ran up and down the carriage, saying "hello" to the other passengers and ate chocolate finger biscuits. She ran her fingers down the windows and watched the streams of condensation chase each other to the bottom. Fred read books to her, but she wouldn't sit on his knee. "Itchy Daddy," she said each time he tried to get her to sit on his lap. The guard's uniform he wore was the culprit.

The rental agreement sat on the desk at the landlord's office. Number seven Bell Avenue would be available the following Saturday for the family to begin their occupancy. Fred pried Dorothy's fingers from his hand and signed the agreement with a flourish. He had no qualms about it. Living next door to his parents in a modern house with running water and a proper bathroom was a dream come true for him. To be able to begin his civilian life in such luxury compared with most of the working class around them was a blessing Fred was immensely grateful for. True, they had no furniture or household items, but they had a roof over their heads and they would gather the other things together when they could.

The landlord's clerk said they could pick up the key on Saturday morning at nine o'clock. Then he shook Fred's hand, gave him a copy of the rental agreement and they were done. Back to London for Fred, leaving Dorothy and Ann with his parents to wait out the week and collect the key.

BELL AVENUE

*T*wo keys were issued to Dorothy on Saturday morning. She held them all the way back to Bell Avenue, feeling the cold striking into the palm of her hand. Keys to her own house—well her own rented house. Her heart pounded with the thrill she felt. She couldn't wait to push the key into the door lock and explore the house. It was exactly the same as number five, but Dorothy wondered if the previous tenant had put down linoleum on the floors, or painted the walls. What condition would the house be in? Maybe dirty! Or smelly! Or infested with beetles!

By the time Dorothy arrived at her in-laws' house, she was full of anxieties about the house next door. She asked May to watch Ann a little while longer and, taking a short cut, stepped over the tiny privet hedge in the front garden to open up number seven Bell Avenue.

The front hall had stairs running straight ahead to the upstairs. On the left was the door into the living room. Without furniture the twelve-foot square room looked big. Dorothy sighed with relief when she saw the linoleum on the floor—not in bad shape! The kitchen looked bleak with the watery sun shining through the window onto the dingy sink, but Mrs. Carmichael had left behind a small gas cooker—a bonus for the new tenants. Dorothy took a peek into the lav and pulled the chain to watch it flush—no more going up the yard to a back house. It made her smile to listen to the flush sound and watch the water whirl around the bowl and disappear. A shiver went through Dorothy as she climbed the stairs to look at the bedrooms. They felt cold and were littered with debris: bits of paper, an old sock, broken crayons, a patch of something sticky where dust bunnies clung. The tiny bathroom, containing a small sink and a bathtub, had the same cold feel, but was reasonably clean and there was a blue and white striped curtain hanging at the window. The only curtain in the house.

"How did it look, duck?" asked May, when Dorothy returned from her trip next door.

"It's just the job," answered Dorothy. "Needs a good cleaning, but there's nothing a bit of elbow grease won't cure. Now I just 'ave to figure out a plan to get a few things together so that we can move in."

"Well you stay 'ere with us until you can get things straight," May said. "We can move Fred's stuff out of the bedroom 'ere —that'll give you a start."

Putting a home together was difficult when money was scarce and ration books had to be used for everything. Every young couple relied on the generosity of family and friends, who gave away the household items they could do without. Dorothy didn't expect anything from her Longton family, but totally unexpectedly Aunt Mary Ann and Aunt Lena pooled their money and bought a utility two-seater sofa. It was delivered by the furniture van one rainy afternoon, and sat in the middle of the newly cleaned living room like a piece of art on display. Once the word was out that May's son, daughter-in-law and granddaughter had rented the house next door, the stream of visitors began. Every day people knocked at May's door with a few things for the young couple.

"It's not much, duck," everybody seemed to say. "But I 'ope it'll 'elp 'em out."

From old pots, pans and dishes to old towels, blankets and curtains, the pile of possessions grew. Dorothy spent all her time at number seven, with Ann as helper, cleaning, polishing and finding a spot for all the second-hand gifts. With her ration coupons she bought a wooden table and four chairs. The table could be folded down when not in use, providing much-needed space in the tiny room. The ladies from May's chapel collected a box full of mis-matched dishes and delivered them one Saturday morning, along with a kitchen storage cupboard to keep them in, donated by one of the old ladies.

Edward sent a money order for fifty pounds, which was a small fortune. The average man's wage was about five pounds a week. Ration coupons wouldn't allow many items to be purchased, but Dorothy managed to equip her house with most of the items she needed, with money to spare. With old used curtains at all the windows upstairs and in the kitchen, she splashed out and bought lovely green curtains for the living room window, with pure white netted curtains underneath. It made the room look bright and warm.

Finally in May of 1946, the Second Battalion of the Welsh Guards was demobilised.

Arriving home after dark, Fred held Dorothy tightly in his

arms before taking her hand and leading her upstairs. The following morning, he awoke early, feeling the warmth of her body beside him. It felt like heaven! Their bed, their bedroom, their house! Fred felt he would burst he was so happy. He cuddled into Dorothy as she slept, remembering the joy of the night before. He was the luckiest man alive. The most beautiful wife he could ever have imagined was lying next to him. She smelled of lavender and had the softest skin. He was home.

Remnants of the six-year war with Germany remained. Haunted faces and horror-filled dreams. Men and women crippled in body and spirit. Victims of the prisoner of war camps returned as skeletons, not able to eat anything placed before them by worried wives and mothers, their stomachs shrunk to the size of a walnut, their guts shrivelled with years of dysentery and malnutrition. They had gone into the war as boys and girls and returned as men and women. Many unable to return to their former jobs because of injury: a lorry driver with no feet, a potter with one hand, a teacher with no memory, a doctor who was blind.

Fred counted himself lucky, escaping with only a slight limp. He probably wouldn't play football again, but he would be able to go back to the job he was trained for.

Walking through the house in his long army-issued underwear, Fred was amazed at all the work his wife had accomplished.

"It's really great, Dot," he said. "How did you do it? You are fantastic."

He took Dorothy into his arms and kissed her tenderly. She was all he had ever wanted. He adored her. Ann pushed herself in between them, gripping her mummy's legs and putting her head between her mummy's knees. She hadn't seen her dad for three months and didn't like the way he held mummy so close. She glowered up at him and when he tried to pick her up, she said "No," and held out her arms to Dorothy. She didn't want anything to do with the soldier she barely remembered.

Fred was mortified and hurt by his daughter's rejection.

"Come on, pigeon," he coaxed. "It's Daddy. Don't you remember me?"

"Go 'way," Ann said, her bottom lip sticking out and her chin beginning to tremble.

"Leave 'er, Fred," Dorothy soothed. "She doesn't really remember you after so long. She'll get used to ya again. Just give 'er some time."

A new Wedgwood factory was being built in the countryside, in a tiny village called Barlaston, four miles from Longton. It was the first pottery factory to be built entirely without coal-fired bottle necked kilns. The building had been started in 1938 and included new, Swiss made, electric kilns, but completion was delayed because of the war. Now it was all systems go, and production was well under way in the finished parts of the factory, which included the Jasper department, where Fred would work.

Fred dusted off his old bike, which had been stored at the back of the coal shed, and worked on making it roadworthy. Off he set, early Monday morning, on his ride into the country to find the new factory. He stopped to ask several people for directions as he sped along the country lanes. There was no sign of anything industrial as far as he could see, but his informants assured him the Wedgwood factory was there.

"Turn right when ya see a long straight road lined with trees," was the instruction.

Farmers' fields lined both sides of the narrow lanes, the smell of newly hoed soil filled the air. The long straight road lined with trees led downhill over a bridge, spanning a long narrow lake. Two swans floated around, their reflections mirrored in the water. Cherry trees lined each side of the lake, covered in pink blossoms. Fred almost lost control of his bike as he gazed at the idyllic setting. The factory was hard to spot, hidden behind a thick copse of trees. No thick black smoke belched from bottleneck chimneys—the kilns were all electric, soundless and spotless.

The office staff greeted the returning young soldier with smiles. It was a daily occurrence for them and the paperwork was laid out ready. Fred had his apprenticeship papers from the Etruria factory with him to confirm that he worked at the Josiah Wedgwood & Sons factory before the war as an ornamentor. The manager of the Jasper division shook his hand and took Fred through to the factory to show him where he would be working. The ornamentor's benches, in the prestige shop, were lined up along a wall of windows, giving them natural light to work in. Fred's two figure makers were already busy working, pressing the soft clay into moulds, then gently lifting them out with the pressure of a flat metal tool. They were working on simple patterns for the ornamentors on the factory floor in the large room next door, but would be figure making entirely for Fred when he started to work. He introduced himself to the two young women and told them he was looking forward to working with them. There were only four men working on prestige ware. They were the master potters and Fred was to be the youngest of the four. He would be decorating the most expensive and complicated of the Jasper ware, placing the white figures onto urns, vases and vessels with precision, something few others had the training or artistic talent for.

"Well, 'ow did it go? Can ya start working? Is the factory nice?" Dorothy bombarded her husband with questions.

"Dot, it was so incredible," Fred began. "The factory's in the middle of a forest of trees in the prettiest countryside ya could imagine. The boss wants me to start tomorra'. I 'ave me own bench and stool and 'ave two figure makers to meself."

Dorothy couldn't stop smiling as she bustled around the kitchen cooking pork chops for their tea. She was living her dream. Fred home from the war sitting on the sofa reading the newspaper, Ann playing in the living room. She vowed to herself that she would never complain, that she would never serve only chips for dinner, that Ann's clothes would never come from a jumble sale. Her daughter would want for nothing.

They settled down to their new life together. Ann's entire universe began and ended with her daddy. He forgot the months of her not wanting to have him near her, revelling in the wonder of his tiny daughter, who wanted to be with him all the time. She wanted him to bath her, to put her to bed, to read countless books to her, to sing his funny war songs to her. She missed him every minute of the day when he was at work, waiting for his bike to appear in the avenue. After their evening meal, she sat on his shoulders and combed his hair while he read his newspaper.

The first twinges of resentment crept into Dorothy's subconscious mind. Did her daughter love her daddy more? Just like she had.

CALLED TO SHEFFIELD

*V*isiting went only one way for Dorothy. She was expected to visit her grandmother, Emma, in Edward Street and take Ann with her. Fred never went. Nobody from Longton ever visited Dorothy and her family in Normacot, although it was only a twenty-minute walk or a short bus ride away.

Usually Dorothy and Ann visited on Friday afternoons, because Nancy Bryan visited then, and she was always kind to Ann, deflecting the caustic communication from Emma. Nor was it every Friday by any means. No matter when the visit, it was always greeted with criticism and sarcasm.

Dorothy wondered why she felt she needed to keep visiting her grandparents. It puzzled her that the ties to them were so strong, despite the years of abuse she had suffered at their hands. Was it because she had no other family? Or because they were the only link with her mother? Did she feel guilty that she lived next door to her husband's parents and saw them daily? She couldn't answer her own questions. She hated exposing Ann to such a hostile environment.

Even so, she still went to Edward Street regularly, with Ann in tow.

It was on one such visit that they were surprised by Aunt Mary-Ann walking into the kitchen. She rarely left the home she shared with her sister Lena, and Dorothy couldn't remember her being in Emma's house for many years.

"It's Dorothy I've come to see," Aunt Mary-Ann announced as she took a seat on the horse hair sofa. "Get me a cuppa, Emma. It was a long walk from Lena's house."

Ann stared at the old lady, all dressed in black. She had very white hair gathered into a bun at the back of her neck, and when she spoke, Ann noticed her front tooth was missing. Her face was very wrinkled, her eyes bright blue.

A cup of tea in her hand, she turned to Dorothy with a sigh.

"Ya mother's sent for ya," she began. "I've been in Sheffield this past six weeks, 'elping out. Gertrude 'as terminal cancer and wants to see ya before she dies. I know she's never been a mother to ya, Dorothy, but can you find it in ya 'eart to go to 'er before she goes?"

Dorothy closed her eyes, as if to shut out the news. How could she go to Sheffield to see the woman who had never cared about her? Ann was almost the same age as she had been when Gertrude abandoned her, and Dorothy couldn't imagine leaving her little girl for any reason. Now Gertrude wanted to see her! Why?

"I won't go," choked Dorothy. "Why would I? She doesn't even know me, 'as never cared about me. I don't want to see 'er, ever."

"Don't speak in 'aste," Aunt Mary-Ann urged her great niece. "She's always regretted the decision she made to

285

leave ya behind. She spent years regretting it. I know, because I'm the only one who ever wrote to 'er. She let me know she was poorly a few months ago and I went to 'er because she needed somebody from 'er family. Now, my girl, ya think again. I can tell ya, ya'll regret not goin' to see 'er."

"Leave 'er alone, Mary-Ann," Emma intervened. "Our Gert was no mother to 'er. A cat would 'ave been a better bloody mother. She made 'er bed, she must lie in it. Even 'er death bed."

Dorothy glared at her grandmother. How dare she speak for her? Did she think she'd been such a great caregiver? It was the comment from Emma that made up Dorothy's mind.

"All right then, I'll go," Dorothy said, between tight lips. "It'll 'ave to be Saturday, so Fred can stay with Ann. I'll take the train Saturday and come back Sunday. Give me the address and instructions 'ow to get there."

Her great aunt wrote down the details and handed them to Dorothy.

"Ya won't regret it, my dear," she said. "Be prepared though. Cancer takes a terrible toll."

Emma said no more. Gertrude was her eldest child and she couldn't help but feel a tug deep inside her gut at the thought of her suffering.

The following Saturday, Dorothy took a taxi from the Sheffield main station to the address she had been given.

The house in Sheffield belonged to Bill Hyden. He had married Gertrude in 1940 after George Owens had died. Dorothy had no information about her mother's life. Even Aunt Mary-Ann hadn't told her details of Gertrude's life in

Sheffield. Now Dorothy was faced with twenty years of history, which included two step-sisters and a step-brother.

"I knew about Mr. Owens, but didn't know he'd died and Gertrude had remarried," Dorothy said, taking the cup of tea Bill offered her.

"Well, luv," Bill said. "I'm actually Gert's first husband. She never married George Owens. Long story. She has nice children though. You'll meet them later on. They're at the hospital with her this afternoon."

Joyce, Barbara and Geoffrey arrived home together and came quietly into the comfortable living room. Barbara ran forward, clasping Dorothy in a warm hug.

"I'm Barbara," she said. "Mam has told us all about you. I'm so happy to meet you. You look just like mam, every bit."

As she paused for breath, Joyce and Geoffrey approached their step-sister slowly.

They didn't hug her, but took her hands and smiled at her.

Dorothy couldn't explain why she started to cry. She never cried, no matter what. Now here she was with the tears running down her cheeks.

"Come on now, you three," Bill said. "Give her some space."

Barbara told their story, with occasional comments from Joyce and Geoffrey. They all agreed they had the best dad in the world, and all shed tears at his loss. Gertrude had been a loving mother and had told them all about Dorothy only a few years ago. They were shocked to find out they had an older sister, born out of wedlock, when their mother was just a girl. But here she was, sitting in their living room.

Dorothy dreaded seeing her mother. A stranger! Edward had

a small picture of her on the wall in his bedroom, never quite giving up the memory of the girl he had loved. Dorothy had seen the picture many times and knew that she looked like her mother. Now she wondered if she would recognize her. The picture had been taken when Gertrude was twenty years old. Now she was forty-eight and at the end of her life.

The Sheffield General hospital loomed dark and dreary. Long corridors smelling of carbolic and bleach slid by. Grey walls, white beds, nurses moving quietly about their work. Bill escorted Dorothy to bed number eleven and, after kissing the head on the pillow, he said he would wait in the corridor outside the ward.

Oh no! Don't leave me! What will I say? You don't know the life I've had since my mother left. I don't remember anything about her. This is a stranger lying in this bed. She looks nothing like the picture of my mother. Please don't walk away! She won't know who I am. We have nothing to say to each other. I want to run away. I want to run back to my family—my Fred, my Ann. Away from this woman who didn't want me.

The panic rose in Dorothy's throat as she stood rooted to the spot beside the bed. Gertrude lifted her head slightly from the pillow so that she could see her daughter.

"Dorothy?" she whispered. "Dorothy? Is that you?"

"It's me," was all Dorothy could manage.

"Come closer. Let me see you."

With legs turned to lead, Dorothy walked a few steps towards the stranger in the bed.

The face on the pillow was gaunt as a skeleton. The skin stretched over the bones. The lips pale. The eyes clouded.

The hair thin and unkept. It bore no resemblance to Gertrude now that the cancer had done its worst.

"Thank you for coming," murmured Gertrude. "I didn't think you'd come."

Dorothy didn't answer. She stood and looked at her mother in a daze.

"I need to ask you somethin'. I don't 'ave the energy or the time to make small talk," the breaths were short and shallow. "Aunt Mary-Ann told me you 'ave a nice husband and a girl. I'm 'appy for you."

Gertrude paused to catch her breath, reaching for a towel to wipe her mouth before continuing.

"I want you to do something for me, Dorothy. You know I'm dying. You know Bill isn't the father of my children. The girls will be all right—they're old enough to manage on their own. It's Geoffrey I'm worried about. 'E's only fifteen. 'E's a really clever boy. 'E needs somebody to look out for 'im."

Dorothy was puzzled. Where was her mother going with this? What did Gertrude's children have to do with her?

It was several minutes before Gertrude could continue. The effort of talking drained all her energy, but she was determined to finish what she had begun.

"Will you take Geoffrey to live with you?"

There, she had said it. She had asked the question. Now the dying woman waited for her daughter's answer, her eyes full of dread and hope.

Dorothy couldn't believe the words she had heard. Gertrude had sent for her, not to say how she regretted she had left her. Not to say she was sorry. Not to beg forgiveness for the years Dorothy had spent with her grandparents. Not to say she had loved Edward and that they had both wanted her. Not to say she had thought about Dorothy through all the years while she was raising her other family and regretted she had never sent for her.

"No, no, no!" Dorothy said, looking directly into her mother's eyes. "Never! Do you 'ear me? Never! Why would I look after your son? You left me behind, not once but twice when I was a little girl. Who looked after me? Not you!"

Dorothy paused for breath, her heart pounding, her head spinning.

"You're right. I do 'ave a lovely husband and a little girl. 'Er name is Ann. She's your granddaughter. Did you ever think about 'er? NO, you didn't. Just like you never thought about me. I will not take care of anybody that belongs to you."

Dorothy didn't remember leaving the ward. She ran past Bill, standing in the corridor, and out of the front doors. Her head felt like it would explode, and because her knees were suddenly weak and wobbly, she collapsed onto a wooden bench and let the tears flow.

It was over! What had begun more than twenty years ago, when Gertrude had left Dorothy in Longton and moved to Sheffield with George Owens, was finally over. Gertrude's life was almost over. Dorothy would never have to wonder about her again.

Bill found her sitting on the bench, staring at the darkening sky. He took her back to his house, where her step-siblings were waiting. Dorothy didn't tell them about the conversation at the hospital. It was too painful to share with anybody, especially Gertrude's children.

"Will you come back for the funeral?" asked Barbara.

"No, I don't think so," Dorothy answered.

"We must stay in touch," Barbara continued. "Now we've met our sister, we don't want to lose you. Will you come and visit sometimes and bring your family?"

Dorothy wanted to say "no," but somehow, looking into Barbara's sincere eyes, she found herself agreeing to visit sometimes. These three people were her siblings after all.

Gertrude died three days later.

Aunt Mary-Ann was the only family member at Gertrude's funeral.

LIFE AFTER DEATH

*H*er mother's death made Dorothy more determined than ever that her child would never feel unloved and unwanted. She would do everything within her power to give Ann the things she never had, but how does a child exist when they don't eat? Every meal Dorothy made, Ann said "Don't like it."

Growing up in the Bryan household, Dorothy had never had anybody to care for her the way she cared for Ann. Why wasn't her daughter more co-operative? Why did she deliberately try to make Dorothy cross? Why did she refuse to eat? Why wasn't she more grateful for the good food Dorothy gave her?

"Please, Mr. Plant," Dorothy begged the butcher. "I know I don't have the coupons, but could you give me a few beef bones to make soup?"

Mr. Plant liked Dorothy, and her little girl was the boniest thing on two legs. He wrapped a couple of bones in brown paper and sneaked them over the counter, giving the young mother a wink as he tapped the side of his nose.

"Thank you," mouthed Dorothy.

The beef bones were put in a pot on the gas stove to boil, the onion and carrot chopped into small pieces were added to the pot. The soup was on its way. It would be a real treat and Ann would love it.

Dorothy set the bowl of soup on the table in front of her four-year-old daughter, with bread sliced into "fingers" on a plate beside it.

"Look at this lovely soup I've made," Dorothy said. "It will taste sooooooo good."

"Don't like it!" Ann exclaimed.

"Yes you will like it," argued Dorothy, dipping the spoon into the fragrant liquid broth.

"NO! Don't like it!" repeated Ann. "Not eating it."

It seemed all the years of eating chips from a newspaper, thrown into the middle of the table, came rushing into Dorothy's mind. She had begged the butcher for bones. She had spent the whole morning making the soup. She looked at her daughter, sitting there with her lips pressed firmly together. Then she picked up the bowl and emptied the contents on top of Ann's head.

Ann screamed and screamed! Dorothy just stared at her. Little pieces of meat, carrots and onions were trapped in the curls and the broth was running down Ann's face, neck and shoulders and progressing onto her dress. It took the better part of an hour to get the little girl cleaned up. She sat in the kitchen sink, filled with warm water, while her mother washed her, picking the meat and vegetables out of her hair bit by bit.

Dr. Livingstone examined Ann while Dorothy looked on anxiously. She had asked the doctor to examine the skinny little girl, telling her that Ann ate nothing and she was afraid she would die.

"She is fine," exclaimed Dr. Livingstone. "Don't worry about her, Dorothy. She'll eat when she's hungry. Children can exist on very little food. She's probably eating more than you think she is."

Dorothy made blancmange in egg cups. She made toast in every shape, putting in currant eyes and buttons. She whipped mashed potatoes and squeezed them through her icing bag to make letters and numbers. The only words she ever heard from Ann were "don't like it."

Grandad Podmore often came home from work an hour before Fred, giving Ann a precious hour with her granddad. She kept watch through the front windows to see him walking up the avenue.

"Here's me granddad," she would yell, running through the house to the back door. "Bye Mummy."

She would be through the door like a shot and into the house next door. Dorothy gave up trying to stop her. She loved her granddad and was determined to see him every day.

Grandma May cooked very differently than her daughter-in-law. She prepared the same food for tea that she'd always prepared. Bacon, cheese and tomatoes, or bacon and eggs or chips and egg, or sausage and mash. With ration coupons still in effect, they were only allowed two eggs and a bit of cheese each week, so bacon, sausage and potatoes were the foods of choice.

George sat in his chair, pulling off his workbooks when his little granddaughter came flying into the house to greet him, running past her grandma in the kitchen. George picked her up for a hug and kept her on his lap, talking about his day and asking her all kinds of questions about her garden, which she loved to dig, and about her "husband" Bill, who was her constant imaginary companion. When tea was ready George moved to the table to enjoy his bacon-based meal. The grease from the bacon floated around the plate, making it ideal for dipping in his thick slices of bread to mop up the fat.

"Come on up 'ere, young Annie Lawrie," he said, every night. "Come and 'ave a dip from me plate."

Ann stood beside her granddad as he tore off a wad of bread and dipped it into the fat, then handed it to her. She could hardly wait, licking her little lips as he prepared the tasty dip. She gobbled it down in delight and asked for "more please," much to George's delight. Every night she dined on bacon dip and bread. Sometimes there was mashed potato scooped up onto the bread with the fat. Sometimes a dip of yellow egg yolk. It was Ann's favourite part of the day, sharing her granddad's meal.

It took Dorothy many months to find out about Ann's tea with Grandad. She went to collect Ann from her grandparent's house one evening as they were going to Normacot Church of England Primary School to meet the teacher. When Dorothy walked into the living room Ann had her mouth full of a bacon dip and Grandad was loading up another piece of bread to feed to his granddaughter.

"What are you doing?" Dorothy asked George.

"What does it look like?" he replied. "Givin' the young 'un a bacon dip."

"She never eats anything at home," Dorothy said, her voice rising along with her temper. "Maybe it's because you've been feeding 'er rubbish like that."

"Wait a minute, young madam," George paused his meal to look at his irate daughter-in-law. "If me young Annie Lawrie wants a bacon dip from her granddad, that's what she's goin' to get. So shut up."

"She's my daughter!" yelled Dorothy. "I make 'er all kinds of decent, nutritious food and you feed 'er bread and bacon fat. Bloody 'ell, you've got a nerve."

"She likes bacon dips. She doesn't like the food ya make for 'er. She shares me meal every night and she loves it, don't ya lass?"

Ann looked from her mother to her granddad. Both of them were red in the face and looked angry.

"I like the bacon dips," Ann stated.

"See," said George. "Now leave us alone and let us finish our meal."

Dorothy grabbed Ann's hand and dragged her out of the house.

"You are never to go to ya granddad's again for those 'orrible bacon dips. Do ya 'ear me?"

Ann burst into tears and ran to the front hall to sit on the stairs and talk to her imaginary "husband" Bill.

When Fred came home, Ann was still talking to Bill with a

sobbing voice and Dorothy was still mad. On hearing the entire story, Fred tried to smooth things over with his wife, but she wasn't hearing him. The three of them set out for the school in a sorry mess. Ann's eyes bloated from crying, Fred with his lips in a line and Dorothy with red splotches on her face and wild eyes.

George was very upset with Dorothy. He told Fred his wife was unreasonable and out of control. The rift lasted for days. Ann, stubborn as her mother, still refused to eat, even when Dorothy actually made her bacon dips.

"They're not like Granddad's," was Ann's response.

"Oh! Go on then you little Miss Muck. Go to your granddad," shouted Dorothy.

Ann ran like the wind into the house next door to hug her granddad and eat his meal with him.

Dorothy couldn't believe she had talked to her daughter that way. The very words of Emma coming out of her mouth. She vowed to begin again, curbing her temper and her tongue. It was a battle she would struggle with for her whole life.

There were only fourteen houses in Bell Avenue, with lots of children between them. There were no backyards. At the back of the houses was a large dusty area of spare ground where the children played together. A fenced chicken run was the boundary, where the children would peer through the fence to watch the chickens scurry about and gaze in awe of the big rooster, who stood two feet tall. The chickens seemed to escape from their run on a regular basis, sending the children scattering in all directions. The two girls responsible for the chickens, Norma and Jean Barker, had to round up the escapees and get them back into the run. The big fear was the rooster!

Ann was playing outside with another little girl when the rooster escaped. They spotted him strutting across the dirt toward them and both of them started to run. Carol ran to her house and Ann ran to hers. The rooster decided to chase Ann. He knocked her down, as she almost reached the path to her back door. Dorothy heard the screaming and ran out to see the rooster flapping his wings frantically, his talons stuck in Ann's hair. Dorothy panicked and ran next door, where she found her mother-in-law polishing silver and singing hymns. Without explanation Dorothy grabbed May and pulled her towards the back door to show her what was happening. May grabbed the first thing she could find, which was the yard brush and swung at the rooster, catching him under his head and sending him flying backwards with bunches of hair caught in his feet. May continued to chase the rooster until he was back in his pen.

Dorothy ran to pick up Ann, who was beyond upset. It took hours for Dorothy to calm her down. When Fred came home he went to see Mr. Barker, who owned the chickens, and told him to repair his fence so that the birds couldn't escape again. The experience left Ann with a life-long fear of anything with feathers, particularly hens and roosters.

May couldn't help but be critical of her daughter-in-law. Dorothy insisted on wearing lipstick, even as a married woman, and short skirts. She smoked cigarettes and wore nail polish and May had heard several swear words escape from her lips when she was mad or frustrated. All unacceptable in May's eyes. The biggest problem was neither Dorothy nor Fred attended chapel. May talked to her son telling him how disappointed she was that they weren't attending, but Fred dismissed it, telling his mother that he'd seen too much during the war to have much faith in God. Sundays were always a tense day, as they heard May slam the door on her way out to chapel and on her way back, twice every Sunday. Dorothy didn't obey the commandment "On the seventh day, ye shall rest," either. She cooked a dinner on Sundays and washed the dishes. May had even seen her hanging out a few things on the line to dry. May did all her work to prepare food on Saturday: cooking the Sunday meat the day before, peeling potatoes, scraping carrots, baking a pie. The only thing she allowed herself to do on Sunday was put a light under the vegetables and serve the food. The dishes were stacked until Monday morning. She read her bible and went to chapel and rested in her chair. That was Sunday.

Dorothy invited May and George for Sunday tea a few times, but May refused to go into the house where the Lord's commandment wasn't being followed.

"Silly sod," remarked Dorothy under her breath. "She's got a funny way of trying to get us to go to chapel. I'll never set foot in the place, I'm telling you."

"She's old fashioned, Dot," defended Fred. "She's always lived like that. Sunday is chapel day, for 'er and all 'er sisters. 'Er father was one of the founders of Newhall Mission, ya know. Let 'er 'ave 'er way. We 'ave to respect what she believes."

In the years Dorothy had known her husband, she had never heard him say a bad word about anybody. He defended everybody's opinions. He never swore or lost his temper. He was the most loving person she had ever known. Even when she was angry and flying off the handle, he remained calm and serene, waiting until the fury had abated, then holding her and telling her he loved her.

In this one family argument, however, May was persistent and Fred finally agreed that, although he and Dorothy would not attend, he would take Ann to Sunday School when she was old enough. Dorothy was furious. He had made the decision without her input and she nagged him about it for days.

"Dorothy," her husband said, after listening to the latest tirade about Sunday School. "Enough. I've made the decision that she will go when she's old enough, and that is the end of it. I don't want to 'ear about it any more. It's not because Ma insists either. It's a good way of life and I want Ann to learn about God, like we both did as children. Do not mention it again."

Dorothy could see his lips were in a straight line and his eyes steely blue. His words were pronounced carefully and spoken slowly. Her first reaction was to fight on, but she thought better of it and walked away. Her husband had drawn his line in the sand and she didn't cross it, this time.

WORK AND PLAY

*M*rs. Brooker, the class one teacher at the infant school, was an immediate hit with Ann. She was old and plump and had spectacles at the end of her nose. She welcomed her new students, all aged five, and asked if they knew any of the other children in the class. Ann knew Sandra Clayton, whose dad worked with her granddad at James Kent. She had been to play with her at her house a few times. Mrs. Brooker sat them beside each other and gave them each paper and crayons to draw a picture of their families.

At lunchtime Dorothy picked up her daughter and took her home. They had barely enough time to eat a quick lunch as the school was a twenty minute walk away. Ann had loved her first morning and couldn't wait to go back in the afternoon. She dragged her mum along as her little legs sped up the hill, towards the school, in record time. The afternoon was even better, with the teacher reading to them from an Enid Blighton book and giving them time to play outside with bouncy balls. Ann talked all the way home about how

301

wonderful school was. She couldn't wait for her dad to come home so that she could tell him all about it. Fred was delighted with the stories about Ann's first day at school, and had to continually remind her to eat her tea as she chattered on and on. After tea, Ann put on her shoes to get ready to go back to school. She was disappointed when she was told school was over for the day and she would have to wait until the morning to go back.

Life as a five-year-old seemed idyllic. Not so for the adults!

The dreaded words "short time" echoed around the neighbourhood. The pottery industry was in decline and laying off workers. A tragedy for the working class. Nobody had money saved. Every penny was spent each week on rent, food and bare necessities. If there was no work, there was no way to live.

Fred showed Dorothy the notice in his pay packet. "Four days a week," was all she read.

"'Ow will we manage?" she asked.

"We'll manage. I've been 'aving five shillings a week stopped for the 'oliday fund. There's a bit of money there. It'll keep us going until we go back on five days. Don't worry, Dot."

"I could get a job cleaning," offered Dorothy.

"No, you will not get a job cleaning," stated her husband, his lips in a line. "We will be all right."

After a month on four days, Fred was dropped to three days and they both knew they would not be "all right." The holiday savings had already been used up. Dorothy knew how to cut corners. She had sewn the flies up on Fred's army underwear to use for herself, she sewed or knitted clothes for the three of them, she bought the cheapest cuts of meat and slow cooked them all day to make them palatable.

"Mrs. Cotton, up the 'igh street, knows of a little "getting-up shop" who needs decorators." Fred's mother told Dorothy. "I'll fetch Ann from school it you want to go see about it."

A "getting-up shop" usually employed only a few women and was temporary. The owner would bid on an order for china and hire the women to complete the order. It could mean a few days or weeks' work at most, but Dorothy was willing to try anything.

"You're lucky," said Jack Fowler, the man with the china order. "I can use a gilder for a bit. Can you start tomorra'?"

He wiped his nose on his already snotty sleeve and looked Dorothy up and down, a drop of saliva escaping from his lips. The small, dirty room at the back of an old disused factory gave Dorothy the creeps, but the chance of earning a few shillings to make ends meet was all she was interested in.

It was arranged with May's sister, Aunt Annie, who lived close to the school, to pick Ann up every lunchtime and after school. Dorothy would take her in the morning and pick her up from Aunt Annie's after work.

Fred was not impressed when he heard his wife's news, but realized they wouldn't make it without the extra money. He felt inadequate at best, not being skilled at anything but being a potter. On the three days he worked, he rode out to the factory in fear that there would be another downturn and he would be laid off all together. He saw other men standing outside the dole waiting for the chance of a job, any job for the day, or even a few hours. Desperate people picked coal on the slag heap at Florence Pit coal mine, or chopped up anything they could find made of wood, even the interior doors of their homes. Anything to build a fire and keep warm.

Jack Fowler was an unpleasant man. The six women who worked in the cramped room painting and decorating the china were well aware that there was safety in numbers. They even went to the "hole in the wall," as they called the lav, in twos. Jack leered and drooled at the women throughout the day. Dorothy kept her head down, concentrating on painting the gold bands around the cups and saucers, not looking at him. She worked for twenty-four hours the first week and soon regained the speed and efficiency of gilding. She was paid piece-work, which meant the more she did, the more she was paid.

"There could be a bonus for ya," leered Jack, catching Dorothy on her way home. "I could make ya an offer. Stay around for a bit and I'll make it profitable."

He stroked the front of his trousers.

"Dirty old bugger!" shouted Dorothy, bringing the other women to the doorway, and leaving Jack no alternative but to turn his back and walk away.

He didn't fire Dorothy the next day, but glowered at her from behind his desk. If he could find another gilder who was more cooperative, he would, he thought.

Aunt Annie Vasey liked having Ann around. Her only son lived in South Africa with his wife and little boy and she had missed out on being a grandparent. She doted on the little girl and hoped Dorothy's job would last a long time, so that she would be able to take care of Ann every day.

Dorothy's job lasted for eight weeks and coincided with Fred's call to go back to work full time. It was a coincidence they couldn't believe. They had been so lucky. They had made it through without falling into debt. Dorothy never told Fred about Jack Fowler's proposition. She was afraid her husband would have killed her lecherous employer.

The savings for a holiday were gone, but they could begin again and maybe next year they could afford a week's holiday in August. Fred was obsessed with the thoughts of a holiday, and when the Jasper department swung the opposite way and began to boom, he worked Saturday mornings and put the money into the holiday fund.

"What do ya think, Dad?" Fred asked his father one Friday night at the pub. "Take the families away for a week shall we? We could ask our 'arry as well. Ma would love it, being with all of us. Me and you would enjoy a pint every day, 'ave a bet on the 'orses, and a paddle in the sea. It's me dream, ya know. I want to take Dorothy away to the seaside, just for a week. Give 'er a good time. She deserves it."

"All right with me, Fred," answered his father. "Sounds just the job. We could go to Morecambe Bay on the train. I've 'eard good things about Morecambe. Lots of sand—sea's miles out."

"There's a 'oliday camp there," chimed in Bernie, who was playing darts with Fred. "Me sister went last year. Said it was great. Shall I ask 'er about it?"

"Aye, do that Bernie. Thanks," Fred said.

Wakes week for the potters was the first week in August and Fred and his family were headed to Morecambe. Dorothy had spent a week packing all their clothes into the big suitcase. Ironing all of Fred's best shirts and Ann's dresses and folding them into tissue paper to keep them from creasing. The men didn't have "casual" clothes, but dressed in slacks and a dress shirt every day, unless they were swimming, and after their swim they changed immediately back into their clothes. Dorothy had two dresses, one with red spots and one with blue spots to wear on alternate days. There were eleven of them going together, including three children. George, May, Fred, Dorothy and Ann walked from their house to Normacot station, Fred carrying one suitcase on his shoulder and his parent's smaller case in his hand. They met up with Harry's family on the train, along with Harry's in-laws.

Middleton Towers Holiday Camp was a fabulous place! Each family had a chalet to sleep in, set in blocks around the showers and toilets. There was an enormous ship at the centre of the camp, housing a huge theatre surrounded by a luxurious lounge containing easy chairs and sofas. The dining room was beside the ship, with a swimming pool and wading pool on the other side. A beautiful ballroom was housed in another building, with an ice cream parlour and a bar attached. There were tennis courts, bicycles for hire, a children's playground, an indoor arcade full of games. It seemed like paradise to Fred and his family.

Dorothy loved every minute. She didn't have to cook or wash a dish. She went dancing every night with Fred. The chalet patrol reported if there was a child crying in a chalet, posting a sign in the ballroom which said, "Child crying in Chalet number X." The days were spent on the beach, or in the swimming pool, or sitting relaxing in the lounge, or playing cards. After their evening meal there was always a great show in the theatre, with comedians, jugglers, dancers, singers performing. Even May enjoyed herself, once she accepted the fact that the food wouldn't poison her, even though other people had cooked it. It was the first time in her life that she had eaten food not prepared by herself. She refused to take off her thick lyle stockings and lace-up black shoes, even when the weather demanded it. The most she did was roll her full-length sleeves up to her elbows, but her neckline remained firmly at her throat. She frowned in disapproval at the "half naked" young women around her as she sat on the beach in a deck chair. *What was the world coming to!* She glanced over at her husband to make sure his eyes were firmly on his newspaper.

If only Dorothy could have remembered where her chalet was, everything would have been perfect. Her sense of direction was so bad. She learned by experience that she needed to pay more attention. She had entered the shower house through one door and thought she had exited by the same door. She knew their chalet had a blue door and was almost facing the end of the shower house. She marched across to the blue door, pushed it open and walked in. Fred was pulling his shirt over his head, getting changed to go swimming, wearing no other clothes.

"Welcome to Middleton Towers," she laughed tickling him under his penis.

"Oh my God!" she gasped as she looked up at the face emerging from the shirt. "You're not Fred!"

The stranger she had just tickled was struck dumb. Had this strange woman really come into his chalet and accosted him? He was rooted to the spot as he instantly covered himself with his shirt.

Dorothy ran!

"Fred, we have to get packed and leave right now," she said as she ran into the chalet with the blue door on the other side of the shower house.

"Slow down, Dot. What are you talking about?"

When Dorothy told him what she had done, he fell on the bed laughing. Ann jumped on top of him laughing too, although she didn't know why.

"You probably won't see him again. Anyway, he probably really liked it."

Dorothy did see the man again, several times, but ducked out of the way and hid behind buildings or trees to avoid eye contact with him.

The week's holiday was worth the penny pinching and extra hours of work. Fred made a decision at the end of the week that, no matter what, they would save for a holiday at the seaside every year, preferably at Morecambe Bay.

THE FIGHTING WALKERS

Mrs. Benfield lived two doors from Dorothy and Fred, at number eleven Bell Avenue. Her husband, Wilf, was a miner at the Florence Pit. They were an odd-looking couple. Gladys was a large woman and towered over Wilf by more than twelve inches. They had four children and, even though Wilf's wage as an underground face worker at the mine was way above the average wage of most potters, they struggled to pay their bills. Not unlike most men living in the surrounding working class neighbourhood, Wilf's first stop on Friday night, after he collected his pay, was the pub.

The Benfield children along with the other children in the avenue would wait for Wilf to come home on Fridays. They would hear him singing before they saw him. Then he would appear at the bottom of the avenue, rolling along, drunk and happy, as he waved to his own and all the other children running to greet him. Every Friday he was welcomed home as though he was a conquering hero returning home from a battle. There was only one reason the youngsters ran to meet him with such enthusiasm. Wilf put his hand into his trouser pocket and brought out a handful of pennies, then scattered them on the ground behind him, sending the children running to pick them up. A penny would buy a bag of sherbet kali or six pear drops, or bubble gum.

"Thanks, Mr. Benfield," all the boys and girls would chime.

"Thanks, Dad," his own children would join in.

Monday was rent day, when the rent man came to collect the ten shillings from each tenant. Monday morning was also the day Gladys Benfield came to borrow money from Dorothy. It had begun shortly after Fred came home from the army.

"Dot, I'm short the rent money," Gladys confided, coming into the kitchen carrying one of her children, with the second holding onto the hem of her skirt. "Wilf spent too much at the pub this weekend. Can you lend us ten shillings? I'll pay ya back Friday, when he gets his pay."

It was a lot of money! Dorothy would have to take it from her housekeeping money, but she felt sorry for her neighbour and knew the family would struggle without the help. Fred's dad would lend them a few shillings if they ran short, but Gladys had nobody else to go to. Her family lived miles away in Yorkshire, and Gladys hadn't seen them for years. A ten shilling note was pushed into Gladys' hand.

The following Friday, as promised, Gladys arrived at the door with a ten shilling note.

On Monday morning there was a knock at the back door and Gladys came into the kitchen.

"Sorry Dot, but can you lend me ten shillings again? I can't make the rent."

After that the ten shilling note became Gladys' money. Every Friday it was returned and put under the clock on the mantle, so that on Monday morning it could be loaned back to Gladys for the rent. Dorothy never touched that ten shillings. As far as she was concerned it didn't really belong to her.

The houses in the avenue were occupied by a diverse group of people. Four middle aged couples with no children, who kept their homes and gardens in immaculate shape, three senior residents, namely May, George and May's sister Daisy; the rest were families with small children, including the "fighting Walkers." The Walker family lived in the house directly across from Dorothy and Fred. Mr. and Mrs. Walker had two daughters, one two years older than Ann and a grown-up daughter, Eva, who lived in the family home with her two small girls. The other offspring, four grown boys, who terrorized the neighbours and each other, also lived there. How they all fit into the tiny house nobody could imagine. Every weekend, when the men staggered home from the pub, there was a fight out in the avenue between the brothers and their father. They liked to fight. They fought about everything and anything; one of the boys hadn't paid his way at the pub, or father had cheated at dominoes, or one of the brothers had knocked the table, spilling everybody's beer. They didn't need much of an excuse to start a fight.

Everybody stayed in their homes, peeking through the curtains at the combat going on outside. The Walker women and children screamed and cried, as the young men gave each other black eyes and split each other's lips. Mr. Walker was knocked out in one particularly bad skirmish and some-body, nobody knew who, phoned for the police.

Eva would usually run across the avenue with her two little

girls and hide in Dorothy's house until it was all over. Dorothy felt sorry for the thin, sickly-looking young woman. She was always tired and had deep purple circles under both her eyes. She gasped for breath much of the time and was often too exhausted to manage the girls.

The screaming and shouting began again one Saturday night just before Christmas of 1949. It was a bitterly cold, wet night and Eva came across the avenue, running away from the fighting with her little girls, in their threadbare pyjamas and bare feet, clutching her skirt. Eva's lips were purple and her breath came in short gasps as she fell into a chair in the living room.

"I'll put the kettle on, duck," soothed Dorothy. "You'll feel better soon."

Eva sipped the hot tea while the girls drank a glass of milk and ate the cookies Dorothy had given them. They were poor little things, thin and pale, with matted hair and teeth already decayed by poor nutrition.

Fred sat by the fire, his lips in a line, wondering how a family became so dysfunctional and treated each other so badly. He already knew the answer though. Drink and poverty. They always went hand in hand. They drank to forget how poor they were and they were poor because they spent their money on beer. A cycle that was passed from one generation to the next. The two little girls he was looking at would probably grow up, get married and continue the lifestyle they'd grown up with.

Eva dropped her cup, spilling tea down the front of her jumper. Her head fell backwards with a thud onto the back of the chair. Her eyes stared ahead unseeing.

Fred jumped out of his chair and rushed to her side, but

there was nothing he could do. Eva wasn't breathing. She was dead.

"Dorothy," Fred called to his wife who was in the kitchen making more tea. "Why don't ya take the girls upstairs and tuck them into our bed. I think they're probably tired. 'Ow about it girls? 'Ow would ya like to sleep 'ere tonight and play with Ann in the morning?"

"Fred, what are ya on about?" asked Dorothy coming into the living room. One glance at Eva answered her question. She tried not to scream or cry out so as not to scare the girls.

"Good idea," she said, taking the little girls hands and leading them out of the room. "What fun it will be to surprise Ann tomorrow. Come on, I bet ya'll be asleep before ya know it."

The little girls looked smaller than ever in the double bed, but snuggled down together with smiles on their faces. They liked Ann's mum. She always took them in when there was trouble at home. It didn't take long for them to fall into a deep sleep, feeling secure and safe.

"Fred, what are we going to do?" asked Dorothy when she returned to the living room.

"I know what I'm going to do," answered Fred. "Something I should 'ave done weeks ago."

He marched out of the front door and into the avenue, where the fighting was still going on. Swearing and punching each other, the Walkers were all after more blood. Fred grabbed the first two lads and banged their heads together, dazing them enough to stop them in their tracks. He pulled Mr. Walker off his eldest son, who was down on the ground and hit him squarely in the jaw, knocking him into the hedge surrounding his front yard. The eldest son wasn't going anywhere, he was too busy spitting out the two teeth his father had knocked out of his mouth. The other boy, lurking in the shadows ready to pounce on his brothers, ran into the house when he saw what Fred had done to the others.

"Now, you lot," shouted Fred. "Stop it! Get inside the 'ouse and be quick about it."

"Who the bloody 'ell do ya think ya are?" Mr. Walker began. "Nobody tells us what to do. Sod off or me and the lads'll beat ya to a pulp. We don't give a rat's arse about ya. Bugger off!"

Fred grabbed Mr. Walker by the scruff of his neck and marched him up the path and into the house, his feet barely touching the ground. The others followed, not wanting the same treatment.

Inside the house Mrs. Walker sat holding the youngest girl on her knee, both of them crying quietly. Fred shoved Mr. Walker into an old ragged armchair, trying not to let the smell of the house make him queasy. He was in the middle of the lion's den now. The Walkers were all around him.

"While ya were busy fighting each other, your daughter, Eva, came to our 'ouse with 'er little girls," Fred said, using a firm steady voice, borrowed from his memories of his sergeant major in the army. "Eva was breathing with great difficulty. I 'ave to tell ya all that she's passed away. She stopped breathing. I've seen enough of death to know there's nothing anybody can do."

The Walkers were instantly sober. They all knew Eva had a bad heart, but they never thought she would die, especially not this young. She was only twenty-eight years of age. Mr. Walker moved as though he was in slow motion as he pushed himself out of the chair and followed Fred out of the house.

Dorothy had closed Eva's eyes and covered her with a blanket. Somehow she wanted to keep her warm. The entire Walker family crammed into the living room at number seven and surrounded the young mother. They would never fight in the street again.

Dorothy kept the girls for a few days while the Walkers made arrangements for Eva. There was an autopsy because she had died at home. It showed her heart was badly damaged, probably from birth. May went door to door in the avenue to collect money to buy a wreath from the neighbours. Eva's two little girls were taken away by a kindly looking lady who said she was their grandmother. Eva had never married and Dorothy had never heard her talk about the father of her girls, but she was relieved to see them taken away. Any home would be better than staying with the Walkers.

FRIENDS AND NEIGHBOURS

*E*very family in the avenue had a story. The Miltons, next door to May and George, were quiet drunks. The house was dirty and the two children neglected. A mentally challenged old aunt looked after Carol and Peter when the parents were out drinking. They frequently ate ketchup sandwiches for meals, with tinned milk sandwiches for a treat. The old aunt set the house on fire one day and was badly burned. Dorothy took the children in and, when Fred came home from work, she went around to the house to help clean up from the fire. She took her own bucket and mop because there was no cleaning equipment in the burned house. Everything was floating in water. Dorothy didn't know where to start. Mrs. Benfield joined in the clean up, along with Mrs. Newban from number four. They opened the back and front doors and swept the filthy water, floating with crud, food, dog faeces and other unrecognizable objects, outside, before attempting to mop the floors with clean soapy water.

The three women worked hard to make the house liveable

again. It was probably cleaner than it had been in years by the time they had finished. Mrs. Milton sat in a chair watching them work. She didn't have the energy or motivation to help them. Her husband and brother-in-law were at the pub, and the poor woman watched her neighbours clean her house in stunned silence. With the old auntie in the hospital, somebody had to stay with the children, and it wasn't going to be the men in the family. Mrs. Milton wished she was at the pub—her life was bearable after a few drinks.

Two weeks after the fire, Mr. Milton knocked on Dorothy's back door late at night. Dorothy was in the kitchen making Fred's sandwiches for the next day's lunch.

"Can ya come to our 'ouse, Mrs. Podmore?" slurred Mr. Milton. "Me wife's in the bathroom and we can't open the door. I think she's sick."

Dorothy followed the drunken man to number three and, once again, entered the dirty unkempt house. Mr. Milton had tears and snot running down his face as he took Dorothy to the bathroom. The door wasn't locked, but something heavy was behind the door, making it impossible for them to open it. Mr. Milton's equally intoxicated brother joined them as they pondered what to do.

"I think your wife may be behind the door," said Dorothy. "We're going to 'ave to push as 'ard as we can to open the door enough to see what's happened. She may 'ave fallen and 'urt 'erself."

As Dorothy spoke, she looked down to see blood seeping under the door.

"Get your shoulder behind it and push. Both of you," she ordered the two men.

They opened up enough of a gap for Dorothy to squeeze through. Mrs. Milton was unconscious on the floor behind the door, with blood coming from her nose and mouth. Dorothy dragged her away from the door, so that Mr. Milton and his brother could get in. They both went to pieces, sobbing and crying and shaking Mrs. Milton.

"I'll get Fred to phone for an ambulance," Dorothy said. "Don't shake her. Don't move her. Don't wake the children."

Mrs. Milton was dead before the ambulance arrived. It was a cerebral hemorrhage. She was only thirty-two years of age.

Harry and Emmy Bridgewood lived at number one. Harry was Fred's cousin. They never had children and their house was considered "posh." They had matching sofa and chairs, a lovely carpet square, a china cabinet full of lovely dishes, and even a radiogram to play records in their living room. Harry had a beautiful tenor voice and sang in an all-male choir and the choir at Newhall Mission Chapel. Emmy sang in the chapel choir too, but with a less than melodious voice. They had an Old English sheep dog named Sheba, who loved everybody. They were the "star" couple of the avenue.

"Our 'arry's going to be on the wireless," his mother, Daisy, told May. "'Arry's going to Manchester next Sunday to sing on The Grand Hotel program. Isn't it exciting?"

"Oh, our Daisy, fancy 'arry on the wireless," her sister replied. "I bet you're as pleased as punch. We'll all 'ave to listen to 'im. Ya must be so proud."

"Aye, I am," glowed Daisy.

The word spread throughout the avenue that Harry was singing on the wireless on Sunday. The folks without a wireless gathered at the homes that had one, ready for the big occasion. The Benfield family joined Dorothy, Fred and Ann at May and George's house for Harry's debut. The children sat on the floor in front of the fireplace with fingers on their lips, having been instructed by their parents that they must stay very quiet during Harry's performance so that everybody could hear him sing. Promptly at seven o'clock, the announcer welcomed listeners to The Grand Hotel to the strings of the orchestra playing their theme tune. Then, the big moment, the introduction of the male voice choir from Stoke-on-Trent, singing Jerusalem, followed by Danny Boy. Everybody in the living room at number five held their breath.

"Here comes 'arry," whispered May.

The choir sang a beautiful rendition of Jerusalem.

"'E must be singin' Danny Boy," whispered May.

It brought tears to their eyes to listen to the choir singing Danny Boy.

That was it. The announcer thanked the choir and the strings of the orchestra continued to play.

"Where was 'arry?" Wilf Benfield asked.

"I would imagine 'e was singing right along with the tenors in the choir," laughed Fred.

"Well, I never," May sighed. "We all thought 'e was singing on 'is own. That's what our Daisy told me."

"Ma, she said 'arry would be singing on the radio on Sunday," explained Fred. "Everybody assumed we would 'ear 'im sing on 'is own, but it was never the plan. 'E's just part of a choir."

"Good job, 'arry," Fred said the next time he bumped into

319

him. "We could 'ear you above all the rest. We all said—that's 'arry that is, we can tell 'is lovely voice anywhere."

The friends and family living in Bell Avenue never let Harry forget the night he sang on the wireless.

The young couple at number nine were in dire circumstances. John worked for the city council as a street cleaner, earning minimum wage. His wife, Cathy, was out of her depth, taking care of two children under the age of two and heavily pregnant with a third child. Dorothy shared what food she could with the needy family, often taking a bowl of mashed potatoes, or a few scones, next door. Cathy couldn't keep the house clean and had no idea how to cook. The cockroaches from number nine would often cross the entry between the houses and get into Dorothy's pantry through the ventilation grid. DDT powder would be the only way to stop them and Dorothy sprinkled the deadly powder liberally along the walls of the entry.

Dorothy's heart went out to Cathy, who was very slow and seemingly unaware of her shortcomings in caring for her two babies. Dorothy made it a weekly routine to bring the two tots into her house on Friday mornings and sit them in her kitchen sink, washing away a week's grime and dirt. Shampooing their hair and dressing them in jumble sale clothes May picked up at the chapel. Every Friday Cathy said the same thing when Dorothy took them home.

"Oh, don't they look lovely," she would exclaim. "They smell so nice, and look at them clean clothes. I can't believe they're mine! Thank you, Mrs. Podmore, for doin' them up so nice."

"Have you made arrangements with the midwife for your new baby?" Dorothy asked.

"Oh yes. Everything's done and dusted," replied Cathy.

"Do you have the things you need for the baby?"

"Just what I 'ad for these two. I'll show ya if ya like."

Cathy pulled a box from under the sofa. A few ragged, stained baby clothes were stored in the box. There were no nappies, towels, face cloths, soap or blankets. No pads or clean nightwear for Cathy. Gladys Benfield and Dorothy went door-to-door around the avenue, collecting the items needed for the new baby. Neighbours willingly gave what they had, and the box under the sofa was soon filled.

"Mrs. Podmore, Mrs. Podmore!" yelled Cathy from her back door.

Dorothy was hanging the washing on the line in her back-yard, with Ann handing her the clothes pegs. She knew by the urgency in Cathy's voice that something was wrong, and quickly took Ann to her grandma before running to number nine.

"Here I am, Cathy," Dorothy announced as she stepped through the dropped food on the kitchen floor and made her way into the living room.

Cathy was lying on the sofa, crying. Her two little ones were wedged in beside her stroking her face, trying to comfort her.

"The baby's comin', Mrs. Podmore," gasped Cathy. "Can ya go phone for the midwife?"

"I'll go ask Gladys to call 'er, then I can stay with ya," said Dorothy.

Gladys was sent off to call the midwife. She had to run to the end of Lower Spring Road to the post office to use the phone box. Leaving her own two toddlers with Dorothy, off she sped.

Dorothy gathered up Cathy's tots and told Benfield's two children to follow her. Somehow she managed to get all four of them to May's house, two doors away.

"Sorry about this, Ma," she said as she bustled through the door with her group of children. "Cathy's gone into labour. Can you watch them until Gladys gets back from the phone? She'll only be ten minutes."

"They'll be fine with me," May answered. "Come on ducks, lets all 'ave a piece of jam."

May cut the bread thinly and skimmed it with butter and jam. Cutting the sandwiches into fingers, she handed out the "pieces" to each child and quickly made more as she watched them cram the food into their mouths.

"I 'ave to push," screamed Cathy, as Dorothy ran back into number nine. "Baby's comin' now."

"Don't push, Cathy," yelled Dorothy. "Ya 'ave to wait for the midwife."

Cathy bent her legs and raised her head and pushed.

"Don't push, Cathy," Dorothy begged.

Water gushed across the sofa. Dorothy peeked under Cathy's nightie and tried not to gasp or scream as she saw the top of the baby's head appear. She pushed a layer of newspaper under Cathy and begged her again not to push.

Don't panic! Don't panic! Don't panic! Dorothy told herself. She had to keep a level head. There was nobody else. She pulled out the box from under the sofa and found a facecloth to wipe the sweat from Cathy's forehead. She found a towel, donated by Mrs. Arrowsmith from number fifteen, and kept it for the baby. She lifted Cathy's nightie as the next contraction made the young mother scream and push. Dorothy instinctively cradled the baby's head as it came out of the birth canal, and quickly moved her other hand to catch the rest of the baby as it slid easily into the world.

Now what?

The door flew open and the midwife took control. She rubbed the baby with the clean towel until the baby let out a wonderful lusty squeal, then she cut the umbilical cord and handed the baby to Dorothy while she attended to Cathy. By the time the afterbirth was delivered there was an ambulance at the door to whisk mother and baby away. The midwife had ordered the ambulance in case of emergency, and when she saw the condition of the house, she thought it best that Cathy and baby should be in the hospital for a few days to give them a chance to recover.

"It seems like we do nothin' but clean up other folks 'ouses," Gladys said as she and Dorothy began to clean Cathy's house.

"Well, that's what neighbours do, isn't it Glad?" said Dorothy.

A VISITOR

*E*very month since Fred came home, Dorothy had been disappointed she wasn't pregnant. She thought there would be more babies, but it didn't happen. Eventually she gave the baby clothes away, but couldn't part with the beautiful pram Edward had bought for her. She covered it with an old sheet and stored it in the small box room upstairs. It was a reminder that she was still young and there was still time.

Madge had given birth to a girl, Pauline, two years after Ann was born and now she had a boy. Both the children were left with Emma while Madge worked. Criticism was levelled at Dorothy because she stayed at home and did Emma out of babysitting money. It would be the last place on earth Dorothy would ever leave Ann to be cared for.

Edward wrote each month, giving Dorothy a glimpse of his life in London. Mrs. Taylor remained his housekeeper and the two of them lived a quiet, peaceful life. Edward still enjoyed the theatre and dining out. He still enjoyed the company of beautiful women. He still visited Amy on weekends and had noticed how frail and weak she had become recently. She was in her mid-eighties and didn't leave the house any more. Dorothy replied, sending him pictures of Ann and telling him how much she missed him. She didn't have the extra money to take the train to London to visit her father, but would never have let Edward know.

"I 'eard from me father today," Dorothy told Fred as they sat down to eat their evening meal together. "'E's coming for a visit."

"What?" asked Fred. "You mean 'e's coming 'ere to see us?"

"'E misses us all and is coming this Saturday to visit. 'E's not staying overnight. 'E'll catch the morning train from Euston and take a taxi from the station, and 'e'll return in the evening."

"It's a long journey for the old man, but knowing Edward 'e never thinks of 'imself as old," laughed Fred. "It will be nice to see 'im again. Ann won't remember 'im of course."

On Friday Dorothy cleaned the house until it shone. She spent a whole month's coupons on buying enough stewing meat to make a meat and potato pie for their dinner on Saturday.

What would her father think of their tiny house? What would he think of the unpaved avenue? What would he think of May and George? What did he think about Dorothy's decision to marry a potter and give up her dream of living in London?

It had been many years since Edward had travelled north on the train. He cast his mind back to the journey north to rescue Dorothy and take her back with him to the cottage in Cobham. He remembered the ghastly meeting with Gertrude out in the dirty street in front of the house in Edward Street, Longton. All traces of the beautiful girl he had loved, gone! He left to return to his cottage empty handed, leaving Dorothy with the Bryan family, filling his heart with despair. It had taken him three years to move on after that meeting. He clung to the cottage and the memories it held until, finally, he could bear to leave it all behind and move to London. To begin a new life.

The rain splattered onto the windows of the train, blurring the countryside outside. Edward dozed for a while and awoke with a start as the ticket collector gently tapped him on his shoulder to tell him Stoke station was the next stop. Edward had given the man a generous tip at the beginning of the line and asked him to let him know when the train was approaching Stoke. It was a habit he had learned from his father many years before. "Always tip the people who will be taking care of you before, not after, they have been of service," Francis had told him. Throughout his life Edward had lived by this one simple rule and had benefited beyond measure from it.

The porter at Stoke station called a taxi for the elderly gentleman. Given the address, the taxi driver set off down Victoria Road towards Longton and then Normacot. The streets hadn't changed since Edward's last visit more than twenty years before. Narrow streets lined by terraced houses and pottery factories. The noticeable difference was the decrease in black smoke from the bottleneck kilns used for firing the pottery. There were only half of the four thousand coal-fired kilns in use, the rest had converted to electricity and the difference was evident. The air, previously thick with choking smoke, was clearer and easier to breath. The pavements, even in the rain, were running with rain water and not thick, sooty sludge. The people, hurrying through the wet weather, were visible and the colours of their clothes weren't all black or grey. As the taxi entered the tiny avenue, bumping over the stones on the unpaved road, Edward could see small trees in the front gardens and small patches of grass growing, surrounded by clusters of bright flowers.

Saturday was usually a lie-in for Dorothy, but not today. She had been up since dawn anticipating her father's arrival. She dressed in her red spotted dress and took her hair out of the curlers she had slept in. She dressed Ann in her best dress and put a newly bought ribbon in her hair. Fred shaved and dressed in his new pullover Dorothy had knitted for him. They were ready way too early and Dorothy had been staring through the window for an hour waiting for the taxi.

Edward stepped out of the taxi, paid the fare and asked the taxi driver to return for him at five o'clock. He pushed open the gate to number seven and looked at the window to see the net curtains stir. His heart fluttered like a teenager in love at the thought of seeing his daughter and granddaughter again. With his usual long strides he was at the door, which opened before he could knock.

"Father, come in," Dorothy grasped his hands and drew him into the small hallway. "How wet and cold you must be. Oh! How I have missed you."

She helped Edward off with his coat and shook off the rain, then hung it to dry on the coat stand. As always he wore a trilby hat, which he removed and hung with his coat, smoothing down his still-thick grey hair.

"Darling," he greeted his daughter. "Darling, how wonderful to see you. My beautiful girl! My angel! You have no idea how I miss you, every day."

Ann stared up at the grey-haired man. He was much taller

than Daddy. He hardly fit through the door into the living room. He talked differently than Daddy too. Should she be scared? No, she didn't think so. Something familiar stirred inside her. Something she was trying to remember.

"There you are little one," Edward said bending down to Ann's level and looking into her brown eyes. "So much like your mother. Do you remember me, sweet child?"

As Edward reached for his granddaughter to pull her into his embrace, she remembered the smell of him. This was somebody she loved. She kissed his cheek and stroked his hair and watched his eyes fill with tears. Had she made him sad? No, he was smiling as well as crying. Just like Daddy did sometimes when she told him how much she loved him.

Fred finally stepped forward to shake hands with his father-in-law, offering him a seat and a drink. Fred had asked his Uncle Jack to give him a small bottle of scotch from his prolific supply. Uncle Jack was a bookie, taking bets on the horses and dogs, which was illegal. He made a great deal of money, and always kept a well-stocked liquor cabinet. He was happy to help out his nephew, who had never asked such a favour before.

Edward gratefully took the scotch and water, drying his tears and gathering his composure after a few sips of the strong liquid.

Dorothy sat by her father's side on the small sofa, holding his hand. He looked older. He was older. Still handsome. Still kind and loving. How happy she was to see him, to touch him, to be near to him.

The midday meal of meat and potato pie was delicious. Dorothy had learned many of her cooking skills from Mrs. Taylor and she was proud of her pastry making. Not everybody could make good pastry, but she had the hands for it and it always turned out flakey and light. The table leaf was swung into place and the sofa moved a few feet to make room for four chairs. Edward never even blinked at the small space or the meagre furnishings. Dorothy seemed happy, that was all he was interested in.

"I have a few things with me that I want you to have," Edward said after the meal. "I have decided to sell the flat in London and move to Maidenhead. It's time. Amy is old and frail and I need to be with her at this time. You, my dear, are happily settled here with your own family. Mrs. Taylor will move to Brighton to live with her niece. Everything is arranged."

Edward reached for the package he had placed on the sideboard. Inside were some of his treasured possessions: opera glasses, scales for weighing mail, a brush with his initials engraved into the handle, and two silver napkin rings. He placed them on the table in front of Dorothy.

"It's not much, but I want you to have something that belonged to me, apart from the Prussian Captain. When I die, I want you to have the ring I always wear, with a cameo of George Washington. It reminds me of my time in America and how I loved living there. I always thought I would go back and make it my home, but it wasn't to be."

"Thank you, Father," said Dorothy. "I'll treasure these. They will remind me of so many wonderful times with you in London. Going to the theatre, your opera glasses always with you, sitting at your desk, weighing your mail every morning before taking it to the post office, brushing the shoulders of your coat and your hat before leaving the flat and the silver napkin rings placed side by side on the sideboard in the dining room."

Ann immediately picked up the tiny weights and placed them on the small flat surfaces of the scale, watching the scales move up and down as she moved the weights around. Edward taught her how to make the scale balance by placing an equal weight on each surface. They went on to weigh the salt shaker, Ann's cup, Dorothy's brooch, and numerous other small items in the house.

Before Edward left, May and George were summoned by a knock on the adjoining wall. Edward, gracious as ever, shook hands warmly with the disfigured hands of George and sent May into a whirl when he kissed the back of her hand. The two tiny Podmores were dwarfed by the tall, elegant gentleman from London. They felt conscious of their broad midland accent, compared with Edward's cultured King's English. Edward and George had both fought in the First World War and shared stories of their combat experiences, until they were chatting away like two long lost friends.

It was hard to say goodbye. Edward knew it would probably be the last time he would see his family. They wouldn't visit him in Maidenhead and he wouldn't make this trip north again. He held his daughter close, imprinting the memory of her into his mind. He lifted Ann into his arms and felt her soft cheek against his, reminding him of Dorothy at the same age, when he had lost her.

"Take care of my special girls, Fred," Edward whispered as he shook Fred's hand. He slipped an envelope into his Fred's other hand and nodded to the younger man.

The envelope remained unopened as Edward entered the taxi, his family waved to him through the rain. Dorothy felt her lip tremble and her throat ached as she watched the taxi drive out of the avenue. Like Edward, she knew it would be the last farewell.

Trying to think of her father living anywhere except the flat in Chillworth Mews seemed impossible for Dorothy. It had been her home for the years before, during and after the war. Edward exuded the atmosphere of London. It was in his bones. In his spirit. He hadn't talked about Maidenhead very often, but when he did it was always with disdain and he often came up with excuses of why he couldn't visit Amy. Dorothy knew Amy was the wife Edward had been unable to leave when Gertrude lived with him. He had chosen Amy over Dorothy's mother. Would Gertrude have stayed with Edward if he had left his wife and married her? What a different life Dorothy would have led. Now her father was to spend the last years of his life with his wife. Maybe the elderly sought a peaceful life beyond everything else. Maybe Maidenhead was where Edward would find his peace.

The envelope contained one hundred pounds. Twenty times the amount of Fred's weekly wage.

GOODBYE EDWARD

*T*elegrams were a rarity. They usually brought bad news. The war telegrams were still fresh in everybody's minds long after the war had finished. The dreaded message stating in as few words as possible that a loved one was killed or missing in action.

A sharp knock on the door of number seven Bell Avenue, just after Dorothy had returned home from walking Ann to school, heralded a telegram. She took the paper from the carriers hand, knowing it was something she didn't want to read.

FATHER DIED 11.00P.M. TUESDAY STOP FUNERAL FRIDAY AT 2.30P.M. ST. LUKE'S CHURCH MAID-ENHEAD STOP MRS. TAYLOR.

Dorothy sat down with a thump on the sofa and stared at the telegram. Edward was gone!

She sat and sat, staring at the clock on the mantle wondering how the time kept ticking away as though everything was normal, when it wasn't. Her father was dead!

Slowly she rose and knocked at the wall connecting number seven with number five. The signal between the two houses that something was wrong and help was needed.

May came hurrying into Dorothy's kitchen. It was the first time the signal had been used by Dorothy.

"What's up, Dot?" the old lady asked, seeing her daughter-in-law's pale face. "Ya look like ya've seen a ghost."

"A telegram came," whispered Dorothy, handing it to May who read it carefully and slowly. She had difficulty with most writing, other than her Bible or a hymn book.

"Oh duck, I am sorry," she finally said. "I'll put the kettle on for a cuppa right away."

Things never changed. The first thing after a shock or bad news was always a cup of tea. Hot and strong and sweet. Dorothy drank it down, feeling the sweet warmth fill some of the emptiness inside. Edward had always been there. Even living apart, the umbilical cord was never between mother and daughter, but between father and daughter. Dorothy somehow had never imagined life with Edward gone. Even when it was years between meetings, he was her ever-present beloved Father. While her mother's death had meant nothing to her, her father's death meant everything. He was her family.

"You must go to the funeral, Dot," Fred said as they sat down together after putting Ann to bed. Dorothy had been to school to collect Ann as usual, made their tea in time for Fred's return from work, as usual. She had shown the telegram to Fred when he came home, raising her finger to her lips and looking at their little daughter. She would wait and tell Ann the news when she was better prepared.

Money from the savings account was withdrawn for the train ticket. Money from Edward's generous gift. May took over the care of Ann during the day. Dorothy made her way, one last time, to London Euston and caught the connecting train to Maidenhead.

The church was cool and dark as Dorothy slipped into a pew at the back. There was a small gathering of people occupying the first five rows singing Abide With Me. Only Mrs. Taylor knew who she was. She was sitting with Edward's friends and associates and didn't notice the dark-haired young woman sitting at the back of the church. John Goodwin, Edward's long-time friend who had taken over the taxi business, read scripture. Dorothy's favourite hymn, "Oh Love That Will Not Let Me Go," closed the short funeral service. As the coffin was carried out of the church to the graveside, Dorothy hung back, lowering her head and shrinking further into the shadows of a stone pillar.

Words were spoken by the vicar as Edward's coffin was lowered into the grave. Dorothy stood under an oak tree watching and listening from afar. Tears of grief spilled down her cheeks as she privately said goodbye to her father. Her memories flooded through her mind like a movie: the London flat, the taxis, the west end shows, the restaurant dinners, the silk underwear, the "Dorothy" bags, the war years, the visit to Bell Avenue, the love poured out on her by her adoring father. She also unexpectedly remembered her mother, seeing her shrunken face on the hospital pillow, hearing again the plea to take Geoffrey. As a result of the union of these two people, Dorothy had been born into a confusing world of poverty and privilege. She had become a strong woman, facing, with courage, everything life threw at her.

As the last of the funeral party left the grave side, Dorothy walked slowly forward, unnoticed. She stood looking down onto the coffin. From her handbag she took a small cloth bag, tied with a blue ribbon. She gently removed the worn metal soldier from its soft resting place and kissed the top of his head.

"You've been my companion since I was five years old," she whispered through her tears. "When I was scared or un'appy, you were my friend, me connection with me father. Now I 'ave a new champion, me real life soldier, who loves me even more than Edward did. I no longer need you, dear little Prussian Captain, so I'm giving ya back to my father."

Dorothy gently slid the precious toy down the side of the shaft of the grave, watching it come to rest at the edge of the coffin where Edward's head lay.

Dorothy placed the Prussian Captain back into the pouch and tied the ribbon. She smiled through her tears as she knelt in the dirt. "Goodbye, dear Father," she said. "I'm returning the Prussian Captain to you. I no longer need it. I have everything I need— a lovely little girl, a new baby growing inside me and a loving husband. Thank you for always loving me, Father. For taking care of me, for guiding and advising me. You set a high standard for me to find my life's partner, urging me never to settle for second best. I found that partner in Fred, who loves me so dearly. I am content and happy in the life I have chosen. Rest now, and know you will be remembered, always."

AUTHOR'S NOTE

I knew when I wrote *The Prussian Captain* that the story was unfinished. I was compelled to write this sequel, so that I could tie up the loose ends of my grandparent's lives and how they had influenced my mother.

The Welsh Guardsman, was a more difficult book to write! An emotional roller-coaster! I laughed and cried as I worked my way through the myriad of stories surrounding my mother's early life.

The story line is based on the true facts of my mother's early life. My mother, Dorothy, was a strong, confident woman in many ways, but she had a harsh, sometimes cruel side. Writing her story gave me insight into her personality and helped me understand why she could be so difficult at times. She was probably bi-polar or manic depressive, but during the era in which she lived there was no such diagnosis. Dorothy struggled through her periods of depression as best she could. I believe her early life formed her personality and influenced everything she did.

I still have Edgar's (Edward in the book) opera glasses, which I still use. My sister, Christine, has the letter scales, the napkin rings and the brush. I also have his metal travel trunk, which now holds our grandchildren's lego and toys. The cameo ring of George Washington, which Edgar wanted my mother to have when he died, was not given to her. It would have been great to have that.

Our grandchildren have used my father's war memorabilia for class presentations on WWII. Our son has his medals, pass book, picture of his tank liberating Brussels, etc. We still have the original telegram of my birth and my little slipper sent to my dad in France. I have the kit bag he threw downstairs, and actually still use two woollen army blankets - from over seventy years ago! Of course I still have the little horse, Flicker, dad made for me while he was convalescing. Many years after the war dad could still sing Bread of Heaven and the Welsh Anthem, in the Welsh language.

My mother, Dorothy, was a product of the two environments she grew up in. I understand her so much better after writing this book. Beneath all the layers of resentment, hostility, anger and fear, there was Dorothy—loving us in a way only she understood. Love was providing a hot meal, with pudding, every evening; never chips in newspaper. Love was sewing or knitting clothes, so that my sister and I always looked well dressed; never going to the chapel jumble sale for our clothes. Love was a holiday once a year. Love was taking us to theatres and museums.

Dorothy was the matriarch of the family. Nobody crossed her without dire consequences. She always spoke her mind, often inappropriately. She didn't need or seek friends. She didn't forgive easily, if ever. She was sharp tongued, had a temper, swore like a trooper, smoked a pack of cigarettes a day. She adored babies and small children, and lavished her affection on them, until they reached about six years of age—around the same age she was when her mother abandoned her! She found it difficult, if not impossible, to give or receive affection. She was fiercely protective of our family, making sure none of us were "put on" by the rest of the world. From beginning to end it was Dorothy against the rest of humanity.

Life is nowhere near as interesting now she is gone.

ALSO BY ANN BROUGH

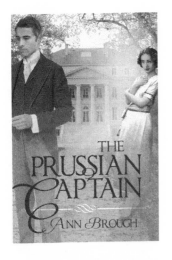

The Prussian Captain is the prequel to *The Welsh Guardsman*. Discover how Gertrude and Edward, individuals from such different backgrounds, came to be together. Read about Edward's early life and adventures criss-crossing the Atlantic, including his family spending time in the Napa Valley, and about Gertrude's heartbreaking upbringing in the Bryan household in the poverty of Neck End. How did Dorothy come to live with her grandparents? How did Edward and Gertrude ever manage to be together, and what finally tore them apart? Find out in Ann Brough's debut novel, *The Prussian Captain*.

DON'T MISS ANY OF ANN BROUGH'S TITLES

You can sign up to be notified by email about her next projects. Visit www.annbrough.com for more details.

ACKNOWLEDGMENTS

I owe such a debt of gratitude to my sister, Christine, for her meticulous research and incredible support. She has been my advisor for both books. She did an amazing amount of research on our father's war record. She also gave me a transcript of a taped interview with Dorothy from 1985, which was full of stories from mum's early life. Thank you Christine. I couldn't have written this book without you.

Many thanks to my faithful proof readers, daughter Tracey Silagy, daughter-in-law Cheryl Brough, sister Christine Podmore and my wonderfully supportive husband David. Each of you pointed out different issues for me to take a second look at and found a myriad of errors and typos.

Thank you Lauren Craft for editing this book and giving me such sound advise and good criticism. You have amazing insight.

Thank you Roseanna White for your work on the beautiful cover. For taking my few ideas and making them into a really special book cover.

Huge thanks to my son, Matthew, who tirelessly guided me through all the technology, supported me at every turn, and encouraged me to keep going. Thank you, Matt, for publishing my book.

David, you support me every day. Thank you for making life easier so that I had time to write. For all the times you made food for me, or did laundry, or brought me a cup of tea so that I could continue to work on my book.

ABOUT THE AUTHOR

My name is Ann Brough, daughter of Dorothy Podmore (nee Bryan or Wrightson?)

I live in Manitoba, Canada, in a wonderful lake community, called Lester Beach on Lake Winnipeg, with my husband David.

I was born in 1944 and immigrated to Canada in 1967 and again in 1978, with a seven year residence in England during that time.

My husband and I have three wonderful children, each married to the very best partners. We have five wonderful grand children, recently increased to six, when our eldest granddaughter married a super young man. Our lakeside home is filled with family, love and lots of sand every summer. It's everybody's favourite place to be!

This book is a sequel to The Prussian Captain, which was my first book. Both books were a labour of love.

For more about Ann and her other books visit
www.annbrough.com

Made in the USA
Columbia, SC
16 August 2018